BROTHER,
BROTHER,

BROTHER BROTHER

CLAY CARMICHAEL

ROARING BROOK PRESS • NEW YORK

To Margaret

Copyright © 2013 by Clay Carmichael
Published by Roaring Brook Press
Roaring Brook Press is a division of Holtzbrinck Publishing Holdings Limited Partnership
175 Fifth Avenue, New York, New York 10010
macteenbooks.com

Library of Congress Cataloging-in-Publication Data

Carmichael, Clay.
  Brother, brother / Clay Carmichael.—1st ed.
    p. cm.
  Summary: After his grandmother's death, seventeen-year-old Brother sets out, with the abandoned son of a friend, on a 200-mile trip to North Carolina's Outer Banks to find his twin brother, of whose existence he just learned.
  ISBN 978-1-59643-743-2 (hardback)—ISBN 978-1-59643-879-8 (ebook)
  [1. Interpersonal relations—Fiction. 2. Secrets—Fiction. 3. Identity—Fiction. 4. Twins—Fiction. 5. Brothers—Fiction. 6. Death—Fiction. 7. North Carolina—Fiction.] I. Title.
  PZ7.C21725Bro 2013
  [Fic]—dc23
                                                              2012041836

Roaring Brook Press books may be purchased for business or promotional use. For information on book purchases please contact Macmillan Corporate and Premium Sales Department at (800) 221-7945 x 5442 or by email at specialmarkets@macmillan.com.

First edition 2013
Printed in the United States of America

1 3 5 7 9 10 8 6 4 2

I love a dog. He does nothing for
political reasons.
—*Will Rogers*

1

FOR THE FIRST NIGHT in months, Brother dreamed of the sea.

The great mother, Mem called it. She'd grown up on the coast, said sea dreams ran in the family. Which explained his dreams, she told him, and why a boy who'd never seen the ocean chased dolphins in his sleep, heard waves crash shores he never reached, woke shaken and soaked in sweat like something half-drowned.

"I swam with dolphins when I was a girl," she'd said. "They're good luck, you know." He did know. She'd told him many times. But last night's dream had been the same vain chase. The dolphin swam ahead of him, just out of reach.

He lay still, breathed deep, and let the dream ebb before opening his eyes. His head throbbed, and the glare from the window showed he'd way overslept. The clock said ten. Even at her sickest, his grandmother rose every day by five, before the sun dawned or the paper thwacked the front stoop. He'd wake to her filling the kettle, hear the scrape and creak of her chair, smell coffee brewing—things that had stirred him since he was three. Until today.

The dead silence jarred him fully awake. He rushed to her room, knocked without hearing any answer, knew before he saw her.

He sat on the bed beside her, took her cold hand in his. She looked upset, whether from pain or anger he couldn't have said. He'd come in late the night before and passed the dark under her door without looking in. Tired after a double shift, too much to drink, and a fight with Cole, he'd spaced her first and second life rules: *Never assume anything* and *Pay attention, pay attention, pay attention.*

At The Elms Rest Home where he and Cole worked, death visited more often than relatives. Jerry had been his first. Brother remembered the old man's utter stillness, his no-one-at-home stare. After that, the names and stony faces blurred. "Dying's what they're here to *do*," Cole had said once, eyeing two dementia patients who paced the locked ward all day, hand in hand. "You couldn't call that living."

Mem was different. Even dying, she'd been so alive. What-ifs crowded Brother's mind. What if he'd come straight home after work? Left Cole's early? Would she still be alive? He shut his eyes till his inner voices quieted, sat for a long while holding her hand.

When he calmed, he found the phone in the bedsheets, the battery dead. He righted the tipped-over lamp and picked up the spilled library books from the floor, along with a crossword book and yesterday's paper. Gideon Grayson scowled at him from the front page. *That scoundrel,* Mem called him. His eyes blazed with some fresh hatred. He pointed a scolding finger at the camera. *Enough to scare a body to death,* Mem had said. Her mother had kept house for the senator's parents when she was a girl, and Mem followed Grayson's career. *Little tyrant even then,* she told Brother, *and not one bit changed, the way he butters the rich's bread, while sending poor boys like you to die in his sort's needless wars.*

She'd hoped to get Brother to eighteen, some months away, before she joined her husband Billy, Brother's grandfather and her true love, killed in Vietnam before Brother was born. *Our generation's war,* she'd said, nodding at Billy's showy urn on her dresser. *Every generation's got at least one.*

Brother studied the urn, the seascape painted there so like his dream. His mother's simpler urn stood beside it, a robin's egg blue. He thought of the rainy night she'd left him and died, his father's identity dying with her. He'd been barely three when she yanked him from the car, thrust him with his belongings at the dumbstruck stranger—his grandmother, Mem. *Don't argue, Mama. I'll be back tomorrow to explain.* His last and only memory of his mother. Hours later a state trooper in a yellow slicker and black hat stood dripping on the stoop and delivered the gruesome news. Brother could still picture the man's long, serious face, the rain pouring off him, his cruiser's hard blue light spinning behind him at the road.

"Brother, Brother," Mem had said, shaking her head, after the trooper left. He was called Brother to avoid confusion, as Billy was his name, and his mother's and grandfather's too. "Brother, Brother," Mem said again, and thereafter whenever life disappointed, words failed. Gazing on her now, he said it to himself.

They'd known she was dying—last visit, the doctor said *weeks*. Still, Brother sat stunned on the edge of her bed, his thoughts morbid and drifting. He wished he'd pressed her more about his family, especially about his mother. But asking about either made Mem cry, so he'd learned early not to. And when her cancer returned, he skirted even everyday questions. "How are you?" invited answers he didn't want to hear, while "You look better today," let him believe what he liked. He was a genius at that.

"What in hell's happened to you?" Cole had yelled at him the night before. "Last year you were the smartest guy I knew, full of fire and plans. Now, you're like the zombies at The Elms. Check into the locked ward, why don't you? You've effing caved."

Brother couldn't argue; it was nothing he hadn't said to himself. Even so, it wasn't like Cole to be so negative or cruel, to lay into his best and only friend. He whined now and then, but mostly their late-night highs were relaxing and a release valve, both.

Like Brother, Cole had left school at sixteen. Before that, they'd run with different crowds, but fell in together studying for the GED. A drunk driver had killed Cole's parents, orphaned Cole and his kid brother, Jack. But if Cole's tragedy resembled Brother's, he wasn't one inch resigned, hadn't let it beat him down like Brother had. In spite of everything, Cole was upbeat and ambitious—if his plan to win big playing cards or the lottery and "rocket out of North-nowhere Carolina" could be called ambition.

Yesterday something had changed though, something major; what, Cole wouldn't say.

Brother supposed he should call someone about Mem, but he couldn't make himself act—a fair description of his entire last year. He willed himself into the kitchen. Mem's foil-wrapped dinner plate sat untouched in the fridge, a small consolation. It meant she'd died before dinner, when he was working and couldn't have been home. He made a pot of coffee in her memory. He brewed it strong and black with a pinch of salt against bitterness, the way she liked it, how he would drink it now.

Afterward, he showered and dressed and walked the half mile up Sutter Highway to Warren Alfred's. The flat, stubbled countryside where he'd spent most of his life looked foreign to him. Time seemed altered, the day too bright. The red dirt might as well have been underfoot on Mars.

He stopped at Warren's mailbox and stood staring at it, reluctant to bear his news. Warren was a nice old guy. He was a widower, twenty years older than Mem and sweet on her, though she hadn't felt the same way. Resigned to Mem's friendship, Warren had kept a watchful eye on them as far back as Brother could remember. Mem's jobs—waitress, cashier—hadn't paid for much, but Warren worked forty years for the county, had benefits and a pension. He'd helped her get her disability and paid for things they couldn't afford: medicines, plants for her garden, her morning paper. He let Brother drive his car.

Brother thought of Mem alone and dead and nearly turned back, but Trooper started barking and clawing behind the door.

To Trooper's glee, Warren opened it. The dog shot out as though sprung from a bow, a gray-and-white blur that nearly knocked Brother down. Trooper was Brother's dog, though he lived with Warren because of Mem's allergies. But Trooper loved Brother best of all, and this morning Brother was glad for his happiness, for the sheer dog joy in him. He smiled and squatted and let Trooper lick his whole face.

"Hey, True; hey, boy."

Warren shuffled out onto the stoop and motioned them in with a toss of his white head. Trooper, an Australian shepherd mix, had to herd Brother, make sure no harm came to him between the mailbox and the door. Today, as every other day since Brother was nine, the dog ran dizzying circles around him, shepherding his flock of one. By the time they reached the house, Warren had lighted a fire in the fireplace. He sat beside it, rocking back and forth, sucking on his pipe stem, scenting the air with cherry tobacco. Warren had a friendly quietness about him that Brother liked. Trooper paced the hearth rug between them, his ice-blue eyes fixing each of them in turn, as though asking an urgent question.

"Trooper stared and paced all night," Warren said, and then, "Mem's gone, isn't she?"

It was said in Schuyler, North Carolina, that Warren had a kind of knowing. No one took it too seriously or held it against him, both because his knowing seemed so matter-of-fact and he was the eldest elder of the Schuyler Baptist Church. When the subject came up, Warren said that any knowing he had was due to the restless way Trooper behaved when something of moment was about to happen. "That dog," he said, "has an instinct for change."

"Last evening sometime," Brother told him, settling in the second rocker.

Warren closed his eyes like he was praying, and Brother let the fire's warmth wash over him. He listened to it crackle and to the jingle of Trooper's license tags as he looked anxiously from one of them to the other.

"There's more change coming," the old man said quietly. "We're not done yet."

Brother eyed Trooper uneasily then. He was used to Warren's claim that Trooper's restlessness predicted things like sudden hail, record snowfalls, found money, or flat tires, but until today, he'd never heard Warren make any connection between the dog and anyone's death.

"I know," Warren said, divining Brother's thoughts. "An old man's fool ideas."

"That's not what I think," Brother said, though it was, more or less.

"Ordinary animal instinct, one hundred percent natural, scientific even. Remember those animals running to higher ground before that tsunami?"

Brother nodded politely. He'd heard this before. He knew animals sensed things people couldn't, but Warren was a missionary on the subject.

"Two hundred thousand people died when that wave hit," Warren went on, "but no animals. They sensed it coming and ran inland, ahead of that wave. Animals feel earthquakes before we do, too. And any child knows animals can smell and hear things people can't. Trooper's instincts are like that—an early warning system to tell you that conditions are ripe for change and consistent with instability and upheaval. I believe that's what he somehow reacts to. Gives us a chance to suit up."

"Suit up?" Brother said. This was new.

Warren nodded. "You know how I feel about Reverend Harvey's sermons?"

"About like Mem," Brother said, making a face. Missing the minister's blistering sermons almost made working Sunday double shifts at The Elms worthwhile.

"He gave one last week that made me sit up in the pew. Said most things that happen are over before we realize. And because they're past before we know what's hit us, we don't experience them while they're going on. Too many folks drift through their lives, experience things in memory after the fact, but that's not the same as being fully aware as things occur. That's been Trooper's gift to me. Being more awake as life happens. When he stares and paces, I listen harder; I open my eyes a little wider and notice more. I don't worry so much about what's going to happen, I just try to notice what does."

"Pay attention, pay attention, pay attention," Brother said.

Warren sighed. "I'm going to miss your grandmother."

"You knew, though. You said, 'Mem's gone, isn't she?'"

"I *guessed*. Trooper kept me up pacing half the night, and then you show up looking like you'd lost your whole world. Plus she's been awful sick. One plus one plus one."

Brother nodded, like this made perfect sense to him, though it didn't really.

Warren set his pipe on the hearth and stood. "I'll phone Bayliss."

Melvin Bayliss ran the Schuyler Funeral Home, one of the few small businesses to survive the closing of the mills and the opening of the chain stores on the highway. With his raven-black hair, pale skin, and white shirt with black suit and tie, Bayliss was starkness personified. He had a black-and-white way of speaking too, and Mem said a metaphor would've seemed as odd as Aramaic in his mouth.

After Warren spoke over the kitchen phone for a few minutes, he sat down again in front of the fire. "He'll call when he's done. You got other kin?"

"Mem said she and I were it that she knew." Brother thought of his father, who, if alive, likely didn't know he'd fathered a child.

"We'll ask Bayliss. He's got a head for family lines, and experience locating kin. Dullness is an asset at times like this. You eaten?"

While they waited, Warren scrambled eggs with cheese and Worcestershire sauce and toasted thick slabs of his own home-made bread with butter, a vast improvement over Mem's frozen dinners and Brother's own cooking. Mem had learned nothing from her mother. Even when she was well, she and cooking were strangers, and she hadn't been much acquainted with housework either. Brother mostly did their chores. *You've been cheated of your youth*, she told him. *You squandered it on a sick old woman.* Maybe so, but he didn't relish going on without her.

After they ate, Warren added a log to the fire. He took the World's Smallest Harmonica, no bigger than half a stick of gum, from its small, so-labeled box. He put the instrument between his lips and moved it from eyetooth to eyetooth, playing "Amazing Grace" without using his hands, and truly, his playing was amazing. If Brother hadn't seen it, he'd never have believed it. Warren didn't miss a note, and it seemed a right remembrance for his grandmother. Trooper paced as Warren played, his tags accompanying the music like a revival tambourine.

"A fine duet, True," Warren said when he'd finished.

The whites of Trooper's eyes showed all round, and Brother thought the dog looked crazed.

Warren patted his head, and Brother remembered the day he and Warren had found Trooper in the hardware store parking lot, how Warren had let Brother name him. True's gray parts were the exact color of that state trooper's cruiser, the one who'd brought the news about his mother.

"After I phoned Bayliss, I took the liberty of calling the nursing home, said you were taking family leave."

"Thanks," Brother said. He'd completely forgotten his shift. His mind was mush.

"You thought about your future? What would happen after?"

Brother shook his head.

"Don't hurry to make decisions. You've got your GED and steady work, more than most have around here. You're a free man. A free man with a good dog. You've got a week left on your rent. After that, you can bunk here till you work things out."

"I appreciate that." Warren's solicitude eased Brother's mind. He didn't have the first idea what was next. He was tired, as tired as he'd ever been.

The phone rang—Bayliss, saying he'd collected Mem. "For her date with the Lord," Warren added, which made Brother picture a red convertible and Mem laughing like a girl as a long-haired, white-robed Jesus helped her into the front seat. Even at her age she'd been a striking beauty, everyone said so, with her easy laugh, silver braid, and large, interested eyes.

Mem had "prearranged" everything, paid Bayliss in advance years ago at the same time as her daughter Billie's cremation. She was adamant: no service. After the diagnosis, she went over this with Brother and Warren many times, making sure they understood what little she wanted following her "demise."

"I've got an emergency vestry meeting about termites," Warren said, "but you and Trooper can stay here by the fire."

Brother eyed Trooper, who had quieted for now. "Thanks," he said, rising, "for everything. But I think I'd like to go home."

Hearing the last word, Trooper's ears pricked and he shot, forever hopeful, to the door.

"No point in denying him now," Warren said. He went to the kitchen and returned with Trooper's bowl, two cans of dog food, and a bag of kibble. "Call if you need me."

Brother walked home in a daze, Trooper panting happily by his side. Once home, he filled the bowl with dry dog food, a stew pot with water, and left the kitchen door ajar so Trooper could go in and out. He got Mem's brandy from the kitchen cabinet, leaned in her doorway, and took long snorts while staring at her bed, empty now, stripped to the bare mattress.

The sound of someone sucking the dregs of a spent drink through a straw made him turn toward his own room. There, he found Cole's five-year-old brother, Jack, and the greasy trash from a fast food burger and fries in his bed.

"What are you doing here?"

Jack pointed to his cheeks full of food with the straw from the empty drink cup.

"Besides that."

The boy shrugged.

Brother tried to remember if he'd agreed to anything the night before. He felt pretty sure he hadn't, but it was like Cole to presume, to drop off Jack with Mem or Brother for an afternoon, even a day or two. The night before, Cole had gotten as high as Brother had ever seen him. He'd warmed up razzing Brother, but then went on a tear about Jack. How he loved Jack, but he was owed his own life. How their parents dying wasn't *his* effing fault. That one day the little bugger might wake up and, brother or not, he'd be-the-hell-gone. Maybe he'd just pack up and park the kid with Brother—who had no life anyway, so what the hell? All of which he shouted with little Jack sleeping in the next room. Usually Jack slept like the dead through their noise, and thank God, because the walls were as thin as Cole's brotherly devotion. But last night Brother had turned to see Jack standing in the doorway, wide-awake and pissing his pajamas.

"Swallow, Jack, then tell me where Cole is."

Jack swallowed but took another bite.

Brother waited. Jack was a sweet kid, but like Cole he had a way of clamming up when someone wanted answers he didn't want to give.

"Where'd he *say* he was going?"

Again Jack shrugged.

"Jack?"

"What?"

"Tell me where Cole is."

"Or you'll tickle me till I puke?" Jack said, and laughed.

Brother set the brandy bottle on the floor. He went to the bed, grabbed Jack's ankles. "I'm not kidding."

Jack squealed like this was a fine game—which it usually was, one Jack loved—but Brother wasn't in the mood to play.

"Tell me, buddy."

"You're choking me," Jack said, laughing more.

"You can't choke somebody by the legs." Brother tightened his hold and looked Jack straight in the eyes. "Listen to me. I'm not playing today, you understand?"

Jack put his hands over his ears, shut his eyes tight, and started humming for good measure.

"I mean it, Jack. Take your hands off your ears and look at me. Something's happened. Something serious."

A sucker for a mystery, Jack's eyes popped open and he uncovered his ears.

"Mem's dead."

Jack stared, processing this, for a long minute. "You mean, like Jeepers?"

Brother remembered the goldfish belly-up in its bowl, how

Jack cried for Brother and Cole to "do something!" when nothing could be done. "Like Jeepers," he said, nodding.

Jack seemed to think on this. "Are we going to bury Mem in the backyard?"

Brother thought of the little funeral, Jeepers shrouded in tissue in a mint-tin coffin and laid to rest in the backyard as Brother, Cole, Jack, and Trooper looked on. Mem had read the Bible story of the loaves and fishes.

"Mr. Bayliss from the funeral home is taking care of everything. He came and got her."

Jack sat up, interested now, while Brother lay down and put one arm over his eyes.

"Is he going to bury her in the backyard?"

"No, he's not," Brother said.

"If you want, you could bury her next to Jeepers."

"Thanks, buddy. That's kind of you. So kind I know you're going to do me a big favor."

"What?"

"Remember how bad you felt after Jeepers died?"

Jack bowed his head, nodded. "Yeah."

"Remember how much you cried?"

"A lot."

"And do you remember how we curled up in your bed and just let ourselves be sad?"

Jack nodded again.

"Do you think we could do that now? Take a little sad nap?"

"Will you buy me another cheeseburger?"

"You bet. But later, okay? When Cole gets back."

Jack seemed about to speak, but didn't. He turned to glance at something by the door. Brother followed his gaze. A little suitcase. What a day.

❊ ❊ ❊

When Brother woke, it was dark and Bayliss stood over him like a giant vulture. "I phoned six times, got worried, and came over."

"I guess I forgot to put it on the charger," Brother said. "What time is it?"

Bayliss looked at his watch. "Eight eighteen."

"What day?"

Bayliss glanced at the empty brandy bottle on the floor and switched on the lamp beside the bed. "Still Wednesday. All day. Whose boy is that?"

Brother sat up suddenly, remembering Jack.

"He's fine, out back, playing with the dog," Bayliss said.

Brother heard Jack squealing as Trooper barked.

Bayliss's brows arched slightly. "They were eating dog food together when I came in."

Brother sighed. "Is Warren with you?"

"Warren's home with a sprained ankle."

"What happened?"

"Fell off a ladder at the church. Asked me to check on you."

"How's he doing?"

"He'll mend. Why don't you splash water on your face while I make coffee? We need to talk."

Brother joined Bayliss in the small living room where he sat before two steaming mugs of coffee. The seascape urn belonging to Brother's grandfather stood between them on the table.

"We've encountered a couple of hitches," Bayliss said.

"What kind of hitches?"

"Before I get to that, you're sure you don't want any service? Reverend Harvey inquired."

"Mem said no."

"Well, begging your pardon, but she's gone and you're not. Sometimes a service lets the living say good-bye and feel that they've done right by their kin. Wouldn't be any charge."

Brother imagined the hidebound eulogy Harvey would deliver. For years, whenever the reverend's sermons expressed views opposed to Mem's own, she hadn't just sat silently and listened. "Don't just spectate, Brother: witness, question, think for yourself." Often, to Harvey's chagrin, she waited until he finished, then stood to politely offer rebuttal. Brother particularly remembered the Sunday Harvey preached on the evils of abortion to a nodding congregation. At the sermon's end, Mem rose in the pew and in her soft, old-lady voice told all present that considering the opinions just expressed, she knew the church adoption rate would rise tenfold in the coming year. She could attest to the joy these adoptions would bring, she said, and ignoring Harvey's glare, took her seat and wiped Brother's snot-crusted nose.

"God, no," Brother said. "She'd haunt me if I let Harvey have the last word."

Bayliss nodded. "I took the liberty of putting the notice in both state papers." He drew a typed page out of his breast pocket and offered it to Brother, who read: "Mem Grace, widow of the late Billy Grace and mother of the also late Billie Grace, died at home on March 23. She is survived by her grandson, Billy Grace.

"Don't know if I'm alive, dead, or my own grandfather," Brother told him.

"It's her precise formulation," Bayliss said defensively. "I never deviate."

"I was kidding."

Bayliss frowned, as if this were no time to joke. "If you didn't all have the same name—"

"Thank you," Brother interrupted. "It's just right. I'm a singular people now, anyway, a family of one. There's nobody to differ."

"Begging your pardon, but relations have a way of surfacing after a death," Bayliss said, "if only to find out if there's money coming."

"They'd be disappointed there." Brother thought of the ten in his pocket, all he had till payday, and his paycheck already owed.

"Even so, in my experience, when there's this much lacking in a family's past, there's a story there somewhere. Bringing me to what we need to discuss."

Brother nodded for him to go on.

"Before I came for your grandmother, I reviewed her directives in the file. She indicated that she wished her ashes to be placed in an urn similar to your grandfather's. I took the liberty of removing the so-described urn when I came earlier. I hope you weren't alarmed."

Brother shook his head. He hadn't noticed it was gone.

Bayliss eyed the urn on the coffee table as if it were a lovely girl. "Porcelain," he said, tipping it to show Brother a date and someone's illegible signature on the bottom. "Italian. 1672. Hand-painted. Probably wasn't made to contain cremains, but for a more general, decorative purpose."

"She didn't get it from you?" Brother asked.

"Oh no. I don't stock anything like this. No idea where she got it."

"No clue."

Bayliss paused and looked around the sparse living room. "Forgive me, I don't know how you're fixed, but I took the additional liberty of sending a photograph of it to a colleague who knows something about antiques. He said he might be able to find something of a similar style and quality for as little as two thousand dollars."

Brother snorted.

"I understand. Normally, since they were married, I might suggest commingling the ashes of the two in the same urn, as many spouses do . . ."

Brother looked at him hopefully.

"But she was specific that they should be kept separate, besides which the urn's too small."

"Of course it is," Brother sighed.

"I'm happy to provide a simple urn, free of charge, as part of the original arrangement."

"Thanks, Bayliss, that's fine until I can manage something else."

The back door slammed, and Jack and Trooper raced nosily inside. Jack stopped short before Brother and looked at the urn, which Trooper sniffed.

"I'm hungry. Are there cookies in there?" he said.

"Ashes," Brother said.

"From a fire?"

"Sort of."

"Can I see inside?"

"No," Bayliss said.

"I don't think he understands," said Brother.

Jack glared. "I understand a lot."

Bayliss cleared his throat. "Actually, *you* don't understand, Brother. The lid's fixed on with some kind of glue. It would take somebody who knew what they were doing to open it without damage, if it can be opened at all."

"Hah!" Jack said, and shot Brother a *so-there* look.

"For your grandmother, I have a simple urn in ash," Bayliss said, without irony. "No charge, as I said. And I'll be happy to tell my friend to keep his eyes open for something similar to the other one. Something reasonably priced."

"Thank you, Bayliss. Is that all?"

"Actually, that's the smaller of your problems."

"How many are there?"

"Time will tell," Bayliss said, and if Brother hadn't known Bayliss to be deadly serious in all things, he would have thought he was making fun, but he wasn't. He drew a wrinkled section of newspaper from his breast pocket and set it folded on his knees.

"When I came for your grandmother this morning, I found a newspaper on the bed."

"I saw it," Brother said.

"I guess you didn't look at it?"

He handed the paper to Brother, who saw Senator Grayson's angry, faultfinding face.

"I saw that too."

"But I guess you didn't look at the whole article?"

Brother shook his head.

"I did only because I opened the paper to wrap your grandfather's urn for transport."

"And?"

"See for yourself."

Brother looked more closely, and underneath the senator's picture, read the headline: *Senator Grayson Criticizes Press Coverage of Son's Overdose. Article, Section B, Page 1.*

"So?"

"Keep going," Bayliss said. "Front page, state section."

Brother turned to the page. At the top, under the headline, *Senator's Son in Guarded Condition* was a photograph of a boy— his school picture from the look of it—a boy who, except that he was well-rested, clean-shaven, and wearing a jacket and tie, was the spitting image of Brother. Someone had circled around the boy's head with a blue ballpoint pen.

"Did you draw the circle?" Brother asked Bayliss, though already he knew the answer.

Bayliss looked affronted. "I did not. I found the pen in the bedclothes. Must've been some shock, and sick as she was . . ." Bayliss stopped, but Brother saw what he meant.

Jack had been setting little pieces of kibble on Trooper's patient head, but the dog shook them off like so much rain, and Jack turned his attention to the newspaper. "Brother!" he cried, proving even a five-year-old could see the striking resemblance. "Why's your picture in the paper? Did you win the lottery?"

"No, buddy. And that's not me," Brother told him, staring at the caption underneath: *Gabriel Gideon Grayson III.* "But I'm pretty sure it's my brother."

2

"COLE!" BROTHER SHOUTED. "Open the damn door!"

Cole was clearly not inside, but Brother kept shouting and pounding away at the mill house front and back doors until his fist throbbed. He had no idea where to find a key—lucky for Jack. He'd arrived determined to park the boy and his bag of burritos inside, Cole or no Cole, and let Jack fend for himself until Cole got back. Determined, until he found the house locked tight and his conscience kicked in, using Mem's voice. *Brother, you can't leave that little boy alone! What if he found matches and burned the house down with him inside it?*

"Sap," he hissed at himself, knowing that if he did ditch Jack, that voice would hound him till he turned around. "I don't need this, Cole, not now. I need to find my own brother, not mind yours."

He heard Trooper's bark and turned to Warren's old black Ford Galaxie, parked at the street. A skulking figure Brother couldn't make out was peering in the far, passenger-side windows, as Trooper yipped anxiously from the shotgun seat. His dog had snored butt to butt with Jack all night, instantly grasping that Jack was part of his herd, his to watch over now. What had happened, Brother wondered angrily, to that instinct in Cole?

"No!" Jack shouted. "I'm not susposed to talk to strangers!"

"Help you?" Brother called, and the figure stood tall. Brother sighed, seeing who it was.

"Who's that little boy?" Reverend Harvey demanded.

Cole's voice and the words *none of your effing business* sounded in Brother's mind, but instead he said, "A friend of the family," then stood mute as Mem had taught him. "Silence makes people uneasy," she said. "When they speak to fill it, they reveal themselves."

Her advice worked too, because Harvey suddenly seemed to remember his manners. "I went by your house, then Warren's. I come bearing spiritual comfort and advice, whatever you need. I mourn your loss," he added, though he seemed more smug than sorry. Brother remembered the Sunday Harvey had told Mem and Brother that much as it pained him to say it, their souls, unless swiftly and locally baptized, were doomed to everlasting hell. Then as now, Harvey looked like someone saying I told you so. But Mem had just burst out laughing. "Satan's much too proud a creature to covet two nobody souls like ours," she'd told Harvey. "It was Jesus who claimed the losers of this world, Reverend; *winners take note*."

"Thank you, sir, I appreciate your concern," Brother told

Harvey, using one of the many polite phrases Mem had taught him. Manners were a refuge, she'd said, a shield against terrible fates and horrible people. She'd drilled him in social niceties and gracious evasions so he wouldn't be caught off-guard, tongue-tied. He thought how pleased she'd have been that her courtesies now sped to the forefront of his mind, at the ready, like eager reservists. "You're very kind to offer, but I'm doing fine."

Brother fell silent again while Harvey lingered uncomfortably. "If you're certain."

"I am, sir, thank you." Brother stood mute, giving Harvey no choice but to go to his car.

"I'll be checking on you and the boy," the reverend called.

Wonderful, Brother thought. He got in Warren's car, slammed the door, and gripped the wheel hard. Trooper's tongue baptized his ear.

"I ate your burrito," Jack said from the backseat.

"It's okay. I'm not hungry."

"I think I'm gonna puke."

Brother took a steadying breath. "Don't puke in Warren's car."

"What if I have to?"

"Get out and puke on the grass."

"Cole'll be mad."

"Cole's not here."

"What if he comes back and yells at me and makes me puke more?"

Brother looked in the rearview mirror. The little bugger was smiling. "Jack?"

"What?"

"You know what." Brother rubbed Trooper's head, gladder for the dog than anything he'd ever been glad for. At least there was one grown-up in the car.

All the way back to Warren's, Jack bobbed and chirped, "Puke, puke, puke, pukey dookey, pukey dookey . . ." over and over, only slipping into a post-burrito coma in the last half mile. Brother cracked a window and locked the dog and Jack in the car. "Guard duty," he told Trooper, who leaped the seat and sat alert beside the sleeping boy.

Back at his house, Warren dozed in his fireside chair, his right ankle raised by pillows on a footstool. Brother sat gratefully in the other chair and closed his eyes. Anger and anxiety had stoked him like amphetamines all night, the new facts of his life racing in his mind: His grandmother was dead. He had a twin brother he'd known nothing about and a famous family besides. Cole had chosen this moment to disappear and saddle him with Jack. And even Warren, once sound, was lame. When Brother had finally drifted off near dawn, he dreamed a nuclear reactor exploded inside him and cleaved him neatly in two. His mirror image stared at him and laughed. The laughter jolted him awake and hurled him shaken and sleep-deprived back into the chaos of his life.

He took the newspaper page with his brother's picture out of his pocket and studied the face, his own and not. Not the barbered hair, the self-assured up-tip of the chin, the suggestion of a smirk about the mouth and eyes.

"How long you been here?" Warren said, waking.

"Not long. How're you feeling?"

"Like a fool for letting Mem's passing rattle me and missing that rung. Damn painkillers make it hard to keep awake. Where's Trooper?"

"In the car watching Jack sleep."

"Cole's not back?"

Brother shook his head.

"He got a cell?"

"Like me, in his dreams."

"Somebody ought to whip that boy."

"Life's already done that," Brother said, and Warren sighed and grudgingly nodded. Warren thought Cole took advantage of Brother and Mem, a point Brother couldn't presently argue. "He'll surface. He always does."

"Crap time to go all shit for brains."

Brother smiled. He'd never heard Warren curse before. "You ought to do drugs more often."

"It's not funny. Child abandonment's a serious thing."

"It's not. He didn't think—"

"You got that right!" Warren snapped. He closed his eyes, seemed to steady himself. "I'm sorry. I'm upset about your grandmother. But everything's changed since yesterday, Brother. *Everything*. Just give me a minute."

Warren shut his eyes, and after a few seconds drifted off again. While Brother waited, he turned the little that Mem had said about their family in his mind. Many times she'd told him of her and Billy's "expulsion from paradise," a story long on romance but short on facts. Billy and Mem had grown up together on an island off the Carolina coast. They shared each other's secrets, much as they had any, inseparable as they were. Billy was the sort of boy fathers warned their daughters against, and Mem, pretty and headstrong, took to Billy like wet to water. When he was near, there was an instant disconnect between Mem's head and heart, and later, her head and her tender regions, when at sixteen Mem had conceived Brother's mother, Billy's child.

They fled west on Billy's motorcycle, lived in shelters and worked odd jobs for money. But Billy was drafted, as happened in those days to boys not in school whose draft numbers were low. Mem begged him to run with her to Canada before the baby was born, but Billy was hardwired for honor, a virtue she couldn't argue with as it was the quality that made him loyal to her. Billy went to war and died. Mem raised their daughter, Brother's mother, alone, until Billie ran off with a boy at seventeen.

"Was the boy my father?" Brother had asked Mem.

"That's what she claimed."

"What was his name?"

"Got me."

"What did he look like?"

"Don't know that either. I only saw the back of his head when they drove out the drive. I'm not even sure she told him, or if so, if he cared. Don't get mixed up with drugs, Brother. They make people do things they wouldn't otherwise."

That was as much as she would say on the subject of his mother, though now and then she tossed him other scraps of her past: a house on the water, a ferry there and back, the swim with dolphins. If he asked her, "Why don't we ever visit?" she looked upset and replied curtly, "Impossible," as if her home were some far, forbidden country and she barred from returning there.

"Damn pills, where was I?" Warren said, starting awake. He winced as he shifted in his chair.

"Want me to get you something?"

"No, I've got things to say before I doze off again. Where'd I leave off?"

"Everything's changed."

Warren nodded firmly. "Everything *has* changed, Brother, and you know it. You have a brother, a twin, the scion of a certain somebody. I knew that woman was hiding something, maybe a lot of damned somethings. Did Mem tell you how we met?"

"She never said."

"Before I retired I worked for the county Register of Deeds. Mem came into the office one day inquiring how to get a birth certificate for an orphaned grandchild who didn't have one. I helped her with that and other things. I'm not suggesting she asked me to do anything inappropriate or illegal, though God knows I let her turn my head, so maybe I did. But she was missing an awful lot of paperwork, and I always felt she knew more than she claimed."

Brother had felt that too, but it was hard to challenge the person he loved most in the world, especially since she was his only family. *Was.*

Then Warren shook his head vigorously, as if shaking off his doubts. "I know you got a few things to close out before you go, but it's time you left Schuyler and sorted out your kin."

Brother had known that the minute he'd seen his twin's picture in the paper, even before the full truth of it sank in. Forward motion was all he lacked.

Warren reached for an envelope on the side table. "I got Bayliss to help me with a few things this morning. I called the nursing home and said you quit your job. I told them you'd be coming by tomorrow to pick up your last check."

Brother ought to have been sorry about the nursing home, but he wasn't. He'd taken the job only for Mem, and none of the residents on the dementia ward would notice he was gone.

Warren held out the envelope. "In here's the title to my car, signed over to you. Old as it is, I don't know how far it'll get you, but there's five hundred dollars cash in this envelope for gas and food and motel or to get you a ride the rest of the way."

"I can't take that."

"You can and you will," Warren said.

"How will you get around?"

"I won't be mobile for a few days and the congregation won't let me want for anything. Time I bought a new car anyway, but you let me worry about all that." Warren looked hard at Brother to show he meant it, and Brother took the envelope reluctantly.

"If Cole's not back, take Jack with you and leave a note on Cole's front door to see me. Anyone asks me or Bayliss, you and Jack went to take care of family business, which isn't but a quarter mile from the truth." Warren's stare fixed him like a bug on a pin. "Well? Did I work things out for the near term?"

"Wish I had."

"I know this last year's been awful, but life's unlocked a door for you, Brother. Don't just stare at the knob. Promise me. Promise *her.*"

"I promise," Brother said, but more from politeness than conviction. He held up the envelope. "Thank you for this." That he meant.

"You're welcome," Warren said. "Now go find your twin."

3

"SQUISH!" JACK CHIRPED, pointing out the car window at a dead possum on the shoulder.

For the first hundred miles, Jack cheerfully toted up roadkills, till it seemed to Brother that death was everywhere, the new theme of his life.

He couldn't bring himself to put Mem's urn or the others in the trunk, so he belted them side by side next to Jack in the backseat. The sight of them in his rearview mirror, along with the raw gray weather and Jack's shrill announcement of each flattened little cadaver, seemed proof positive of the unrelenting hopelessness of life, of unrealized potential squashed mid-lane, of a spiteful, road-raging god and the pea-brained stupidity of every living thing. Why did the raccoon cross the road? Who the hell knew? But he was doomed to be mashed flat as a hairy hamburger when he did, never to reach the other side or see his ring-tailed kin again. Even the road signs seemed to read like one of Reverend

Harvey's despairing sermons, warning of the mortal perils just ahead (Crosswinds/Falling Rocks/Blasting Zone); the swift, damning, and eternal justice to follow (One Way/Dead End/No Exit); and the impossibility of consolation (No Shoulder).

"Watch out for grief," Warren had told Brother on his way out the door. "You'll feel like there's no good or lightness anywhere, and every breath requires work of a heroic order. That's how I felt twenty years ago after my wife died. You'll want to throw yourself off a high bridge or walk in front of a bus or take up drugs or alcohol or some other stupid such, but just remember Jack's counting on you, and True needs you to open his can."

The bleak feelings would ease in time, Warren assured him, and Brother was relieved to know it, because he'd have been scared otherwise. He'd hardly slept and crazy ideas, like letting the Galaxie drift into the oncoming lane or crash into a bridge abutment, constantly caromed through his head. He glanced at Trooper—head out the open window, biting at the chilly air—already enjoying his new life; and then at Jack, who left off his litany of roadside dead to belt out a sea song Cole had taught him:

> A sailor went to sea, sea, sea
> To see what he could see, see, see
> But all that he could see, see, see
> Was the bottom of the deep blue sea, sea, sea.

Likely Cole was off somewhere similarly seizing the day, using his fake ID to lush and yuck it up. Maybe he'd gotten lucky and finally hit a lottery number, or maybe he'd really beaten the odds and there was a girl involved.

"People always think *everybody else* is having more fun, making more money, and having better sex than they are," he heard his friend's voice say. "Lighten up, man." That was Cole's mantra, his counter to every tragedy, setback, or too-serious thought. Brother teased him that the end of the world could come, the destroying angel blow down their mill house door, and "Lighten up, man," would be all Cole said.

Put out as Brother was about Jack, he missed his friend's raucous chatter, the dreamer-wheeler-dealer who'd have gone on endlessly about the opportunities, angles, ironies, and weirdness in Brother's new situation—none of it remotely useful, but that wasn't the point. Brother craved distraction. Unsettling questions nagged him like gnats. How were he and his brother separated? What had their mother done and why? What did Grayson have to do with any of it? And had Mem known more than she'd let on?

Kind Bayliss had delivered her ashes, but it had been all Brother could do to go down the rest of his list: Clear out the rental and store the little worth saving in Warren's shed. Return the keys to the landlord, pay and cancel the utilities, leave Cole a note. Drop off Mem's books and look up the Grayson family home at the library. Bagging Mem's still Mem-scented clothes for the thrift shop had nearly felled him. Everywhere, memories or judgments jumped him or some chain of derailing associations lay in wait.

"Mem kept me busy," the librarian said, handing Brother

printed directions to Winter Island, North Carolina, along with a ferry schedule. "Such a lively mind. Always wanting history, biography, and political science." None of them Mem's interests, Brother knew. After he'd left school, Mem had pleaded illness and made him read to her, but she'd chosen the books for *him*, his continuing education. He'd been so tired, the words had barely registered, though Mem held out hope he might one day win a scholarship, study law.

At The Elms he picked up his check. He said good-bye to each of the patients, who either aped his words or stared vacantly back. It seemed wrong that Mem was gone while they lingered. The staff expressed sympathy and envy both, wished him luck. Some smirked as they asked about Cole or expressed irritation at having to cover both their shifts. On his way out, he passed the kitchen and caught sight of Del, who looked quickly away, like he wasn't there.

She was twenty-some and had a son, but in Brother's first months at The Elms they'd spent happy nights together, first talking and then more. But she'd flipped the morning her four-year-old woke early and found them together. The boy stood staring, so close Brother could smell the peanut butter on his breath. "Are you my daddy?" he asked, after which Del chased off Brother like a stray.

At the bank Brother cashed his check and closed their account at the bank. The manager pushed the $280 and change across the desk brusquely, as if it confirmed Brother's worth. As first-ever sophomore student body president, Brother had briefly caught the eye of the man's pretty and popular daughter, who quit returning Brother's calls after he quit school. "Stuck up little bitch," Mem had snapped, adding cryptically, "If she had any idea what she's throwing away."

So many things he wouldn't miss about Schuyler. Warren was right about a door having opened, if only a crack. *I have a brother, I have family*, he said to himself over and over. For twenty or thirty miles he actually enjoyed the rearview sight of the last year receding behind him and started to feel thin slivers of optimism and adventure piercing his gloomy mood. For maybe thirty whole minutes he allowed himself to think that his luck might be turning. He even joined Jack in a chorus of the sailor song, until Jack suddenly stopped, pointed at two bloody lumps on the left shoulder, and cried, "Double squish!" shattering Brother's fragile, lighter mood.

Brother willed himself not to look, forced his gaze to the opposite shoulder, but worse than roadkill, he found himself abruptly eye to eye with the super-sized, smiling face of Gideon Grayson on a Grayson for Senate billboard. Grayson's head was huge and craggy, like something chiseled on a cliff. The words RIGHT FOR AMERICA! blazed under his chin in fiery capitals and a giant pink finger pointed straight at Brother like a hex. The sight so startled him he veered off the highway onto the rutted shoulder. But just as he regained the road, Trooper started to bark, the Galaxie engine shrieked, clouds of smoke and steam began billowing out from under the hood, and Jack set off wailing like a siren, all at the same time.

4

AT A REST STOP HOURS LATER, Brother sat at a picnic table and studied a map. He found Winter Island on the fragile spine of the state's easternmost shore, a pinprick near the whispers of land known as the Outer Banks. As best as he could figure, he, Jack, and Trooper had two hundred miles to go on land, but then would have to board a ferry at a place called Satterfield Point.

He now had no clue how they'd get there, and no firm idea what he'd do when they did. He'd managed to coax the Galaxie a mile or so more, but it took the extra distance hard. First, smoke and steam grew to an enveloping cloud. The noise under the hood grew shrill, and vibrations rattled the frame. After that, the oil light burned with a deep red finality, and a few seconds later, the car just stopped. He coasted it to the shoulder. They walked miles to the rest area—he had no idea how many—with Jack unaccountably triumphant atop Brother's shoulders. Granted it was Sunday, but not one passing car or truck had stopped or even slowed. Would hitchhiking be easier or harder with a kid and a dog? A rhetorical question, he now thought. If they made it to a bus station, did buses allow dogs? The way things were going, probably not.

"How do you feel about ferries?" he asked Trooper, who lay calmly alert at Brother's blistered feet. The dog turned to the sound of Brother's voice, but then went back to watching Jack play with another boy while the boy's parents finished eating at a nearby table. In the late daylight, Trooper's eyes were soft, expectant, blue as deep water, but they told Brother nothing. He wished the dog could talk, tell him what to do. He missed Mem's guiding spirit. Even having Cole to spar with would have been better than no one at all.

Sometimes, late at night, he'd heard Mem talking to his grandfather's urn, asking for advice or otherworldly intercession.

"What do *you* think?" Brother tried whispering to the chilly air, but he felt like an idiot. Despite Mem's efforts—or maybe because of them—he was a crap believer. Heaven was just a story, the dead forever gone.

It would be dark in an hour or two. He wondered where they'd all spend the night. If they started out now, they might get back to the car before dusk, sleep there. They'd have to go back sometime to get their stuff. Or maybe they could beg a ride from somebody at the rest stop to a nearby cheap motel where he could put Jack to bed, and rest himself. The thought of the effort either choice required made him doubly tired. He craved sleep and real food. His eyeballs ached in their sockets. He'd let Jack play a few more minutes, feed Trooper from the bag he'd somehow re-membered to put in his pack, then make up his exhausted mind.

He nursed his third Coke, watching cars and trucks come and go. Couples, parents, sisters and brothers, grandmothers and grandfathers filed in and out together, quick-stepping in, saunter-ing out. They argued, laughed, and teased each other as families do, the children pushing and shoving, the couples holding hands, everybody with places to go and people they knew to see. He envied all they had for sure and all he didn't. Would his own family be pleased to see him? Mem hadn't thought so and kept as much distance as she could.

He looked across the empty picnic table and tried to imagine his twin sitting there. Better educated and dressed, his look-alike, *that* Brother could conjure, but beyond that, his imagination failed him. His twin blinked back at him, his insides a cipher. Was he otherwise like Brother? Like the senator? If the news-papers were right—and even the senator hadn't disputed the overdose—Gabriel's situation was as serious as Brother's in its own way, and Brother was about to make it exponentially more complicated. *Senator Grayson's not your father, our father,* Brother rehearsed silently, but then he thought: Maybe Gabriel already knew that. Maybe he knew everything, whatever everything was. Maybe Brother was the one in the dark.

Probably it was the grayness of the day and his lack of sleep plus all the Cokes, the two packs each of peanut M&Ms, cheese waffles and nacho-flavored chips, but he started to feel shaky and sick, and it struck him like a hurled brick that Mem was really and truly dead. He'd left steady work and Schuyler without strategy or plan. He'd never *really* soloed, not like now. What did he know about running his whole life? What the hell had he been thinking? Bringing Jack along was nuts. What if they slept in the car and the police came along and asked questions? He couldn't believe he'd thought any of this was a good idea.

More and more families set up picnics at adjacent tables or hit the vending machines, calling out to each other: *You want a Coke or a Crush? They don't have MoonPies, how about Nabs? Chicken salad or tuna fish?* Only truckers came and went alone, but even they came and went with purpose; they had places they were headed, somebody or something waiting for them at the far end. What did he have? Maybe four hundred dollars after gas and necessities, no job, a kid that wasn't his, a strange dog, and a crap car with three powdered dead people strapped in back. No cause for jubilation by any standard.

Warren had been right about grief, because the longer he sat there, the more he wished Cole was here and that they were drunk as skunks and passed out where nobody could find them. Despite his brother's overdose and what Warren and Mem had told him, getting as wasted as he could seemed like the best idea he'd had in his life. Genius, in fact. And being just seventeen wasn't an insurmountable obstacle. Plenty of adults were willing to sell alcohol to kids, and if not, plenty of others were willing to buy it for them. Didn't he have American dollars? Didn't he have cause? All he'd have to do is tell his sad, orphan story and somebody'd oblige. Why shouldn't he get high? Didn't he deserve a little fun?

A break from death, responsibility, and depressing thoughts? By God, he did. Oblivion sounded like just the ticket, and he wondered what it would take. Not much, tired as he was. A six-pack? Twelve? A bottle of wine? Two? Whiskey might be quicker. Maybe his brother had the exact right idea. And even if he and Jack and the dog had to trek longer to an exit with both a store and a motel, that didn't matter now that he had a relaxation plan. But seconds after the idea jelled in his mind and he stood to call Jack over, Trooper stood up too, moved right in front of him and stared, like he knew.

"Quit that," Brother told him. But the dog kept right on staring and began to pace anxiously back and forth.

"I mean it, True. I'm tired of you staring at me every time I get a decent idea," Brother said, even though Trooper'd never stared down any idea he'd had, and decent wasn't at all the appropriate adjective for his intended behavior.

The dog only seemed to pace faster and stare harder then, and if Brother moved, Trooper moved to cut him off.

"Come on," he cajoled, trying to reason with him. "Stop being selfish. Lighten up for once and quit sounding the tsunami alarm. I need a break. I need to stop thinking and feeling and paying attention, just for a few hours. I'll get you some biscuits and Jack some cookies and milk. It'll be fun. I won't be driving. We'll get a room somewhere, watch TV. You and me and Jack.

But Trooper kept staring, a dog possessed. So Brother sat down. And the second he did, Trooper quit staring and pacing and trotted over to some trees to take a pee.

"Sometimes I don't like you," Brother muttered, and at that moment he had the darkest of all the dark thoughts he'd had since Mem had died. One that made the idea of getting stupid drunk seem like a lark by comparison: What if I left you and Jack right here? What if I went inside to pee and just strolled out the back? Trooper would keep watching Jack, none the wiser. They trusted Brother. All he'd have to do is walk through the trees to the trucker lot and hitch a ride. Alone, hitching would be easier. Trooper'd be all right. Hadn't he been on his own before? Yes, he had, and he'd done fine. Maybe he'd scan the rest stop looking for Brother for a while, sniffing at cars. But he'd get the message sooner or later. And Jack? *Cole* had abandoned Jack, who was, technically, not Brother's problem. Jack might cry when he realized, cry like Brother had when his mother had left him at Mem's. But he'd get over it, Brother had, and Trooper wouldn't let anything bad happen to him. Somebody responsible would step up, maybe the mother and father of the kid Jack was playing with. They'd give him a better home than Cole ever had. They'd both be fine, better off without some depressed and scared-shitless seventeen-year-old at the broken wheel of their lives.

It took only a minute for these thoughts to seem perfectly sensible to Brother's worn-out mind. But as he stood to trash his empty wrappers and cans, he noticed Trooper staring hard at the little blond boy Jack was playing with. The boy was maybe thirty feet away, his mama's back turned while she fussed with the boy's daddy over something on a map. The boy and Jack were laughing and playing like mad with a red ball, the kind used for jacks,

41

taking turns throwing it into the air and then squatting under it with their hands splayed open, trying to catch it, though neither did. They tried though, laughing and carrying on as they threw it and dropped it over and over again. Then the blond boy finally got his chubby fingers around the ball, but as he tried to fist it, it popped out and dropped to the top of his shoe, where he kicked it straight toward the parking lot. He zoomed after it, laughing in delight the whole way. His mama whirled around too late to stop him, screaming, "Caleb! Caleb!" while she took off after him like a sprinter running a dash, the boy's daddy and Jack right behind her. But the kid was deaf and blind to everything but the ball, running like something greased across the grass. The ball bounced between two minivans, then across the path of a Mercedes. One split second later, a hair's width of time, Trooper streaked past everybody, running so full out his belly hair grazed the ground, then arced his body like a bow—curved it in a way Brother would have never thought possible—to slam Caleb sideways onto the grass. He hit hard, shaken, but sound. Inexplicably, Trooper veered the other way, sped into the parking lot and shot in a gray blur in front of a moving red pickup. The truck's brakes squealed. Brother went sick with fear and only then noticed that every person in that rest stop was standing as if frozen—men, women, and kids—everybody watching the unfolding tragedy in helpless horror, and how they all suddenly thawed, ran screaming and cheering toward the now-wailing boy, his relieved and sobbing parents, a laughing Jack, and the suddenly reappearing, red-ball retrieving, heroic herding dog.

His dog.

5

"THAT WAS THE MOST AMAZING thing I've ever seen," the girl said.

Brother opened his eyes and squinted up at her: black-haired, pony-tailed, pretty, about his age. He sat leaning against a tree, at the far edge of the admiring crowd giving Trooper his due. Jack stood proudly at Trooper's side while anybody with a camera or phone snapped a picture. Others patted Trooper and told him what a great dog he was. He soaked up the attention like warm sun.

"Why aren't you over there?" the girl asked.

Shame, Brother thought. *Because I don't have any right to be.*

The girl waited, her gaze and manner direct.

Finally he said, "Trooper's the hero, not me."

"That's pretty humble of you. Most people? They'd be right alongside him, taking all the credit themselves."

Brother sighed, bowed his head between his knees.

"You all right?" she said, squatting down beside him. "The little kid said you were here because your car broke down."

"On the highway. We were on our way to . . ." His brain seized; he couldn't remember the name. "The coast."

"Your car black? Real old? Six or eight miles back?"

He nodded.

"I saw that car. You waiting on a tow?"

Brother shook his head at her sensible idea, one that hadn't even occurred to him. "I was thinking—" He trailed off again, trying without success to put a complete, coherent sentence together before he spoke.

"I'm Kit," she said.

"Brother, Brother Grace."

"Some guy videoed the whole thing with his phone." She stopped, studied him hard. "You're really not doing so well, are you?"

Jack skipped over then, a burly, determined man in a red shirt behind him. "His," Jack said, pointing to Brother.

"Son," the man said, "I'll give you five hundred dollars cash for that dog."

"God, no," Brother said, covering his eyes with one hand.

"Six hundred, then," countered the man. "All I got on me."

"He's not selling his dog!" Kit cried, looking at the man as if he'd lost his mind.

"Seven-fifty," the man said, ignoring her. "But I'll have to give you a check."

Kit stepped between the man and Brother. Her eyes narrowed and her tone grew sharp. "He. Is. Not. Selling. His. Dog!"

The man backed up a step, unsure. He peered around Kit, who stood firmly rooted.

"Sir? Are you hard of hearing?" she said, and the man looked peeved but reluctantly moved off.

Brother looked up. "Thanks."

"You're welcome. It's hard to deal with half-wits when you're all in." She stared daggers at the man's back. "My dad's got a sign on his scrap yard: *No haggling. No custom jobs. No idiots.* Wishful thinking if you ask me."

Brother actually smiled a little and suddenly hoped this girl wouldn't hurry off. Beyond the crowd fawning over Trooper, another group of onlookers stood craning around the man who'd captured Caleb's rescue on his phone, and Caleb's mother tended to her son, his father kneeling beside her. The boy was whining about his ball. Caleb's father caught Brother's gaze. He said something to his wife, and then started Brother's way. Brother took a long breath, and a second later watched Kit step up again and hold out her hand to Caleb's dad. "I'm Kit, Kit Scripps. Brother's done in from all the excitement."

The man nodded like he knew. "Roger Thurman," he said to Brother. He offered his hand, which Brother shook. "My wife said you didn't want any notice, but I had to say thank you. Caleb owes his life to your wonderful dog. I can't even bear to think—" He stopped, choking a bit, and put a trembling hand to his mouth. "Words can't—I—we can't tell you how grateful we are."

The man's earnest eyes grew misty and he nodded firmly as if to say he hoped Brother understood, because he couldn't say anymore.

"I'm glad your boy's all right," Brother managed. He nodded as firmly, hoping to put a stop to all the gratitude.

The man stood uncomfortably for a few moments more and then said, "I'd best . . ." and gave a little wave before he went back to his family, rubbing Trooper's head as he went by.

Jack raced up, holding out the little red ball, pitted where Trooper's teeth had left marks. "Can I keep this?"

"That doesn't belong to you. Go give it back to the boy," Brother said firmly.

"Why?"

"You know why, Jack."

Jack glanced at the girl.

"I'm Kit," she said.

"I'm hungry." Jack pouted.

"You're always hungry," Brother told him. "Go do what I said."

Jack ran off to give Caleb his ball.

"You're good with him," Kit said. She took a phone out of her jeans' pocket and pressed a key. "Hey, Charlie . . . Oh no, I'm good, but I got a young guy here needs a tow . . . Frankie's fine, in the car sleeping it off . . . At the rest stop. The guy who needs the tow's here too, with his kid brother and his dog, but his car's seven or eight miles east. And wait till I tell you. The guy's dog saved a little boy from getting run over, which is what got my attention. Most amazing thing I've ever seen . . . His car's black. What's the make?" she asked Brother.

He told her, and when Kit repeated it into the phone, he heard the person on the other end whistle.

"Yeah," Kit laughed, "ancient artifact."

She listened, then said, "Thanks, Charlie. I'm going to ride them up to the pancake house. The little kid's hungry. Bring you something?" She listened again. "Will do."

She slipped the phone in her pocket. "We have a plan."

Brother thought those might be the four sweetest words he'd ever heard.

When Jack came running back, he, Trooper, and Brother trailed Kit like ducklings toward a white pickup with the name *Scripps' Scrap* on the doors.

"Charlie knows somebody who works on old cars," Kit said over her shoulder.

"Charlie?"

"My dad. I've always called him Charlie, I don't know why."

"You're not afraid to give rides to strangers?"

"You're way too tired-looking to be dangerous, and besides, Frank's here." She pointed to a big black Labrador retriever watching them closely out the rear window. The dog whined and trembled all over with excitement at the sight of her. "Anybody lays an unwelcome hand on me, Frank'll take his face off."

Brother couldn't tell if she was kidding or not.

"Frank's had a hard weekend, though. Mixed it up with a raccoon. Had to take him to pet emergency this morning for stitches and a rabies booster."

"He has rabies?"

"'Course not. He's had his shots. Booster within seventy-two hours, that's the law." She opened the passenger door, moved a thermos and a leash, then let an antsy Frank out the back. "Get acquainted, ya'll! I don't want any roughhousing in the car."

"Two dogs!" Jack said, elated.

Trooper and Frank did the dog-meets-dog stance and dance, sniffing and wagging. They hit it right off, and Jack laughed and waded in like one of the pack, getting his face and hands licked, first by one dog, then the other, then both at once.

Brother noticed several lines of fresh stitches on Frank's head and snout.

"Been down this road before, haven't we, Frankie?" Kit said. "Raccoon didn't make it, though. Frank doesn't take many prisoners."

"Shotgun!" Jack called, breaking free of the pack.

"No, sir! Dogs and Jack in back!" Kit ordered, and all three scrambled onto the rear seat. Brother got in front and buckled up, while Kit turned to Trooper, Jack, and Frank and pointing a finger at each in turn, ordered, "Sit! Seatbelt! Sit!" Each instantly did as he was told.

The crowd in the rest stop clapped, hooted, and waved as they drove out of the lot. Kit rolled down her window, smiling and waving like a queen.

✳ ✳ ✳

"So did you remember where on the coast you're headed?" she asked, once the pancake house waitress had taken their order.

Brother settled back into the vinyl booth and remembered the road map in his pocket. He spread it on the table. "There. Winter Island."

"Frank and I ride to the coast every chance we get, but we've never been there."

"Me either."

"So, why? I mean if you want to go to the beach, there are a lot easier places to get to."

Brother took a huge breath and let it out slowly.

"Okay," Kit said, "I'll mind my own business."

"It's not that," he said quickly. "It's just that it's so weird and complicated."

"Well, once you've got food in you, if you'd like to tell it, I'd like to hear."

After two cups of coffee, a large orange juice, and a four-egg western omelet, he told her everything—the short version—though he left out the part about almost abandoning Trooper and Jack. The food and telling her made him feel better. As Brother talked, Jack inhaled a dinner-plate-sized blueberry waffle with extra whipped cream and afterward fell asleep with a purple smile, his head in Kit's lap.

"God, I'm sorry," she said, when he told her about Mem, and "Poor little guy," when he sketched out Jack and Cole's story. Otherwise she sat silent, rapt, as her untouched scrambled eggs got cold.

"That's sad, but not so weird," she said, dabbing the worst of the blueberry stain from Jack's mouth with a damp napkin.

"I saved the weird for last," Brother said. "In Mem's bed we found the newspaper from the day before. There was an article with a photograph that looked exactly like me. Mem had circled the picture, like it surprised her too. But it wasn't my picture, wasn't me. It was a picture of Gabriel Grayson, Senator Gideon Grayson's son. His son—and, I'm pretty sure—my brother."

Kit didn't say anything at first. Brother drew the wrinkled clipping from his pocket and set it in front of her. Her eyes widened slightly. She read the short article, glancing up between paragraphs to compare the photograph to Brother.

"Here's what else I know," Brother said. "Mem's mother worked for the Grayson family when she and the senator were kids. Mem and my grandfather ran off when they were our age, and Mem was pregnant with my mother."

"What about your father?" Kit asked.

"Some young guy my mother ran off with, Mem said. She didn't know his name or if he knew he was a father. She mentioned drugs. That's all I know."

Kit glanced again at the paper, then back at Brother. "Don't take this the wrong way, but just me asking: you believe your grandmother, right?"

"I do," he said, and nodded.

"Which means at minimum there's a huge mystery," Kit said, raising her eyebrows. "And maybe Gideon Grayson's a big fat liar."

Brother wasn't sure what to say. The waitress brought the check and he reached for it, but Kit snatched it first. "I've got that."

She handed Brother the truck keys. "You take Jack out to the truck and let the dogs out while I splash some water on my face. Frank'll mind you, and he knows *sit* and *stay*."

He watched her make her way to the restroom at the back of

the restaurant, then he gathered up Jack and carried him out to the truck. He opened the door for the dogs and lay Jack on the backseat, taking off his flannel shirt to cover him. Kit was gone a good ten minutes. Brother started to worry that he shouldn't have told her or said so much, that she didn't believe him, or all of it at once, but finally she joined him on the strip of grass next to the parking lot and split her cold eggs between Trooper and Frank. She didn't say anything at first, but studied him, as though retaking his measure.

"Are you sorry you asked?" he said.

"Oh, gosh, no. It's just a lot to take in."

"It's that, all right." He looked down the highway, at the fast-food places, gas stations, and taillights of traffic in the dark. This time last week he'd been changing old men's diapers and that was his future as far as he could see. Now, he didn't know what the next five minutes would bring.

"I'm really sorry about your grandmother," she said. "She sounds like a wonderful person. All the time you talked, I sat there thinking what I'd do if anything happened to Charlie, how *that* alone might derail me. I can't even imagine." She closed her eyes, shook her head. "Plus a brother you didn't know about and Gideon Grayson and all the rest. It's all so . . ."

He waited, wondering what her word for it would be.

"Confusing," she said finally. "I mean, if I lost Charlie and at the same time found out that everything I thought I knew about myself and my family maybe I didn't? Plus I got stuck minding a kid that wasn't mine and I hadn't slept and then my car blew up?

You know, I'm a strong person, but that might push me right over the edge."

Brother laughed, he couldn't help it.

"You think that's funny?"

"No, I think it's *true*. I almost *did* go over the edge. Right before True saved that little boy." He looked at his feet. "I thought about leaving them both in that rest stop. That I'd catch a ride with a trucker and bolt."

She snorted.

"What?" he said, looking up. "You think *that's* funny?"

"I think it's *human*," she said. "You wouldn't have done it, though."

"I might have."

"I don't believe it."

"You don't know me."

Kit shrugged. "You're right, I don't. I've known you all of two hours. So call it Kit's intuition, but I don't think so. I think you're a stayer, like Charlie, like me. Besides, know the man's dog, know the man, that's what I say. I do have to tell you something important, though, before we take Charlie some dinner, tuck you and Jack in our spare room, and all get eight or ten hours of sleep."

"I couldn't ask you—" he began, but she held up her hand and he waited.

"There's a lot of bad feeling around here toward Gideon Grayson," she said, "no love lost. People here used to fall all over themselves loving that man, like the folks you talk about where you come from. Not anymore. Not since a few years ago when he got the idea of putting a landing strip for the Navy on top of a lot

52

of local people's farms and businesses. People here fought it for a long while, but nothing came of their fighting until a bunch of environmentalists, crusading to save some bird, forced the senator to consider moving his runway someplace else, to wipe out some *other* people's businesses and farms and birds in some other part of the state. But the fight's not over by a long shot. And people here have long memories. Doesn't sit well with them that he came after the little that was theirs, what they'd worked for all their lives. So, my advice? Till people get to know you, maybe don't mention you might be related, you know?"

"I shouldn't have told you."

"Oh no, you did right telling me. My mother cut out when I was a baby, so I learned early not to hold people's kin against them. And if I heard you right, you're headed to the coast to *sneak up* on Gideon Grayson—whose spare bastard kin you likely are—and yell, 'Surprise!' Is that right?"

Brother smiled. She actually made it sound fun. "Pretty much."

"*That* I would pay real money to see." She turned to her dog. "Whaddaya say, Frankie? Feel like a little ride?"

Frank sprang to life then, as if he'd understood, and gave a resounding triple yip. "Frankie loves riding. Only one thing he likes better"—Kit lowered her voice—"and that's the w-a-t-e-r."

"You have to spell in front of him?"

She nodded. "That one word in particular."

"Or?"

"You ever seen a candied-up four-year-old the day after Halloween? Like that."

"I couldn't ask you to drive us."

"One, I'm offering. And two, after the last twenty-four hours, Frank and I could both use a treat. Just what the vet ordered."

"Don't you have school?"

"I take a day now and then."

"Won't your father mind?"

"We're going to stop and get him a heart attack on a bun at the drive-thru. But just between you and me and the road signs, Charlie'll be sacked out in front of the TV by now. He's hard-working weekdays, but pretty much sleeps and watches sports, nights and weekends. It's just him and me. Liza only stayed long enough to squeeze me out and hand me off to Charlie."

"Liza?"

"The person momentarily my mother. You and I have that in common. Anyway, Charlie can find me anytime by cell. Frank and I drive to the beach all the time. He lives to swim."

"Isn't the water cold now?" Brother asked, and the words weren't out of his mouth when Frank started to quake and whine. His black eyes grew wide and glazed over, and after a few seconds he alternated his whining with short, joyous barks and yips. The barking and yipping grew steadily louder as Frank started to pace from side to side, straining at his leash. People in the pancake house gawked at them out the window. Even Trooper moved off a few paces, sat down, and stared.

"Now you've done it!" Kit said.

"Done what?"

"Lit the fuse, that's what. Honestly, what did I *just* say?"

Brother didn't answer, afraid he'd make things worse—not

that Frank would have heard anything over his yapping and whimpering. Kit heaved a testy sigh.

"Frank!" she shouted at the frantic dog. "Frank!"

Frank suddenly stopped and sat abruptly down, looking like a sheepish, hyperactive child who'd been called out by a parent. He sat squirming and trembling on his butt, barely able to contain his excitement. He looked from Kit to Brother to Trooper, quivering like something spring-loaded. Brother thought it wouldn't have taken much to send him rocketing into space.

"Now, *Frank*," Kit said firmly. "You listen to me. Are you listening? We'll get to the w-a-t-e-r in due time, but we are going to sleep first and then ride for a while. So calm down."

Frank shook some more and yipped softly.

"Stop that right now, Frank, or I'm leaving you home. *Home*, you understand me?"

And it seemed to Brother that Frank did understand. The dog kept shaking and yipping for maybe ten seconds more while Kit stared him down, but then, by sheer force of dog will, he lay down with his head facing front between his paws, his pathetic and pleading eyes looking from Kit to Trooper to Brother to Kit again.

"I'm sorry," Brother said.

Kit sighed. "Watch you don't do it again, especially while we're in the car. Frank's a junkie for H_2O. We'll make it up to him by buying him a b-u-r-g-e-r when we get Charlie's. That'll put him out of his misery for tonight so we can all get some sleep. Frank's form of doggie downer."

Brother regarded Frank, who was still looking hopefully from one of them to the other. "I've caused you enough trouble."

"I'm sorry, but there's no option now that you've spilled the Adam's ale. Besides, what goes around comes around, right, Frankie?" she said, smiling at both dogs. "We're agents of serious karmic forces fixed on Gideon Grayson and Trooper the wonder dog."

✳ ✳ ✳

Kit drove faster than even Cole driving The Elms's old ambulance, careering around pokey traffic, accelerating through caution lights, and pushing the yellow-lined limits of passing zones, but Brother sat back, closed his eyes, and for the moment put himself in her so-far capable hands. He must have drifted off, because what seemed only moments later, Kit pulled into a driveway behind a larger, black pickup with *Scripps' Scrap* also written on its side. Brother glanced at the bag in his lap.

"I try to tell Charlie that two double cheeseburgers, a soda, and a pint of Rocky Road do not constitute a nutritious dinner, but does he listen?" She made a resigned face and shook her head. "C'mon in. We'll give Charlie his grub, put you and Jack in the spare room, and head out first thing in the morning. I need a shower. I feel like I'm covered in dog."

They both grabbed the burger bag at the same time.

"I've got this and the dogs," she said. "You get Jack."

"Thank you," he said, keeping hold of the bag for a second longer to hold her attention.

"You're welcome." She tugged it away and opened the truck's

double door. The dogs poured out, shoulder-to-shoulder, fric and frac, leaving Jack curled up under Brother's shirt on the backseat. Brother gently lifted him and followed behind.

"Hey, darling," said a sleepy man from his recliner, without glancing away from a basketball game on the largest TV Brother had ever seen. Charlie was a portly fifty-something in sweatpants and a flannel shirt, with a head of thick silver hair. "How's our Frank?"

"A-1 again," Kit said.

"That's good," Charlie said absently.

"That's Brother, by the way, standing behind your chair. His dog's out back with Frank, and the little boy's Jack. They're staying the night in the spare room."

"Brother Grace, sir," Brother said, shifting Jack to his left shoulder. He stepped to the side of the chair and extended his free hand to Kit's father.

"Charlie Scripps. Pleased to know you," the man said, realizing he had company and heaving himself up to a semi-sitting position. He shook Brother's hand warmly, though his eyes cut back to the game.

"Here's your supper," Kit said, setting the sack on his lap.

"Bless you," Charlie said. He slid out a sandwich. "You didn't let them put any of that rabbit food on it, did you?"

"Nope," Kit answered, motioning for Brother to follow her with Jack down a short hall. She pointed Brother to a room on the left. "All nutrition-free, just how you like it. *With* fries."

"Have I ever told you you're the best child anybody could ever have, and that I thank the Lord you don't believe in that you were born?"

"Every day."

"Well, it's true."

"Back at you without the Our Father."

Brother put Jack on the bed, and followed Kit back into the living room. It was a clean, comfortable ranch that smelled of coffee grounds and sleeping dog, with pictures of father and daughter at various ages, places, and seasons on the paneled walls: Kit, maybe seven, building a lopsided snowman with rebar arms; Kit and Charlie, say two years later, laughing in the seat of a junked Ferris wheel, and Kit at maybe thirteen grinning atop a hillside of crushed cars. Brother had not one family photograph and looked at Kit's feeling he'd missed out.

"Your car's at the Burnett Brothers' shop," Charlie told Brother. "Kit knows where."

"We'll stop in there tomorrow to see if they can get it going. If not, Frank and I'll drive them on to the coast."

"It's really kind of you to offer," Brother said to both of them, "but I really can't let you—"

"It's decided," Kit said sternly.

"Might as well argue with a cyclone," Charlie said. "She and Frank go coastal all the time, so you're in good hands. A good guard dog's the best thing the father of any teenage girl can buy. Best decision I ever made."

"Yeah, except that we didn't buy him and I decided to bring him home from the yard," Kit said, then pecked her father lightly on the cheek and headed down the hall. "I'm taking a shower."

"Just call me when you get there," Charlie called after her, then glanced at Brother. "In about twenty minutes, the way she drives."

The man knew his daughter.

"Hush now," Kit called, "you're scaring him."

For the first time Charlie looked squarely at Brother and laughed. "You scare easy, you better bail now."

6

MITCHELL BURNETT ROSE FROM UNDER the Galaxie's open hood and stepped back in wonder. "This car's got original parts!"

Burnett Brothers' Garage stood alone at a sleepy crossroads, a white-framed building with a single bay. Vehicles of every kind—tractors, dirt bikes, golf carts, trucks, and cars—were parked pell-mell in the surrounding gravel lot, but what most drew Brother's attention was a white, vertical dotted line dividing the garage roof in two, and the shallow splintered gash at the line's very top.

"When their mother died, the Burnetts argued over the property," Charlie explained when he dropped Brother and Trooper off. "One night, the abler Burnett got drunk, climbed up there with a brush and a bucket of paint and drew that line. Then he climbed back up with a chainsaw to carve off his half."

Brother considered this. "What was he going to do with it once he finished?"

"That's what the judge asked him," Charlie said, shaking his head.

"So I guess they worked it out?" Brother asked.

"You'll see. The Burnetts are odd, but they can fix anything you can break."

Kit, Jack, and Frank had gone for supplies and would swing back by for Brother and Trooper. A night's sleep, a hot shower, and Kit's breakfast smoothie served with her entertaining talk had lifted Brother's mood. As she put it: "Sure, there's a lot scary, strange, and sad about your deal, but how many people get to start their lives all over again?"

He liked the way she saw things. She was tough-minded and pragmatic, cut to the beating heart of the matter, but scrounged the humor and light in even the worst situations. Unlike Cole's jokey, hit-the-jackpot optimism, she found the true upside. After breakfast, they'd searched the Internet for any information or update on his twin but found only the newspaper article Brother already had, plus a short follow-up plea from the senator's family to respect their privacy at this difficult time. "On the one hand," Kit said, "it's weird there aren't any family pictures, but when you think how most politicians trot out their kids like trained ponies, it's kinda nice Grayson doesn't, you know?"

Mitchell Burnett chattered amiably while he worked under Brother's hood, relating bits of his and his brother Carl's personal history. Their garage had limped along for thirty-some years serving local drivers, farmers, and homeowners, as Mitchell made no distinction among machines. If a thing broke, he made it whole—whether car, tractor, or washing machine—after his brother Carl scoured the Internet for parts. "Only 27,000 miles on this engine," Mitchell marveled. "Not even."

"Somebody's fooled with that odometer," snarled a voice from a small office marked with a hand-lettered sign: *Jesus is NOT coming.*

"Carl's so distrustful," Mitchell told Brother. "Always has to be something nefarious where he's concerned."

A guffaw came from the office and an older man in coveralls rolled out the door in a wheelchair. He resembled Mitchell plus ten years, wire-rimmed glasses, fifty pounds, and a scraggly gray ponytail. "*Nefarious,*" he said. "Never heard Mitchell use a word that big before."

"I'd like to see *him* fix this engine," Mitchell said. "Claims he's my kin, but I say he was switched at birth with a water moccasin."

Carl ignored this, sized Brother up. "What's your name, son?"

"Brother Grace, sir."

"Where you from?"

"Schuyler, North Carolina."

"Where you headed?"

"Winter Island," Brother said, instantly thinking he should have kept that to himself.

"Never heard of either one," Carl said. "You a preacher?"

"He's no preacher," Mitchell sneered, before Brother could answer. "He's a kid."

"What other kind of name is Brother Grace, I'd like to know?" Carl asked Brother, and it dawned on him that they weren't so much speaking to him, as to each other *through* him.

He started to say that it was the only name anybody'd

ever called him, but Mitchell was quicker. "Carl spent two semesters at the university in Chapel Hill. Thinks he knows everything."

"More than some." Carl sniffed.

"And ever since he got that computer, he thinks he's God Almighty," Mitchell said.

Carl rolled in front of Brother and twirled himself 360 degrees. "You see any computer?"

Mitchell snorted. "Probably got the cord up his ass."

Carl rolled his eyes, and Mitchell turned back to the Galaxie's engine. Their testy back-and-forth made Brother dizzy. When they didn't have an audience did they talk at all?

"Don't see many carburetors anymore," Mitchell said, changing the subject. "Nowadays everybody's got fuel injection. Lucky you pulled off the highway when you did. Shape these belts and hoses are in, don't expect this car's done distance in a while. Guess you don't have triple A?"

Brother shook his head.

"Cell?"

"No, sir."

"Too bad. This thing's a relic."

Brother saw Carl squinting through the Galaxie's side window at the backseat. He pointed at the urns. "Those what I think they are?"

"My family's ashes, sir," Brother said. "It seemed disrespectful to put them in the trunk."

Carl scowled. "Why don't you put them in the *ground*?"

"Not every family has a plot," Mitchell said, glaring at his brother. "Maybe it's nobody's goddamned business."

"My garage, my business."

"*Our* garage," Mitchell corrected.

"Only because Mother died before she made a will," Carl told Brother. "But she said it was mine. I was her favorite."

"He dreamed that," Mitchell countered, shaking his head. "Takes too many painkillers."

"Do not," Carl said fiercely. "He'd sing a different tune if he'd had to fight in Vietnam like I did."

"Oh, here we go." Mitchell sighed and shook his head.

Brother was about to say his grandfather had been in Vietnam, but Carl cut him off.

"Like he knows dick about anything!"

"Now *there's* a fancy word," Mitchell told Brother pointedly. "At least I know enough not to quit college like a dumbass and get myself drafted into the war."

"Yeah, like quitting high school did wonders for *his* prospects," Carl shot back, and rolled furiously into the office.

Brother sighed and reached in through the open passenger-side window to pat Trooper's head. The dog's muzzle rose to his gentle touch, and he softly licked Brother's hand. He tried to imagine where his own brother might be at this moment. Home? Back at some fancy school? Still recuperating in a hospital somewhere? If he and his twin had grown up together, would they be as sniping as these two? Before now, he'd imagined only what he and his brother's separation had cost them, never considering what they might have been spared.

Carl rolled back out the office door. "Winter Island," he said, actually speaking *to* Mitchell this time, pointing to a printout. "Never guess who owns half of it."

"Who?"

"Who do we hate more than taxes, war, and dry counties?"

"You're kidding me."

Carl nodded forcefully. "That Gray*son* of a bitch himself."

Mitchell turned to Brother. "The one thing we agree on."

"That S.O.B. wanted to put a landing field on top of Burnett Brothers' Garage," Carl said. "*Right smack dab on top.*"

"Before that, we actually voted for that piece of crap," Mitchell said, disgusted.

"Before we knew he'd turn on us like he did," Carl put in. "That landing field really opened our eyes. We sat out the last election."

Brother remembered Mem saying how people so often voted against their own self-interests and thought how she'd have approved of the Burnetts' wising up. "You said the senator owns half of the island," he said. "Who owns the other half?"

Carl studied the printout. "Says it's a nature preserve Senator Asshole donated to the state. Probably just to put his name on it, protect his own property, and get himself a big fat tax deduction. I'd like to know why he didn't put his landing field there. Let those navy boys land in his own backyard."

Kit pulled up then in Charlie's bigger black truck, and Brother went outside before Mitchell and Carl got around to asking him why he was headed where he was. He supposed he could say he was going to the nature preserve, but he was a terrible liar and worried Mitchell and Carl would see right through him.

Kit hopped out of the truck wearing a red baseball cap and sunglasses, followed by Frank in a yellow bandanna.

"What's with the truck?"

"I switched with Charlie. More room in the crew cab."

"Did Warren call?"

She shook her head. "Not a peep."

At her suggestion, he'd left her cell number with Warren and Bayliss in case Cole showed.

Jack slid out of the backseat wearing swim trunks over his jeans and a yellow diving mask, a snorkel, and flippers. He said something that sounded like, "Wook itta tool tuff hit sot me."

"What?"

Jack lifted the mask. "Look at the cool stuff Kit got me."

"Did you thank her?"

"Thanks," Jack said, and slapped off to explore the junk in the lot.

Kit opened the truck camper, showing off dog food and towels. "You can put the rest of your stuff in here. Your car fixed?"

"Nope."

"Worth fixing?"

"We didn't get that far."

"They're chatty and you're too polite. C'mon."

Kit strode inside with purpose, Brother trailing behind.

"Woo-woo, boy," Carl said to Brother. "My estimation of you just went up two hundred percent. You're the first male besides Frank she's ever brought in here. I know boys who'd give their right arm if Kitten here even noticed they were alive. She doesn't take up with anybody.

"It's plain Kit, Carl, like I've told you a hundred times. K-I-T, like Kit Carson. Plus, it's not like that," she said, and it surprised Brother to feel his heart sink.

"You'll always be Kitten to me," Carl said.

Kit smirked and looked at Mitchell. "What's the verdict?"

"Depends," he said.

"On?"

"What the customer wants to do," Mitchell said to Brother.

"What he means, Kitten," Carl said, "is just because it can be fixed doesn't mean you'd want to."

"Don't be saying what I mean," Mitchell told him. "I mean it's up to Brother."

Carl sniffed.

"So you *can* fix it?" Kit asked Mitchell.

"Darling, anything can be fixed," Mitchell said.

Kit looked exasperated. "Well, what would *you* do if it were *yours*?"

Mitchell waved a hand at the machine-littered lot. "As you see, I'm not one to give up on things, except maybe Carl, but even I'd probably put her out of her misery in your daddy's yard."

"You?" she asked Carl.

"I was going to say that, but now Mitchell's said it, I've got to think of something else."

Kit sighed.

"Tell you what," Mitchell said. "We'll keep it here while you think on it. You decide you want it fixed, Carl'll order the parts. You don't, we'll tow her over to Charlie's."

"Thank you," Brother told them. "Thank you both."

"Either way, you take your family remains with you," Carl said crossly, and went back into the office.

Brother took out money to pay for the diagnosis and the tow, but Mitchell waved him off, said they'd settle later, and slipped him a card with their phone number on it, saying softly, "If you decide to fix it, I'll give you a good price on the work."

But there was nothing wrong with Carl's hearing, and as Brother shifted the urns and his and Jack's belongings from the Galaxie to the truck, Carl carped that somebody's bleeding heart was going to put them in the poorhouse. Mitchell groused back that even a crippled junkie cheapskate could see that the Galaxie and its contents were all in the world Brother had. They were still going at it as Kit, Brother, Jack, and the dogs pulled out of the lot, Kit smiling and shaking her head, Jack starting up the sailor song, and Brother musing on chainsaws and dotted lines and what life with his own brother might soon be like.

7

IT SEEMED ODD TO BROTHER THAT the Winter Island ferry slacked off in the season of the same name. The last ferry had left Satterfield Point at four that afternoon. The next didn't run until the following morning due to the seasonal schedule and budget shortfalls, as the dock sign said.

While Jack tried his new swim mask in the nearby shallows and Kit threw tennis balls for Trooper and a water-drunk Frank, Brother stood on the ferry dock, taking in the Atlantic, as dark and unsettled as his life.

The afternoon was gray and cold, the incoming tide hypnotic. He watched it mesmerized, lulled by the current, as if under a spell. The great mother, Mem's name for it, seemed right, the sea both vaster than he'd ever imagined and as mysterious and un-knowable as his own mother, really his entire past. Before it, all his recent tragedies seemed far off and his worries, in the wide, watery scheme of things, small. Near the shore the waves crested and broke, rose and broke again, the sea like a restless, living thing. He thought he understood what the ancients must have felt at their first sight of the sea: awestruck, astonished that they had arrived at the end of the world.

He thought of the church story of Jonah and the whale. He wondered what waited out there for him. His thoughts ebbed and flowed as the sea spoke to him in its watery tongue. Time slowed and seemed a puny construct. He'd never understood why people became preachers or poets, but he had an idea now. And he felt something else. Something about the view, the water, the dock, the sharp salt air made him wonder if he'd been here before.

Trooper and Frank raced to him and shook off, and the cold shower brought him back to the present.

"You okay?" Kit said, coming to stand beside him. "You look a little overwhelmed."

"I'm fine except for being soaked," Brother said.

"Jack's hungry."

The boy ran up, wet through from the knees down, and shouted, "Pancakes!"

"First we gotta get dry clothes on you, buddy," Brother said.

"Noooo!" Jack said through chattering teeth, and they all laughed.

Once he was redressed and dry, they headed into Satterfield, which they'd skirted earlier trying to make the ferry. Nearest the water they passed fishing boats, weather-beaten and businesslike, then neighborhoods of squat wooden houses on overgrown yards.

For the first time all day, Jack was tuckered out and quiet.

During the nearly three-hour drive to the coast, he'd jabbered or sung songs, making long conversation hard. Brother had managed to find out that Kit was headed to college in Chapel Hill after she graduated in June and that she proudly maintained a 4.0. Every hour or so, her phone rang. She glanced at the screen but didn't answer it while she drove. He'd enjoyed her full attention for a day, but he saw now that she had a wider circle, a future, a full life, and despite what Carl had said, likely a boyfriend to go back to. Just as well. What did a carless, jobless, phoneless, hard-up boy with few prospects have to offer a girl like that? Nada. Less.

Even so, he couldn't keep himself from hoping she felt otherwise. At one point in their drive from Bailey to the coast, Brother had dozed off and woke to see her glancing repeatedly out her driver's side window, saying to Jack, "And that one says, 'Hurry home, Angel, we miss you.'" Brother took in the long chain-link fence hung with homemade signs drawn or painted on what appeared to be bed sheets. Sign after sign, brightly lettered and illustrated, fluttered or ballooned in the breeze. "My Daddy Is a Superhero!" said one in orange block letters, next to a child's drawing of an airplane. "Welcome Home, Dale!" said another in rainbow colors. "We Love You, Petey Boy," said a third in army green.

"Oh, geez. Those things get me every time," Kit said, seeing that Brother was awake. She wiped away tears with the back of her hand. "Reach me a tissue, will you?"

It took him a second to realize they were passing one of the military bases that crowded this part of the state. He thought of his grandfather, who, unlike Dale and Petey Boy, had not come home from his war. He handed her a tissue from the box at his feet and held the wheel while she blew.

The town of Satterfield was maybe five miles from the ferry dock. It wasn't any metropolis, but it was two stoplights and a warning signal up on Schuyler. Brother saw a hardware store, a realty company, and a post office with a faded flag, in addition to a number of businesses—a surf shop, an ice-cream parlor, a seafood restaurant—closed for the off-season. Kit parked on the street near a small, dimly lit diner. She, Brother, and Jack got out, leaving the dogs in the car.

The diner was spare and empty except for a girl hunched over a book behind the cash register. "Ya'll sit anywhere. Menu's on the chalkboard at the back," she said without looking up. She was about Brother's age and pretty in a scrubbed way, at least he thought so before she glanced up. Her face instantly hardened as she spat, "You got a lot of nerve coming in here."

"Excuse me?" Kit said.

"I wasn't talking to you," said the girl. She looked at Brother. "I *said*, you got a lot of *nerve* coming in here," she repeated, raising her volume a notch. "Don't act like you don't know what I mean."

"I'm sorry, I *don't* know what you mean," Brother said. "We just got into town and we'd like to get some dinner, please."

The girl stared at him in furious disbelief. "Well, you can get it somewhere else!"

"Why's she so mad?" Jack asked, and hugged Brother's legs.

"Could you maybe watch how you talk around the little boy?" Kit said quietly.

The girl stood and slammed her book on the counter, making them jump. Her face was all outrage, not the least bit pretty anymore. "Don't you even think you can talk to me like that, girlie."

Kit's eyes widened like Frank's might before he lunged, and Brother put a steadying hand on her arm.

"Please," he said to the girl. "You've mistaken me for someone else. I've just today come into town, a town I've never been in before."

The girl reared back. "What kind of idiot do you take me for? I'm not like those airheads you date," she said, glaring at Kit. "*I* have a brain in my head. So get your sorry ass out of here. You and your friends can starve for all I care. You're not eating here."

"She thinks you're *him*," Kit said.

"I don't think anything, girlie, I know exactly who he is."

"Look—" Brother began, but the girl cut him off.

"Look nothing," she snapped. "You thought a bad haircut and some old clothes would make it so I didn't know you?"

"Miss, please," Brother said, searching for something to say that might calm her, but this time Mem's lessons failed him.

"Don't you dare *Miss* me. Just get outta here before I call the police."

"Let's go, Brother," Kit said, tugging on his arm. "You're not going to change her mind." She looked at the girl. "You don't know how wrong you are."

The girl stood firm. "Get out! Get out now, and don't ever come back!"

Jack seemed about to burst into tears. Brother picked him up and strode straight to the truck, his face burning, but burning with what? Shame? How could he be ashamed of something he hadn't done? Rage? How could he be mad about an obvious mistake? Even so, he was mad at the outright injustice of it, but also at his brother for being the cause. He opened the truck door, waking Trooper and Frank. Trooper looked at him questioningly, no alert in sight.

"Thanks for the warning," Brother told him.

"Why's she so mad at you?" Jack said, climbing into the back.

"She's not mad at me, buddy."

"She looked real mad."

"That was intense," Kit said, getting in. "Guess Satterfield feels about junior the way Bailey feels about senior. Sure you don't want me to stick around tonight, ride over with you on the ferry? Maybe you ought not face these people alone."

Right then, he wanted her to stay about as much as he'd ever wanted anything, but he shook his head. "You've done enough. Way more than I can ever repay. If I haven't said thanks—"

"You've said it plenty. But if I leave here and something bad happens to you before Frank and I can get back, I'll tell you this: There will be *hell to pay*."

Kit seethed as she started the truck and gunned it past the diner for good measure. She pulled into a convenience store in the next block. "Shall I get us all some highly delicious and nutritious dinner after I gas up?" she said with a fake smile.

Brother took out his wallet and handed her some bills. "Thanks. I'm not sure I could go through that again tonight."

"You want to come?" she asked Jack.

But Jack was facing the rear seat with his feet on Frank and his head on Trooper's haunch. The boy shook his head. "I'm not hungry."

Brother and Kit exchanged worried looks.

"I'll bring you a surprise," Kit told him softly, but he didn't answer.

Brother watched her pump gas and head inside, as sure and competent as someone twice her age. She had Mem's sense of outrage and decency, as well as her foolhardy confidence that the world couldn't hurt her unless she let it. He barely knew her, but he'd miss her when she was gone. Jack sniffled and Brother turned to the backseat. "What's going on, buddy?"

"Nothing."

"Not nothing. Did that girl scare you?"

"No."

"What then?"

Jack buried his face in Trooper's belly and said something too muffled for Brother to hear.

"Say again?"

"Is Cole ever coming back?"

Brother sighed. Both dogs lifted their heads, but Jack kept his face buried in Trooper's fur. Curled up between the dogs with his knees to his chest, he looked so small. Brother had been so mired in his own problems, he hadn't been much use to Jack since Mem had died, hadn't thought how Cole's disappearing and Mem's dying and everything that followed might have shaken the little boy. Brother thought now of all the times Cole had dropped off

Jack "for a few minutes," leaving the boy for hours. Jack had downed cases of cereal and gallons of milk, while Mem told him stories she knew, after which she'd tucked him in Brother's bed. Jack had lost a lot, too.

He reached back, put his hand on Jack's leg. "Yes, buddy, he's coming back."

"Why isn't he here now?"

"He's having some Cole time—you know, like he's done before. He just hasn't caught up with us yet."

"He's never been gone this long."

"I know. But we've been on the road. He'll catch up."

"When?"

"I don't know," Brother said. "But soon, I bet. And wherever he is and whatever he's doing, I bet it's something to make life better for you and him."

"What?"

"I don't know, something good."

"What if he doesn't *ever* come back?"

Brother's heart sank. Mem wasn't ever coming back, or Jack's parents either. *Don't ever come back!* the angry girl at the diner had said.

"He will, any day now," Brother told him, and petted Trooper. His dog eyed him calmly. *Please let your calm mean Cole's okay. Please you and Cole don't make me a liar.*

Kit stayed inside the store a long time, walking up and down the aisles, taking items off the shelves, heating something in the microwave, and then chatting up the man at the checkout.

When she got back to the truck, she passed Brother a big plastic sack, saying, "Best I could do," then cut her eyes to the rear seat, lifting a questioning eyebrow.

"I'll tell you when we get to the dock," Brother said.

"I've got news for you, too."

"News from who?"

"The mini-mart guy."

"The mini-mart guy?"

"Okay, not the *New York Times*. But better than nothing."

They rode in silence back to the ferry dock, where Kit threw the ball for Frank while Brother and Trooper saw to Jack. He whined when Brother tried to coax him to eat a little of the mac and cheese Kit had heated up at the store. He flung the pirate eye patch she'd bought him into the dirt, then threw a kicking and punching tantrum, howling over and over how he wanted to go *home*, wanted *Cole*, wanted both *now, now, now*. He wouldn't be calmed or consoled. Finally Brother left him in the truck to wear himself out. Brother set up Kit's tent behind some scrubby bushes in sight of the dock. She thought of everything.

Afterward, he coaxed a quieter Jack to pee, then zipped him inside the sleeping bag. He ducked out of the tent as Trooper ducked in and lay across the doorway. "I'll be back soon, I promise, okay buddy?" Brother said, but Jack didn't answer, turned away, even from Trooper.

"I could really hurt that waitress," Kit said, as she and Frank joined Brother near the truck. Night was falling fast and her cheeks, lips, and nose were ruddy from the cold off the water.

"I guess she's got her reasons. And Cole's being gone isn't her fault."

"Has he ever been gone this long?"

Brother shook his head. "I've had so much else to think about I haven't let myself worry. He's not the most reliable person, but he's usually good where Jack's concerned. I just keep telling myself he didn't consider Mem might die. Sick as she was, I didn't."

"You're nicer than I am," Kit said quietly, glancing at the tent. And then, mock sternly, "I want that tent *back*."

Brother smiled, hearing it as a promise that he'd see Kit and Frank again soon. "I'll take care of it," he said, continuing to speak in code.

"You'd better," she said. "I don't like leaving."

"I appreciate that, but you should get on the road."

She sighed, got a towel out of the camper and squatted to dry Frank. The dog looked longingly at the water, but she opened the truck door and said, "Get in the back now," and he reluctantly did.

"So what did the mini-mart guy say?"

"God, I totally forgot. Your brother's off somewhere hush-hush, recovering."

"Where?"

"The guy didn't know. But he did know what from."

"What?"

"Heroin."

"He overdosed on *heroin*?"

"That's what he said."

"The mini-mart guy?" Brother said doubtfully.

Kit smiled a little back. "Yeah, so maybe not gospel?"

She took out her phone then and pressed a button. "Hey, Charlie . . . I'm fine, just starting back . . . I'll tell you all about it when we get there . . . I will . . . I love you, too."

They stood awkwardly, looking at each other, the sea, the tent, and each other again, not saying anything. A hug or a kiss seemed presumptuous, a handshake too formal. Then he realized. "What about the urns?"

"I've already thought about that. I'll keep them for now. You got enough to keep track of."

Which was true. And it meant he would definitely see her again.

"You don't mind?"

"Frank and I'll take good care of everybody. Call me if you find a phone."

"I will."

And a moment later, as if to avert any more awkwardness, she got in the truck, gunned the engine, and drove off. He watched her taillights until they disappeared in the dark, half expecting and half hoping she might turn around and come back. But she didn't, for which he was relieved, because she'd done too much for him already, and sorry because it wasn't nearly as much as he wanted.

He checked on Jack, asleep now, and patted Trooper's head. He used his duffel as a pillow and lay on the dock. He watched the ocean and ate the cold mac and cheese and a bag of corn chips, washing them down with a quart of milk. He wondered about what the waitress had yelled, if what the mini-mart guy said was true, what Kit was thinking about as she drove, and where his brother was and where Cole was and what they were doing. His thoughts surged in waves from Kit to Gabriel to Cole to Jack to Mem to Gabriel again, returning to Kit—until he slept and swam all night after the dolphin, toward what he could not see.

8

Two blasts of the ferry's horn woke them.

An early morning rain had chased Brother off the dock and into the tent with Trooper and Jack, where they slept in a heap, like a litter. At the sound of the horn, Trooper shot through the tent flap, Jack stumbling out sleepily behind him. The two of them raced to the dock and barked in chorus at the ferryman. Hooded in a gray poncho, he was an ominous sight in the rain and fog, like something from a myth, until he laughed at the barking pair and shouted to Brother in a friendly drawl, "Sorry I'm late. Want help with your gear?"

"Sure, thanks," Brother called.

While Jack and Trooper made pit stops in the dunes, Brother stuffed Kit's sleeping bag into its sack and packed the box of granola bars—the last of their mini-mart supplies—in the top of his duffel. Kit would be finishing her breakfast with Charlie or at school by now, back in the rhythm of her normal life. He envied her and missed her, both.

The ferryman deftly collapsed the tent and slung it over his shoulder.

"I want to drive the boat!" Jack yelled, running up.

"Can't let you drive," the ferryman said, glancing at Brother, "but you're my only fares, so you can ride up top if you want."

"Up top!" Jack shouted, and Brother nodded.

The ferryman led them up the stairs from the lower deck to the pilothouse above it. The ferry was small, with room for ten or fifteen cars, but spacious with no other passengers aboard.

"I want to see sharks!" Jack said excitedly, scrambling onto the window seat.

Brother sat beside him, thankful the tantrum of the night before had passed and that the ferryman didn't seem to recognize him. Trooper jumped on the seat and scanned the water for someone to save.

"I want to see man-eating sharks!" Jack said.

"Don't be too sure about that," the ferryman said, smiling. "We don't get those around here if we're lucky." He started the engines and steered them away from the dock, which receded swiftly behind them. Trooper whined softly, and Brother patted his head as the shoreline vanished in fog.

"If you go on deck, you'll want to put life jackets on," the ferryman said, pointing at orange vests heaped under the seat. Out of his poncho, he looked hardly older than Brother. "It's four dollars, round-trip, whenever. We collect on the front end."

"Are there whales?" Jack asked, as Brother paid.

"I've never seen one," said the ferryman. "Might see dolphins, though."

Jack and Brother both looked out the window then, Brother thinking about Mem and his dream, but the weather obscured nearly everything. After a few minutes, even Trooper tired of watching fog and empty gray water and hopped down to sniff at the tools, ropes, and mechanical parts on the floor. Brother got out Trooper's bowl and fed him.

"There's cocoa in my thermos." The ferryman pointed to a knapsack on a forward bench. "Help yourselves."

Brother thanked him and poured steaming cocoa into the thermos cup, not seeing any other. "You don't mind us using this?"

"Not if you don't. I've had my fill."

Brother gave the cup to Jack with a granola bar. "How long's the trip?"

"Half an hour, if the weather holds. Taking care though. Wasn't so squally where I live."

"You're not from here?"

"Nope. Live in Doyle, twenty miles north. I'm Jimmy, by the way."

"That's Jack and Trooper, and I'm Brother." He studied Jimmy's angular face. "So I don't look familiar to you?"

"Should you?" Jimmy said, looking Brother's way, but quickly turning back to the water ahead. "I'm bad with faces. Walt, my boss, says there's always somebody famous coming through here, but I guess I don't notice. Sorry if I'm supposed to know who you are."

"I'm not anybody," Brother said, relieved.

Some staticky voices traded information over a radio, but Jimmy ignored them.

"What can you tell me about the island?" Brother asked.

"Again, Walt's the one to ask. Talk your ear off about it. Not many live there. Half the island's a refuge—you know, for wildlife, and there's just the one family on the private side. No full-time ranger anymore since the cutbacks. No hunting or camping. Stays pretty empty in the off-season, though a fair number come for the day once the weather warms."

"You know the family?"

"The Graysons?" Jimmy snorted. "Not hardly. I mean, the senator shook my hand once, but don't guess that counts. I know they've lived there a while. Got a big house, to hear Walt tell it, and a couple of smaller houses, I think. Walt says there's always stuff going on."

"Stuff?" Brother asked.

Jimmy seemed wary then. "I mind Jimmy's business, you know? Don't watch the news. Don't vote. You're not from a newspaper, are you? If so, be sure and spell my name right: N-O-B-O-D-Y. First and last."

Brother smiled. "Yeah, that's me, Clark Kent. And that's my newsboy and newshound," he said, pointing to Jack and Trooper.

Jimmy chuckled, and any wariness Brother had felt from him passed. True to his word, he minded the water and the boat, leaving Brother to wonder what Jimmy's boss had meant by *stuff*.

Jack downed every drop of Jimmy's cocoa and one by one ate

the whole box of granola bars, while Trooper curled up on the floor and slept. The rain, the rocking motion of the ferry, and the rumbling engines lulled them all into a kind of trance from which Jimmy's two blasts on the horn abruptly woke them. A great hazy mound began to appear in the fog before them.

"Sea monster!" Jack said, in an awed whisper.

Jack was right: the large, prickly shape rising out of the water ahead called up the craggy spine of a dragon or the hairy crown of a submerged giant's head.

"Winter Island," Jimmy said.

The engines slowed. As they drew closer, the island's ragged shoreline and squat trees grew more distinct and ordinary, if no more welcoming. Jimmy maneuvered the ferry smoothly into the small dock. Jack and Trooper ran behind him, out the pilothouse door and down the stairs, eager to explore. "Wait for me," Brother called, and grabbed their gear while Jimmy tied up.

As Brother stepped off the ferry, he checked if Trooper was on alert. But his dog just sniffed, pawed some weeds and took a road-side pee. Brother smiled, shook his head, heard Cole tell him to lighten up, grow a set.

"Till Memorial Day, last ferry's at four thirty," Jimmy called.

"Thanks," Brother said, waving, as Jimmy cast off. Once the ferry left, there'd be no quick or easy turning back.

The narrow road inland was lined on both sides with live oaks, salt-stunted and blown as bent as old ladies. Brother had pictured something grander; a guardhouse maybe, at least a gate. Pocked with potholes and sprouting devil grass, the asphalt

seemed more an abandoned trail than the way to a rich and powerful family. He and Mem had lived on a dirt road better than
this.

"Looks scary," Jack whispered when Brother and Trooper ran
to join him. He leaned into Brother, held on to his shirttails.

"It's just the rain," Brother said, thinking not scary so much as
lonesome, maybe the loneliest place he'd ever seen.

Only Trooper seemed unaffected and trotted off ahead, pausing to mark this bush, that shrub. After a short distance, the road
turned north. A bit farther on it forked, and at the split Jack and
Brother found Trooper barking up at a craggy tree, its branches
draped in hanging moss. High in its limbs, a large bird flapped
huge wings and took slothful flight.

"T. Rex!" Jack gasped.

Brother squeezed his shoulder. "Pelican."

"Which way?" Jack asked. He pointed at two signs nailed to
the tree trunk. "What's it say?"

"You tell me."

Because of Mem's patient teaching, Brother had learned to
read when he was four. Mem had worked with Jack too, when she
was well enough. "But he's not as quick as you were," she'd said.

Jack shook his head. "I can't."

"Try."

"It's too long."

"Okay, I'll do the long one and you do the short."

The top, larger sign pointed to the right. "WINTER ISLAND
WILDLIFE REFUGE," Brother slowly sounded out, pointing to
each syllable. "Now you do the other one."

This smaller sign looked handmade, the three words crudely carved as if by a kid with a penknife. Jack spelled the first word. "E-D-E-N."

"That's right. Now sound out the whole thing together."

"E-duh-e-en," Jack said.

"That's right, Eden."

"What does that mean?"

"You've never heard of the Garden of Eden?"

Jack shook his head. Jack's parents might have taken him to church when he was a baby, but Cole sure never had.

"Eden's a place where people are happy and nothing bad happens to them," Brother said, keeping the end of that story to himself. "You read the other words. I know you know them."

"Keep Out!" Jack shouted proudly. "That's on Cole's door at home!"

"And what does it mean?"

"Don't come in, or I'll kick your little butt!"

"That's exactly right," Brother said, and Jack beamed.

Brother peered down Eden's dreary driveway. So this was the road to the paradise Mem and Billy had fled. *Pay attention*, he heard her say. *The Eden part may sound inviting, but pay heed to the p.s.* He was tempted to see his family right away, but something told him to wait. He took Jack's hand. "C'mon, True," he said, and led them down the refuge road.

After a hundred yards they came to a chain across the road and another sign: *No Non-Resident Vehicles Beyond This Point, Permit Required.* An arrow pointed left to an empty gravel lot marked *Refuge Visitor Parking.* Beyond the trees at the back of the lot, Brother heard waves crashing ashore. Trooper took off in that direction, ears pricked, as if he heard someone calling him. Brother let him go, Jack too. It was a small island; how far could they get?

He left their gear at the lot's edge and followed a faint, overgrown trail to a high dune overlooking the sea. Even on this gray day, the vista was grand. The sky was starting to clear. Here and there, patches of blue peeked through. At the dune's edge, dense, tall grass swayed back and forth as if to its own music. Trooper yipped beyond it and below, and when Brother got where he could see, he saw his dog running circles in the sand around a girl of maybe fifteen. She wore a windbreaker and rubber boots and her hair was tucked up into a man's felt hat, the brim of which flopped in the stiff wind. She laughed and held the hat to her head with one hand, while reaching for Trooper with the other, trying to catch hold of him as he ran. Finally, she gave up on the hat, let it drop on its neck cord down her back.

"Silly dog! Hold still, so I can pet you," she said, but he kept circling her ecstatically, doing what he did best.

"Trooper, quit!" Jack said.

Finally the girl knelt and let Trooper lick her face. "Hello, Trooper," she said, and looked at Jack. "I'm Lucy. Who are you?"

Her blond hair, loose now, swept across her face.

"I'm Jack! Trooper's a shepherd and thinks everyone's a sheep."

Lucy laughed again, the sound like the tinkling of chimes.

"Silly dog. I'm no sheep. I'm a girl. Aren't you cold, Jack?"

"No!"

"You look cold. Are you here by yourself?"

"With Brother!"

"Your brother?" The girl looked up and down the beach. "Where?"

"He's coming," Jack said, and pointed vaguely toward the dune. Remembering the angry girl in the diner, Brother kept back, out of view. "But he's *not* my brother! Brother's his name. Trooper's his dog. We just came on the ferry. It was cool!"

"It is cool! I love riding the ferry. Did you come over this morning?"

"We just got here!"

"So Brother's your friend?"

"Brother is Cole's friend. But sometimes I stay with him. Like now."

"Cole?"

"Cole's my brother," Jack said, tiring of her questions. He looked toward the sea. "Can I swim now?"

"Gosh no, the water's still freezing."

"I went in it yesterday," Jack said. "Me and Frank."

Lucy's face lighted up, as though she finally understood. "So you're here with your brother and lots of his friends. And you're all visiting the refuge?"

Jack scowled. "No! Cole's not here. We don't know where he is."

"This *is* confusing. So where's your friend Brother now?"

"He's . . ." Jack pointed up the dune. "Up there." Then he ran off toward the surf with Trooper barking at his heels.

Lucy looked where Jack had pointed. "Hello!" she called. "Is anyone there?"

"I'm sorry they bothered you," Brother called.

"I'm not bothered, I'm Lucy," she said, laughing again. "Are you coming down?"

"We had a bad experience last night in Satterfield. Some girl thought I looked like someone she knew and didn't like. She got upset and made Jack cry."

"Did not!" Jack hollered from the shore.

"Okay, sad."

"She yelled mean things!" Jack shouted. "And told us to go away and never come back!"

"How awful!" Lucy said. She looked at the dune, raised her right hand, and said, "I, Lucy, solemnly promise by all I hold dear that even if you're as scarred and ugly as Frankenstein, even if you are the most disgusting, fish-faced monster in the whole universe—"

"Hah!" Jack laughed.

"—I will not yell or scream or get mad or react in any but the most welcoming way. I've been bred to be as poised as the Queen of England. Which means that even if someone throws up right in front of me, I'm not allowed to do anything but smile."

Jack laughed again.

"All right," Brother called back, and began angling his way down the dune. He tried to move sideways and keep his face turned inland, but the dune was steep and unstable and neither was good for looking where he was going. His foot slipped in the sand and he felt the dune give way underneath him. He slid down on his rear, landing nearly at Lucy's feet.

At first she laughed her chiming laugh, but when he looked up, straight at her, she drew breath sharply, despite her promise. Her light and easy mood suddenly vanished. To Brother's great relief, she didn't look angry, but he read a half-dozen other emotions in her expression: shock, caution, fear, and worry among them.

"Despite what your eyes are telling you, my name is Brother, actually Billy—Billy Grace," he said. "But everyone calls me Brother. I'm pleased to meet you. That's Jack," he said, pointing, "and that's Trooper. I'm here looking for my family. My grandmother grew up on Winter Island a long time ago."

Lucy kept staring in stunned silence. Still flat on his back and not knowing what else to do, Brother took his wallet from his back pocket, opened it to his driver's license, and held it up to her. She looked from the license to his face, studying it and him, but still didn't speak. He took in her pale skin and fragile features.

They kept staring at each other, until Jack's laughter and Trooper's barking from the water's edge made Brother glance away. The sky was almost completely blue now, the last bank of clouds moving off, revealing the sun, which warmed the air and varnished everything in golden light.

A resolve seemed to possess Lucy then, and she regarded him more decisively, though her eyes were full of questions. She tipped her head. "There's a difference, if you look."

"I beg your pardon?" Brother said.

Lucy sighed. "You've been brought up as I have, to be excruciatingly polite."

"My grandmother said manners were a refuge—"

Lucy cut him off. "And a shield?"

The words, Mem's exactly, astonished him. He waited, not knowing what to say, hoping Lucy would know.

She looked at the ocean, thoughtful. "Does your grandmother also say that silences tell you a lot if you know how to listen to them? In my family there are a great many silences, and almost everything's left *unsaid*, at least around me." She turned back. "More than I ever imagined, I now see. Is your grandmother—?"

"She died last week."

Lucy's face fell. "I'm so sorry. God, this is awkward." She closed her eyes, breathed deep, and opened them again. "No good. Still here. Still awkward."

"For both of us," Brother said. "She was all the family I had. Or thought I had. Until I saw Gabriel's picture in the paper."

At the mention of Gabriel's name, Lucy looked crossly away, heaved a heavy sigh. "It's Gabe, by the way, if you want him to answer. Only Senator and a few other grown-ups call him Gabriel."

"Senator Grayson's your father?" he asked, trying to draw her attention back.

"Stepfather," she said, distractedly.

"You call him Senator?"

"Everyone does, even my mother. She says it's his first name. Everyone except his sister Mamie, and my stepbrother Gabe. Mamie calls him Giddy, if you can believe it."

"And Gabe?" Brother ventured, eager to know more about his twin.

Lucy smirked. "Sir, to his face. But behind his back, Gabe calls him *God*."

"Where—" Brother began, but Lucy raised a hand to silence him.

"I need to think." She scanned the beach, empty in both directions, the smooth sand marred only by her footprints from the direction of Eden. "He doesn't know about you, does he?" she said with a sly expression.

"Gabe?"

She swatted the air dismissively. "No, *Senator*."

"I don't think so," Brother said, and just as he was about to press her once more about Gabe, she looked at him in wonder and clapped her hands.

"This is perfect! Something *I* know and *he* doesn't. We'll show him. We'll show them all. You have to tell me *everything*."

She took a phone out of her pocket, looked at the time, and scowled, "But later," she said. "I have to go dress for breakfast with the she-monster."

"Who?"

"Caroline." She pronounced the name with a long, mocking *i* in the last syllable. "Senator's second wife and my mother. At least she claims she's my mother, but I'm sure there was a terrible mistake and I was changed at birth with another baby girl who will never know the sacrifice I've made for her. My real father's a jackass, but he's a distant memory, thank God. You said your grandmother was all your family. Is your father dead too?"

Brother shrugged. "I don't know. My mother died when I was three. My grandmother raised me. She didn't know anything about him either."

Lucy smiled triumphantly. "This just gets better and better."

The phone in her pocket rang, but she ignored it. "That would be Millicent," she said without looking.

"Millicent?"

"Eden's resident cook, housekeeper, and majordomo." She started backing away, waving to Jack, who waved back at her with both arms from the shore. Trooper saw and raced up to her, excited and whining. Lucy patted his head.

"Listen carefully, Brother," she said quickly. "I have to go tame the she-monster for a while, but I must hear all. There's a little house about half a mile up, right on the beach. Wait a few minutes—in case Millicent's trolling for me on the walkway to the house—then come up the shore and you'll see it. It's not far and not locked. Make yourselves at home, and I'll meet you there in an hour or so. If I'm later, it's only because Caroline's especially unhappy today, but I won't be longer than I have to. Millicent's a wonderful cook. She makes scads of food whether anyone's here to eat it or not and no one is, so I'll bring us a feast!" She looked at Trooper, who had begun to whine and turn in anxious circles beside them. "Is he all right?"

"He does that sometimes when something's about to happen," Brother said truthfully.

Lucy threw back her blond head and laughed. "Well, I'd say! I'd say all hell's about to break loose! In Eden, no less!"

Before Brother could say anything more, Lucy phone rang again. This time, she glanced at it, whirled around, and yelled up the shore at the top of her lungs, "Oh, for God's sake, Millicent! You'd wake the honored dead!" and went storming up the beach toward Eden.

9

BROTHER WATCHED THE WHIRLWIND that was Lucy head up the shore and exhaled a long, slow breath. A stepsister. Beyond Gabe and the senator, he hadn't had time to imagine other immediate family, much less any extended or step kin, but now that he'd met—collided with—Lucy, it struck him that intensity must be a dominant Grayson family trait. *We'll show them*, she'd said. What did she mean? Once, during her first chemo, Mem had told him, "Take care you don't drown in other people's storms." At the time he'd thought she meant storms he knew about—her cancer, his mother's dying—but now he wondered if she'd meant far more.

In the time it took Lucy to shrink to an agitated speck, Brother fetched their gear from the refuge parking lot and piled shells at the base of the dune he'd slid down, marking a back door escape route in case he needed one. He called to Trooper and Jack.

"Look!" Jack said, running up from the water's edge. He nearly tripped he was staring so hard at what was cupped in his palms. He parted his hands to show Brother the sand dollar, barely the size of a quarter, perfect and white.

"A real treasure, buddy," Brother told him.

"Yeah, treasure!" Jack said, his eyes widening. "And there *were* sharks!"

"Where?" Brother scanned the water, saw nothing but ocean.

"Out there!" Jack shouted, pointing.

"Whatever you saw's gone now, buddy. C'mon. We're going this way."

He started up the beach in Lucy's tracks. Jack lagged behind, his eyes glued on the sand for more treasure, while Trooper ranged and chased whatever moved: crab, bird, or tide. Brother took his time, pausing often to watch the waves break, crash, foam, and then retreat as if expressing his own ambivalence about what was ahead.

Soon he heard Trooper bark and saw him atop a flight of wooden stairs leading inland from the shore. The steps went to a walkway that turned at the dunes, paralleled the beach to form an overlook, then turned again, he guessed, to Eden. Tucked beneath the balcony, at a right angle to the stairs, was a small, squat house on pilings. It was weathered gray but solid looking. Steps led from the beach to a porch with bamboo railings and a central door between two green-shuttered, sea-facing windows. Seeing Brother, Trooper shot to the beach house and stood alert on the porch as if the place belonged to him.

The door was open, as Lucy had said. Brother wiped his feet

and rubbed the sand off Trooper as best he could. Inside, the one fair-sized room was a larger space than looked possible from outside. There was a square wooden table with four chairs, two old recliners beside a small woodstove and an unmade bed. On the left was a tiny kitchen, the sink piled high with empty beer cans and cups. Behind it, in the back corner, was a tiny bathroom with a toilet, sink, and shower. Rustic, but it had the basics, though when he looked for a phone to call Kit, he found none.

Cole would have told Brother to screw waiting and charge the main house, demand his birthright and news about his twin, but Brother, like Mem, preferred to wait. Waiting was their own family trait, even to a dangerous fault. She'd foolishly waited months to call the doctor when her symptoms returned, at first saying nothing, and later, when even Brother grew alarmed at her fatigue and thinness, protesting, "I'm afraid he'll find something." Irrational, they knew, but like them both to believe that until it was certain, it wasn't so.

"Wow! Is this ours?" Jack said, running in barefoot and sand-dusted to jump on the bed.

"For now." Brother lifted him to the floor. "You know better than that."

"I took off my shoes!" Jack protested, and fell backward and spread-eagled on the bed. "You're no fun!"

"You're right," Brother said, thinking of Jack's meltdown the night before. "Let's see how much tickling you can stand."

Jack shrieked with delight but wriggled away and burst back out the door.

After that, Lucy could have taken all day and none of them would have minded. Jack found and piled treasure after treasure on the steps while Brother sat in the porch swing, lazed on the sand, skipped smooth pieces of shell on the water, or wandered the shore one way or the other. Trooper nosed crab holes, barked as pelicans flew low over the sea in close formation, or tried to herd small birds that scurried on stick legs before taking flight. Though the water was numbing cold, Jack stripped to his T-shirt and skivvies and waded till he was shivering and sticky with salt but happier than Brother had ever seen him. If anyone had asked Brother, he would have said without pause that Eden was perfectly named.

Lucy's hour passed, then two. The sun peaked at its noon zenith and began its slow descent. Brother took her at her word, made himself at home and unpacked their gear. He opened Kit's tent to dry in the sun and aired the sleeping bag on the porch rail. He even managed lunch with a jar of stale mixed nuts from the kitchen cabinet and two bottles of Coke from the fridge.

Jack was filling plastic cups with wet sand and unmolding the results around Trooper in the shape of a huge, toothy lower jaw. Brother sat and put the lunch between them.

"I'm making a shark," Jack told Brother. "He's eating True."

"I see that."

Trooper wagged, not seeming to mind. Brother hand-fed him bits of his kibble and watched a fishing boat on the water, a lone fisherman leaning precariously over its side.

"Jack, can you swim?"

"I can swim the whole ocean!" Jack said, unmolding another tooth. "I can swim two oceans! Are we going way out in the water?"

"Show me how you move your arms when you swim."

"I don't want to right now," Jack said, sculpting the tooth to a point. "I can, though."

"I believe you," Brother said. "It's too cold now for way-out swimming. I just want to make sure you know the best way, so when it's warmer, you'll be ready and super fast."

That last part got Jack's attention, as Brother had known it would. "How fast?"

"Mem swam with dolphins, that's how fast. And she taught me."

Brother must have been about Jack's age when a Schuyler teenager who'd never learned to swim had drowned one night in a pond where kids skinny-dipped. "That boy didn't even know how to dog-paddle!" Mem had snapped. Senseless tragedy made her furious, and after reading the account in the paper, she was as angry as Brother had ever seen her. The next day she'd called Warren and made him drive them twice a week for three months to the nearest public pool where she gave Brother rigorous lessons, barking like a drill sergeant: "Kick harder. Move those legs! Bend your elbows! Tread five more minutes!"

"I want to swim fast!" Jack said.

"Okay," Brother said, "first fast rule of the dolphins. Never go in the water by yourself. Trooper doesn't count. Got to be another person or somebody watching you, a person who can swim. Promise me."

"Why doesn't Trooper count?"

"Because I'm not sure he could pull you out of the water if he had to," Brother said, thinking it had been so long, he wasn't sure if *he* could save Jack.

Jack's eyes got big. "You mean if a shark had me by the leg?"

"Promise me, Jack."

"And another shark was biting off my head?"

"Promise."

"Okay." Jack sighed and went back to his sand teeth.

"That's the lesson for today. We'll do lesson two tomorrow. I'm going inside to see if the shower's working. You stay here, okay?"

Jack nodded, saying, "Chomp, chomp, chomp."

Brother took a long, hot shower in the little stall, where a mildew colony was thriving and the water smelled like rotten eggs, but the pressure and hot steam were wonderful. He found cleanish towels in a hamper and stood at the screen door drying off, when he noticed neither Trooper nor Jack was in sight. Panic rose in his chest. He grabbed his shirt and jeans, toppling a chair and nearly falling twice misstepping in one pant leg and then the other. He flew out the front door and down the stairs. Shielding his eyes, he looked one way, then the other and saw them. Jack was talking a mile a minute alongside a dark figure—a man, Brother thought—who was hobbling resolutely up the beach from the refuge end of the island. The man was very old or crippled or drunk or all three from the odd way he walked, pitched forward and without swinging his arms, as if he might at any second fall face-first into the sand. Even Trooper gave up his usual herding circles and paced watchfully at the man's side. The man wore a black watch cap, an unbuttoned brown overcoat far too big for him, and a neck scarf that flailed in the wind behind him. He looked like a great, grounded pelican with broken wings.

"True! Jack! Come here!" Brother shouted. Jack whirled around and ran back toward Brother, but Trooper ignored him and sat respectfully as the man finally stopped, bent stiffly, and patted his upturned nose.

"True!" Brother shouted again, and both the dog and the mysterious figure looked his way. Brother waved and the man stood a long, confused moment, as if he didn't understand the gesture, after which he turned around awkwardly and started back the way he'd come.

"Who's that?" Jack asked, running up.

"I was going to ask you. What did he say?"

"He didn't say anything. He's kinda weird."

There were slow, heavy footsteps on the walkway above them. Lucy, breathing hard, called out, "Gosh, I forgot to tell you about Amos. He wanders up here sometimes. He's got some kind of brain disease and he's odd, but harmless. He's lived on the refuge since before it was a refuge, and now he's grandfathered in, as Senator says."

Trooper raced up to Brother, caked in sand. Brother just managed to grab his collar so he wouldn't trip Lucy as she came down the stairs.

"I bet you thought I'd never come!"

Brother met her at the steps and saw what had slowed her

progress: a large wicker hamper she held in front of her with both hands. He took it from her.

"Wait till you see!" she said, clapping. "I've got scones and roasted chicken and carrot and celery sticks, both, and deviled eggs and even pecan brownies. I'm a regular Robin Hood, I am," she went on brightly. "And Trooper, I have a special surprise for you!"

"I want brownies!" Jack shouted.

"And brownies you shall have!" Lucy told him. She was flushed, her hair pulled back with a big barrette at the base of her neck. She wore an overcoat, a tan wool sweater and slacks, and a lot of makeup. She was what Mem called "put together," though Brother thought she'd looked prettier that morning without any paint.

He carried the hamper to the inside table and helped Lucy unpack the food, plastic plates, and utensils. Brother and Jack were hungry, but even so, several more people could have been stuffed full by what she'd brought—including bones from a beef roast for Trooper, which he gnawed steadily, one after the other. Brother gratefully ate his first meat and vegetables in a week. Lucy was right about Millicent's cooking; everything was delicious, the best food he'd ever had, and he and Jack had seconds and thirds while Lucy picked at a single scone.

"You're not hungry?" Brother asked her, between sizable mouthfuls.

Under her apparent cheer, her face was puffy, her eyes rimmed in red.

"I'm due back soon. At which time Caroline will whine and

bitch some more." She rested the back of one wrist on her fore-head and tipped back her head, the picture of a long-suffering damsel. He laughed, he couldn't help it.

"What's funny?" Jack said.

"I am," Lucy told them. "I'm being theatrical, to cheer myself, but it's no lie. When Caroline's unhappy, the world's unhappy. She hates it here, wants to be in New York and Washington, shopping and seeing her friends, but Senator wants us here right now, out of the public eye. Enough about her! I don't have much time, and I want to hear about you."

Brother hesitated. "I'd like to know more about my brother. *Please*."

Lucy pursed her lipsticked mouth and looked down at the floor. "Gabe, Gabe, *Gabe*," she said furiously. "He's all anyone talks about anymore or wants to." She drew herself up and looked full at him. "I'm sorry," she said crisply. "Of all people, you're the most entitled to know, but you can't imagine how it's been. I'm not allowed to do anything even remotely fun. 'Your brother almost died, Lucy. Things are very serious for Senator, Lucy. What would people think, Lucy? Think how it might reflect on Senator.' All because of Gabe. He's the reason my life is shit, and I'm a pris-oner in my own hellish home."

"She said *shit*," Jack said with his mouth full.

"My ears are working," Brother told him.

"I found him," she said quietly, this time without drama. "Right there. It was horrible. If I hadn't . . . He nearly didn't . . . he almost . . ."

Brother glanced at Jack who was watching them warily, then followed Lucy's gaze to the nearest recliner. It was ordinary and brown and told him nothing, but he stared at it anyway, as if it carried a fatal disease or might suddenly explode. The room felt crowded and stuffy. The thought of his twin lying there, nearly dead, was like imagining himself that way.

"What was horrible?" Jack said. "Was it a monster? A ghost?"

"No, buddy," Brother said. "A person you don't know."

Jack looked bored. "Can I go outside now?"

Brother nodded, stood. "We'll all go."

He and Lucy sat on the porch swing, rocking as the sun sank into the water and the sea breeze grew chilly. She said the ferry side of the island gave the full effect, but Brother thought the westerly sky spectacular with broad strokes of burnt orange, pink, and rose.

"Oh, yes," Lucy said with a sigh when Brother asked if Gabe would recover. She seemed disappointed. "I'm sorry. Ask your questions. I'll steel myself and answer them."

And to her credit she did, mostly without smirks or bitter commentary. Though Gabe had nearly died from the overdose—heroin, snorted because needles scared him—he was young and strong and his physical recovery hadn't been much in doubt. His mental health? Who knew? She had few specifics. He was finishing rehab, but from what she'd overheard Senator and Caroline say, it hadn't gone well. He might need a second round.

This was all she claimed to know, though as she talked, Brother began to feel she wasn't telling him everything. She said she didn't know where Gabe was or when he was coming home, but from the evasive way she said it, Brother didn't believe her. Probably she didn't want him running off to find his twin and spoiling her surprise.

"The prodigal son will come home soon enough," she said, when Brother pressed her, "and the father will embrace him. Once again, he's fallen like Lucifer in Senator's graces, but as Senator's namesake and heir, I promise you, the son *will* rise."

She heaved a great, gloomy sigh. "Enough. I don't want to talk about him anymore. Your turn."

Brother told her about Mem and Cole and his exodus from Schuyler. He described the Galaxie's breakdown, Trooper saving the little boy, and the furious waitress in Satterfield. But he left out Kit. He'd thought Lucy open at first, but when she seemed coy about Gabe's whereabouts, he started to think she was forthcoming and honest when it suited her purposes, whatever they were. Better to be careful what he told her until he knew more, keep a few things to himself, and be sure to stay in her good graces, if only to keep the house on the beach, the food, and a little information coming.

After he finished his story, she said, "There's only one person who could know your story, Brother, and that's Senator. That saying about manners from your grandmother is his, too. He's the one who'll know the truth, if anyone does. He isn't here now, but he will be."

"When?"

"Soon," she said vaguely, dropping her gaze. Again, Brother

sensed something off, even strategic, in her reply. "In the mean-time, it's only right you be extended every courtesy, and keep making yourselves at home. What's left in the basket should hold you till tomorrow when I'll be back with more. Light a fire if you want. There's wood in the box out back. It's not likely anybody will notice the smoke, but if they do, I'll say I came down here and got cold. Millicent and Caroline avoid the beach. If you want to be sure Amos doesn't wander in, latch the door."

"Thank you," Brother said. "May I ask one more favor? Could I use your phone to leave word in Schuyler about exactly where we are? For Cole. Jack's worried."

Lucy stood abruptly and spoke too fast. "Oh, gosh, and I left it at home!" A lie, this time he was sure. He'd seen the outline of it in her pocket. For some reason she didn't want him to use it to tell anyone exactly where he was. Did she think Warren might call the media or the senator and spoil her surprise—a laughable thought—or was it something else? "I have to get back now, any-way. But if you write down the name and number, I'll phone from the house."

She hurriedly put on her coat while he wrote Warren's name and number on a paper plate. She slipped it into her coat pocket without looking at it, smiled sweetly, and hurried out the door.

He was sure she'd never call.

10

AFTER LUCY LEFT, Brother shook off his anxiety about her by doing what needed to be done. "Right foot, left foot; breathe in, breathe out," Mem had said, whenever the news from the doctor was bad or money ran short. Brother told himself the same.

He found split seasoned wood in a firewood box behind the house, as Lucy had said, and carried enough for the night to the porch. Matches took a half hour of searching for before Jack found a partial pack under the bed. After that, Brother started a list of things they needed. Angry waitresses or no, he'd take the ferry into Satterfield in the morning to get necessities so they weren't entirely dependent on Lucy or anyone else.

He put the uneaten food in the refrigerator, kindled a fire with the dirty napkins and plates in the woodstove, then stripped off his and Jack's damp, sandy clothes. He shook them outside and hung them on kitchen chairs to dry. By then, Jack was sacked out on the braided rug, his head resting on a spent Trooper's belly.

Brother carried him to the bed and covered him with the sleeping bag. Trooper immediately hopped up and lay down at his side.

Jack and Trooper slept soundly, but Brother sat wide awake opposite the empty recliner, where Lucy said she'd found Gabe. The more he stared at it, the more power it gained, like a black hole that might suck him in. He tried closing his eyes—but that was worse because then he pictured his twin lifeless in the chair. Did he and Gabe fail alike? Did they have the same faults? Fear the same things? Would they die the same way?

He wondered what kind of person he was that he didn't remember his brother. Weren't twins supposed to have some special connection, a fraternal ESP? What did it say about Brother that he had no sense of Gabe, only a half a state away? Why didn't he know Gabe was in serious trouble, that he'd almost died? His dog had better instincts than he did.

A stiff wind rattled the window glass so hard Brother thought it might break. He went to the porch for wood and closed the shutters. A sharp sickle moon hung over the water, and the blast off the sea was cold and cutting and rushed him back inside. He hooked the screen door to keep it from banging and bolted the inner door behind him. Even shuttered and latched, the house creaked and swayed as if it might fold flat with them inside it.

He tried to calm himself by thinking of Kit, what she was doing and where, but his thoughts were so negative that he kept imagining her with other guys or laughing with her girlfriends about the loser she'd rescued and, thank God, ditched two hundred miles away.

A loud thump on the porch startled him, and then a second and a third. Was Amos back? But even Trooper slept on, oblivious. He thought of the golf driver Mem kept for security under her bed, imagined her wielding it, scolding him, "Now, Brother, you haven't been five years old in a long time." After that he was able to sleep.

The next morning was clear and warm, and the fair weather and calm winds buoyed his spirits and made his night dread seem silly. After breakfast, Jack put on the pirate patch Kit had bought him and found a driftwood sword. The three of them walked the back way to meet the morning ferry right on time. A smiling Jimmy waved to them from the dock.

"I'm a pirate!" hollered Jack.

Jimmy laughed. "You gonna make me walk the plank?"

Before Jack could answer, a voice boomed from the ferry, "Yo ho ho and a bottle of Stoli!"

"Cole!" Jack cried. He flipped up his eye patch, dropped his sword, and sped to meet his smiling brother. Cole's auburn mop blew this way and that like a flame. Brother had never thought of Cole as dapper, but that's exactly how he looked as he came off the boat in a long tweedy overcoat, gray neck scarf, and sweater over a button-down. "Thrift shop, twenty-two bucks. Not bad, eh?"

He held up a bottle of vodka in one hand and set down the backpack and shopping bag he held in the other to scoop up Jack. "Hey there, Jackaroo! Miss me?"

"We rode the ferry, and I saw a million sharks!" Jack gushed.

Jimmy raised a concerned eyebrow, but Brother shook his head.

"Good to see you too, Jackrabbit," Cole said, then looked at Brother. "Sorry about Mem, Brother-man."

"Brother-man nothing," Brother snapped. "Where the hell have you been?"

Cole grinned. "Chasing a hot girl and the American dream."

"How nice for you. Where is she?"

"She cooled and I woke up."

"You mean she ran out of money."

"Ever the killjoy. Nice of you to meet my ship."

"We're headed into town to get a few things."

"I just got here! Besides, I just might have what you need."

"Sure," Brother said crossly. "Like you've got a phone."

Cole smirked. "Hold this and don't drop it," he told Jack and passed him the vodka bottle, which the boy took in two hands. Cole reached into his coat pocket, pulled out a cell. "Ta dah!"

"Where'd you get that?"

"In due time, Bro. What else?"

"Matches."

Cole shook his head. "This is too easy." He reached into his breast pocket and took out two lighters and three spliffs.

"Put that away," Brother said.

Cole reluctantly replaced the matches and weed, took the bottle from Jack, and bent to slip it into the shopping bag. He reached deep into the sack. "Nutritious snacks?" He held up a bag of trail mix. "Water?" He lifted a gallon jug. "Dog food?" He looked at Trooper and showed the top of a pillow-sized sack of dog chow, then a small box, which he shook. "*And* biscuits?"

Trooper's ears pricked and he wagged his tail. Cole had thought of everything.

"And presents for everyone!" Cole said smugly.

"I want mine!" Jack cried.

Cole drew a fat pack of bubble gum from his side pocket, which Jack snatched. "More soon, Jacktopus."

"How did you—" Brother began and stopped. "Where is she?"

"Of whooooom are you speaking?" Cole said, smiling affectedly.

"Kit."

"Whooooom?" Cole said, turning to Jack and making an owlish face. Jack cracked up.

"*Where?*"

"Taking exams. Writing term papers. Like you, your girlfriend's ridiculously conscientious," Cole said, "though for a genius, she's a fox and damned entertaining. What'd'ya do? Set Jack on the roadside with a little bowl and a sign around his neck that said, 'More, please?'" Cole made a pathetic face and a now gum-smacking Jack broke up again. "Before I forget, she says it's a scrap-yard phone, so don't lose it, and you owe her for the supplies."

"How'd you find her?"

"The messages she left with Warren. Who says hello, by the way."

Brother forced himself not to smile. He didn't want to give Cole the satisfaction, but it really was good to see him and good to hear from Warren and Kit, even secondhand.

Cole suddenly wrinkled his nose as if he smelled something awful. He sniffed Jack's neck and drew back. "You need a bath, Jackster." He looked at Brother, feigning outrage. "When *is* the last time you *bathed* this boy?"

"Bring the bags."

"What?" Cole gasped. "No limo? No valet?"

Brother growled and started down the road, Trooper beside him. Cole set down Jack and the boy ran happily after them. Brother looked back. Cole stood for a moment with a martyred look, then shouldered the backpack and heaved up the shopping bag like it weighed a ton. "A person quits his job," he muttered, trudging behind them, "the only income for his orphaned little fidget, leaves the cozy hovel they call home, rushes—bearing gifts—to the aid of his best pal without regard for his own welfare, and how is he treated? Like a rented mule."

"Shut up, Cole," Brother said.

"And 'Shut up, Cole' is all the thanks he gets. I ask you," Cole told the trees and an amused Jimmy, watching from the dock, "does the loyal Cole-ster deserve this shabby treatment—"

"Cole," Brother warned.

"Is there at least cable and a pool?"

"The whole effing Atlantic's in the front yard."

Cole sighed heavily and droned, "I sup*pose* that will *have* to doooooo."

✳ ✳ ✳

"Well, thank god he got there with everything," Kit said over the phone after they got to the beach house, "because with a friend like that, I was thinking you might as well shoot yourself in the foot."

"He's not that bad once you get to know him," Brother said, though Cole had bellyached all the way back to the refuge lot, through the woods, down the dune, and up the shore to the house. But once they'd arrived, the spectacular view seemed to impress even him, and after he'd passed on Kit's directions about how to use the phone, he'd settled right in to being Jack's devoted brother, best pal, and responsible guardian. From the beach house porch, Brother could hear him wrestling Jack into the shower and their pleasant bickering about slimy mildew and the soap in Jack's eyes, both of them excited to be together again.

"You didn't drive him down here, did you?" Brother asked Kit.

"I'll thank you not to insult me."

"Sorry."

"He hitched to the scrap yard. I helped him shop and took him back to the highway, but he thumbed it to the ferry. Tell me everything and be quick. I've got class in ten minutes."

Brother filled her in.

"Your stepsister sounds a lot like her stepdaddy," she said, when he finished. "Be careful."

"Tell me something I don't know."

Brother wished they didn't have to exchange news so fast. It was good to hear her voice, especially the competent certainty in it, which renewed his hope that some things might work out.

"I'll let Cole tell you about Cole, which if you ask me, you should take with the bottle of aspirin I sent and two tons of salt. But here's the big news: I know where your brother, Gabe, is. He's in some country club rehab in Virginia. Ask me how I know this."

"Because you're psychic?"

"Because it was all over the TV. And I mean *all over*. You won't be taking one step off that island without somebody knowing. Which is your own fault."

"Why's that?"

"After you showed up at that diner in Satterfield, Senator Selfish had to produce Gabe to prove where Gabe was. That waitress we met? She swore up and down that Gabe Grayson was on the loose and haunting her place against legal order. Something about her kid brother being injured in a wreck Gabe caused. You should've seen how smug his daddy was proving her a big fat liar and then twelve-stepping all over himself about how seriously Gabe takes his recovery and the consequences of his actions, which anybody with two eyes looking at Gabe could see was a crock. That boy stood beside daddy dearest like the walking dead and didn't say pea turkey. Probably they had his lips sewn shut so he couldn't dig his hole any deeper. You still there? There's a lot of noise in the background."

"It's just the ocean," Brother said. He and Trooper had wandered down the beach toward the refuge.

"*It's just the ocean*," Kit mocked. "Well, I'm so glad you're having a posh vacation, while yours truly is playing operator, banker, and travel agent, and busting a gut on the home front."

"The little house we're staying in is right on the beach. If you come—"

"Oh, *pleeeese*, and *if* nothing! I'm coming all right, but I've got things to do before I can. So don't do anything stupid like go back into town or get it in your head to hitchhike to Virginia before Friday night. That's the soonest Frank and I can get there. Besides which, now that you're on TV, you won't be able to sneeze without getting arrested. So promise me."

"I promise," he said, thinking she'd read his mind, because the first thought he'd had was how he could get to Virginia with no car. It was only Wednesday. So much had happened already in such a short time that he didn't like to think what could happen before Friday. He told her where to park and how to get to the beach house, just in case he couldn't meet her ferry on Friday afternoon. "I'm planning to be there, but—"

"Trust me, I know," she said. "Charlie's favorite saying: *If you want to make God laugh, make plans.* You ought to have that tattooed on your forehead."

A bell sounded at her end.

"Gotta fly. We'll talk later. Try to enjoy it while you can. Your stepsister's right about one thing. Real soon, all flaming hell's gonna break loose, and I really hope I'm there in time to see it!"

11

ONCE HE HUNG UP WITH KIT, Brother set off with Trooper to wander the refuge, glad to have a break from minding Jack. He left a message on Warren's answering machine to say he was fine and thank him for steering Cole his way. He said he'd been thinking about Warren—a lie, but the kind it was good to tell. Then he shut off the phone and strolled the refuge shoreline savoring the sun, the water, and being with his dog.

He'd stuffed his pockets with the small colored dog biscuits Kit had sent, and doled out one whenever Trooper nuzzled his hand. So he wouldn't be easy for Cole and Jack to find, he walked inland at the first path. It was little more than a foot-wide break in the sand and scrub, though the trampled vegetation made it appear steadily used. Trooper zigzagged into the undergrowth, from one side of the path to the other, but the dog treats kept him returning. Brother followed the trail, thinking sooner or later they'd arrive on the island's far side. Sometimes, when he and Mem had been out in Warren's car, she'd point down an unfamiliar road and say, "Why don't we go that way, see where it goes?" And they would. In the same spirit, he went where the path took him.

Soon the trail split, though, the wider part continuing straight and a narrower path turning squarely right. Trooper stopped and looked at Brother.

"You choose," Brother said, and as if he understood, Trooper sniffed each option once and immediately shot right, down the narrower way. He flushed two red-winged blackbirds from a thicket and then sped out of sight, his collar tags jingling. Brother climbed a short rise and at the top found a frame house in an overgrown tangle of oaks. The house was the smaller twin of the one on the beach, more a playhouse for children. Trooper sat out front enjoying the full attention of the odd old man they'd seen on the beach, the man Lucy had called Amos.

"Sorry to bother you," Brother said. "We didn't know this was private. C'mon, True, let the man be."

But Trooper stayed put and the man said nothing, though he seemed to register Brother's presence with a slight sideways jerk. His gaze, though, remained fixed on Trooper, and the dog ignored Brother too, his eyes blissfully closed as the man patted his head.

"He likes you," Brother said. Still, the man didn't speak or turn. He sat pitched forward in a green metal chair. He wore the same too-big brown overcoat Brother had seen him in the day before, the same boots and black watch cap over his shaggy, unshaven head. His face was gaunt, leathery, deeply lined, and a torrent of drool leaked from the right side of his mouth to his chin, a steady flow he did nothing to stop. At the nursing home, several stroke victims had drooled like that, and Brother remembered what Lucy had said about Amos having some type of brain disease.

"He likes these," Brother said, approaching slowly. He held out several of the dog treats from his pocket and touched one to the back of Amos's hand. He stopped patting Trooper, turned up his hand to receive them, then offered the biscuits to the dog in his cupped palm, like a bowl. Trooper ate the biscuits gently, one at a time, and seemed to enjoy Amos feeding him as much as the treats themselves.

His palm empty, Amos looked to Brother, his head cocked oddly on his neck. Whatever was wrong seemed to afflict every part of him but one. His eyes, a piercing blue, almost the same color as Trooper's, were oddly youthful and lively in his old head.

"He usually won't calm unless he knows you," Brother said, handing over the last of the treats from his pocket. "Give him the rest if you want."

And Amos did, every one. Afterward, Trooper tenderly licked the trembling hand, saying thank you the only way he knew.

"Good dog," Brother whispered, and squatted to pet Trooper, but as he did, Amos stood up and began to shuffle toward the house, Trooper instantly beside him. When Amos stalled at the bottom of the stairs, Trooper nudged his hand, which started Amos moving again. Two steps up, Amos stopped, and once again, Trooper nudged. The scene reminded Brother of a wind-up soldier Mem had given him when he was small. When wound with a key, the soldier would go, go, go then slowly rasp to a stuttering halt, at which point Brother could prod him to go a bit more before he stopped for good and needed winding again.

Brother followed them, worried that Amos might fall, but Trooper seemed to know all that Amos needed. He matched the old man's robotic pace and, when necessary, switched him on again. His dog continually surprised him. Once, Brother had taken Trooper to The Elms to visit the old people. He'd sat next to each resident in turn, until the resident tired or moved him along. Even the stoniest faces had softened, the glassiest eyes came to life, until the manager, afraid of accidents or lawsuits, made Brother take him home. Seeing Trooper go, one elderly man had cried.

Amos scaled the stairs at such a glacial pace, he might have been climbing a mountain, but Trooper shadowed him every step, prodding him when he waned. When Amos finally gained the porch, Brother found he'd been holding his breath. Even Trooper seemed relieved. Effort in everything seemed to be a way of life for Amos. He shambled across the porch and went inside, while Trooper sat outside the door. Five minutes passed, more, and just as Brother thought Amos wasn't coming out, he backed out the door holding a bottle of Coke, which, after the minute it took him to ratchet around, he shakily held out to Brother.

Brother hurried up the stairs so Amos wouldn't start down.

"Thank you, I don't need anything," Brother said quickly. But

Amos kept holding out the bottle, so Brother took it and held it to be polite. He wondered where Amos got his Cokes, and everything else he needed. Maybe he was more able on other days, but even so, Brother doubted he was ever well enough to negotiate the ferry, get to a store, buy things, and return home. Someone else bought his supplies.

Brother and Amos stood staring at each other until Trooper, impatient, barged past Amos into the house. Amos, reactivated, went inside and Brother followed. Like the beach house, there was a single room and a tiny bathroom, but instead of a kitchen, there was a squat table and two kid-sized chairs. The floor was strewn with leaves and trash and scattered with the last three of an empty package of Oreos.

"I like this place," Brother said, wondering if Mem had played here as a child. "It's nice and quiet," he added, and the drooling corner of Amos's mouth lifted slightly.

"I'm Brother and that's Trooper." Amos's eyes sought out the dog, who sniffed at one of the cookies. Before Brother could say no, Trooper gobbled it down. "True!" Brother cried, but the old man laughed suddenly, or that's how it seemed to Brother, though it was little more than an out-forcing of breath. Trooper took it as permission to gobble the rest.

"Sorry," Brother said, but Amos not only didn't seem to care, he looked like he was waiting to see what entertaining thing Trooper would do next. But Trooper lay down, and Brother tried to think what else to say or do. Amos kept staring at the Coke that Brother held, staring at it hard while he pressed his lips together, until Brother suddenly thought, *like he's thirsty.*

"Jesus, I'm sorry." Feeling like an idiot, Brother twisted off the cap and handed the open Coke to Amos, who gazed at the bottle as if it were a holy object. He lifted it to his mouth, but his hand shook and the Coke spilled down his front. Brother moved to steady the bottle so Amos could drink, something he'd done hundreds of times for the old people at The Elms. Amos drank easily then, his eyes closed, in a kind of quiet ecstasy.

"Do you need anything else?" Brother asked when Amos was done, but the old man didn't or couldn't answer. Brother reached for the empty bottle, but Amos gripped it hard. His blue eyes bore into Brother, seemed to be challenging him or asking an urgent question, though Brother had no clue what it was. The urgency passed, the intensity of Amos's gaze faded. He seemed suddenly far away, to have forgotten that Brother and Trooper were there.

"Amos!" A man's worried voice sounded outside and Amos started. Trooper barked, burst out the screen door and Amos shuffled out behind him. Brother stayed put. He didn't want to show himself and risk somebody recognizing him again unless it was absolutely necessary.

"Thank heaven! Twice in two days! What's got into you?" the man said, like he was scolding a beloved child.

"You found yourself a friend! Hello there, boy. Who do you belong to? You've got tags, so your master must be close by."

Brother peeked out the dirty window and saw a balding, middle-aged man patting his dog. The man squinted at the house as if trying to decide if anyone was inside. He seemed to think not, and hurried to help Amos down the steps, afterward winding a wool scarf he'd brought around the old man's scrawny neck.

"What would I do if something happened to you? I know you like it here, and you know I'll bring you, but you've got to wait for me to come with you. What if a snake bit you? What if you fell down the steps and broke your neck?" The man's anxious voice retained its good nature, and Brother understood that the man must either be Amos's keeper or kin.

"Good thing I brought wipes," the man said, pulling a plastic bag from his jacket pocket. He took one out and rubbed Amos's mouth and the front of his coat. "I see you had yourself a Coke. Damned if you didn't open it all by yourself! I can't be upset about that! That's progress! The new pills must be doing some good. Wouldn't that be wonderful? I could use a week off to see Gina in Florida before spring's out. You can't be this kind of trouble to whoever takes my place."

Brother couldn't tell if Amos understood what the man had said or if Amos even knew who he was. There were plenty of dementia patients at The Elms who'd treated Brother's appearance each morning as something entirely new. Even minute-to-minute they forgot him. Maybe Amos was like that too.

When the keeper finished tidying him, Amos tipped the bottle to drain the last drops of Coke, then let himself be led down the path, away from the house. Sensing he'd been relieved of duty, Trooper relaxed and watched them go.

"At least you weren't trying to swim like last time!" the keeper said, and laughed. "But this going AWOL won't do. What on earth will you do next?"

And as Trooper looked Brother's way, this suddenly seemed to Brother the very question Amos had been silently asking him.

12

BROTHER WATCHED FROM the window until they disappeared in the trees, then sat in the yard chair and waited with Trooper until he was sure they were gone.

After that, he and Trooper took the first trail inland. While Trooper ran ahead, Brother lagged behind, feeling rattled and inside his own head. Maybe meeting Amos had brought home Mem's sickness and death, along with other recent shocks he'd barely had a chance to register or absorb, but the old man troubled him in a way he couldn't entirely explain.

It didn't help that the unmarked path kept dividing and was as convoluted and confusing as his thoughts. In places, the dense evergreens closed in, blocked any vista, and halved the light until he and Trooper went single file and Brother wasn't sure he was on any path at all. After walking in what seemed like circles for an hour or more, they finally came out on a beach. Brother breathed the sea air, glad to be out on the sunny, open shore again, until he realized he was completely lost. He wasn't sure where he and Trooper were in relation to the beach house, the ferry dock, or anywhere else. Even Trooper looked up at him as if asking, *Where to now? What next?*

"I was about to ask you," Brother said, but the dog just stood there, wagging and waiting.

He could follow the shoreline and, as the island was small and essentially a circle, sooner or later he'd come to the ferry or the beach house or an access road where he could get his bearings— that seemed the easiest thing to do. Beyond picking right or left, he wouldn't have to know where he was going. He wouldn't risk making wrong turns or hazard taking short cuts or chance getting lost again in the labyrinth of trees and brush. But what if the coastline had rocky or otherwise impassable places? His ignorance was total. It might be safer to steer by the sun and make his way back by the few paths and landmarks he knew. He didn't know which to do. As he stood staring out at the sea and then at the empty beach in one direction and the other, it struck him that down deep, what he really wanted was not to have to think about it at all. He wanted someone to come along and find him standing there looking lost, someone helpful and kind who'd say, "No worries. All you have to do is X, Y, and Z" or, even better, "Follow me and everything will be fine."

That's when it hit him that Cole was right. He *had* caved in the last year, but that wasn't the half of it. Worse, he'd let others pick his path, followed any man, woman, child, or dog in front of him rather than decide for himself where he was going or why or if he even wanted to go there at all. His habit of waiting for somebody else to tell him what to do next, to rescue him, and his way of just going along had gone from being a makeshift measure when Mem was sick to a permanent state. He'd forgotten how to live any other way. He'd followed Mem's life rules or Warren's advice, or let Trooper herd or Cole distract or Kit drive, even let a stepsister he'd just met dictate where and when he'd see his own twin and family; and all this made him feel about as autonomous as old Amos, who needed somebody to jumpstart him up a flight of stairs or just take the cap off his Coke.

The thought irritated him, but it energized him too. He found the sun in the sky, and keeping it over his shoulder, headed resolutely east. When he came to a path, he kept to it until it joined a wider, eastward trail. He paid attention to the trees and shrubs, to where his dog was, and to where he planted his feet all the way back to the ferry dock, the main road, the parking lot, his backdoor dune, and finally, the house on the beach. His feet and head hurt, and he thought he might have walked ten miles by the time he got back, but for the first time in a long while, he'd followed his own compass. Maybe he'd just walked across a map-speck of an island, but he knew where he'd been and where he was and how he'd gotten from the one place to the other. Vigilance was exhausting, but it was good.

Trooper raced joyfully to Jack, who was playing alone on the beach, building a big-finned shark half-buried in the sand. His hair and clothes were soaking wet.

"Aren't you cold?" Brother asked him.

"No!"

"Where's Cole?" Brother demanded.

"They're inside," Jack said, pointing.

"They who?"

"Cole and that girl from last night."

"Did you go in the water?"

"Not over my head. Cole said I could," Jack said, adding in a smart-alecky voice, "He says you're not my daddy," as if he knew exactly what Brother was about to say. He squinted at Brother smugly. "And I saw sharks. So, hah!"

"That's really smart," Brother said. "Swimming alone, *with sharks.*"

Trooper stayed with Jack as Brother stormed up the steps into the house. Lucy and Cole were lazing in the recliners drinking beer and sharing a spliff, a mostly-eaten plate of chocolate chip cookies between them. They looked sleepily at him as he burst through the screened door, glared at Cole, and shouted, "He can't swim!"

"Swim?" Cole asked, smiling sleepily.

"Jack! Are you nuts?"

"A fair question," Cole said. "But calm down. He's fine. I'm watching him through the door."

Lucy gave Brother a don't-believe-everything-you-hear look.

"You and Jack are going home on the next ferry," Brother told Cole.

"*Au contraire, Frère,*" Cole said. "Lucy's just invited us to stay, and I quote, 'As long as we like.' Since nobody here even knows you exist, I think *her* invite trumps your boot in my butt."

"That's about to change."

Lucy frowned. "What is?"

"Everything," Brother said, and began stuffing his belongings into his duffel.

Lucy sat up, looking alarmed. "Where are you going?"

"Wherever I like."

"What are you going to do?"

"First thing?" Brother snapped. "Pick off the leeches."

"You have *leeches?*" she asked.

"He means us," Cole said.

Lucy rolled her eyes. "God, and people think I'm dramatic. Sit *down*, Brother. You're not making any sense. You don't know the situation or who the players are."

"You're right, I don't. And I'm pretty sure I'm not going to find out what it is from you. We're not players, Lucy, we're people."

"Don't be a literal-minded child," she said irritably.

Brother stopped packing. "That kind of talk and tone may work with Gabe when he's wrecked, but not with me."

She took a deep breath and tried to scowl at him, but her red eyes undermined her anger. "I'm trying to help you, Brother, to prepare you. You don't know these people like I do, especially Senator, how ruthless he is. Talk to him, Cole."

"Oh, I think he's doing fine," Cole said.

"Do you?" Brother said.

"Better than fine, actually," Cole said, and took a deep drag on his joint.

"What do you mean?" Lucy said. She looked at Brother, exasperated. "What's happened to you?"

"Nothing's happened to me."

"Don't be idiots," Lucy said to them. "We have an opportunity here, and if you go off half-cocked now, you'll ruin it."

"*We* have an opportunity?" Brother said, tensing.

"Careful, Lucy," Cole told her.

Lucy looked from one of them to the other, as if she knew she was losing ground. "Talk sense into him, Cole."

"Wouldn't dream of it," Cole said. "Not when he's like this."

"Like what?" Brother snapped, glaring.

Cole smiled broadly. "Yourself."

"What?" Brother said, surprised.

"Welcome back, Brother-man," Cole said, and laughed. "Good to see you again. Been a long time."

Lucy stormed out, slamming the screen door behind her, and Brother heard her stomping up the walkway.

"She'll be back," Cole said.

"I don't care."

"Don't get all stupid again. It's fine you lost your temper. Siblings do. Hasn't Jack taught you anything? You have a brother *and* a sister now. You're going to lose it every five minutes."

Cole was stoned, but he had a point.

"And it's not like you have a million friends," Cole said. "You could do worse."

Brother shot him a doubtful look.

"Okay, you could do better. But not at the moment."

"Because?"

"You're on an effing island?"

Brother smirked.

"Fine. You're right. I haven't been the best friend lately. I peeled off at a bad time. I'm sorry, all right?" Cole said, testy. "But one last request before you throw us overboard? Give us the weekend. After that, we'll do whatever you want. You want us to go, great. I get it that a piss-in-his-pants kid and his homeless brother aren't real plusses in your fancy new life."

"That's not how I feel," Brother said. He looked out the window at Jack, still building his monster out of sand. "What do you mean, homeless?"

"No lectures, okay?"

"*What* do you mean?"

"I lost it."

"Lost what?"

"The house. I let it go back."

"What does that mean? Back where?"

"To the bank."

"What are you saying?"

"I couldn't keep up the payments," Cole said, all seriousness now. "I was stupid to try. I thought: we lost them, but we didn't have to lose the house too, everything else. I was a sap, okay? It's not like I was beating the scratch-off or there's a living in eldercare. That's why I split. One last toot before the bank locked us out."

Brother stood silent. Cole sometimes chose what truth he told selectively, but Brother had never seen him like this. All his usual confidence had left him. A big, garrulous guy, he didn't often look deflated, but he slumped forward in his recliner—Gabe's recliner—head bowed, his hands folded between his legs. He seemed smaller and supplicating, not the grandiose schemer he usually acted, but the seventeen-year-old kid-with-a-kid he was.

"Why didn't you say something?"

"Nothing you could've done. Not like you needed something else to worry about with Mem so sick," his friend said quietly. Cole, who had little shame, was ashamed of this.

"We could've gotten drunk and depressed together."

"You mean *more* drunk and *more* depressed than we already were?"

"Yeah," Brother said, smiling a little.

Cole looked up. "I'm sorry about Mem. She was a great lady. I'm sorry I dumped Jack on you and skipped at a bad time. I was actually thinking Jack and I could help you and Mem more when I got back, maybe in exchange for a few weeks' use of your couch, until we found something."

Brother thought how he'd nearly ended up on Warren's couch, and might still. "I'm really sorry about your house," he said.

"Yeah, well." Cole sighed. "Now could we stop being sorry? Because if we don't, I'm going to have to hang myself."

Brother leaned on the jamb and looked through the screen at Jack and Trooper. They were playing a game. Jack was mounding cups of sand that Trooper instantly toppled with his nose.

"C'mon," Brother said. "Let's rescue this day."

Cole wouldn't go in the water. He sat with Trooper on the sand, cheerleading, telling Jack that Brother was his swim-daddy and to do everything he said. Brother gritted his teeth against the numbing water, but Jack reveled in the cold. Brother showed him how to float on his back and gave "fish-boy"—as Cole started calling him—the general idea of moving his arms and legs to keep his head above the water. Then Brother hauled a reluctant fish-boy to land and chased him up the beach, making crab claws with his hands toward a hot shower, both of them laughing and blue as corpses.

"I can swim!" Jack cried as he ran.

"And what's the first rule of swimming?" Brother called after him.

"No swimming alone!" Jack yelled.

"And what's the second rule?" Cole shouted.

"No swimming with sharks!" they all shouted together.

After Brother and Jack showered, Brother built a fire in the stove and they finished the cookies and what was left of the food from the night before. Cole produced a pack of cards and dealt a hand of Go Fish.

"You haven't asked what Lucy and I talked about."

"Don't care," Brother said, though he did. He couldn't afford not to.

"Well you should," Cole said. "Gimme all your jacks, Jack."

"You looked! You cheated!" Jack said, forking over two.

"Even morons don't cheat at Go Fish, Jackarini," Cole said. "I just wanted to say 'gimme all your jacks, Jack,' and got lucky." He set down his foursome and said to Brother, "Be ignorant if you want to. But you'll regret it. Gimme all your threes."

Brother gave him one. "Why's that?"

"Gimme your threes, Jackapoo."

"You peeked!" Jack said, pouting, but grudgingly handed him one. Cole put aside his second quartet.

"Tomorrow," Cole told Brother, "is G-day. That's what Lucy calls it. Gimme your twos."

Brother handed him a pair. "Because?"

"Because," Cole said smugly, "tomorrow your brother Gabe is coming home." He paused for dramatic effect. "They're *all* coming home."

13

THE NEXT MORNING, rain came down in relentless gray sheets. Trooper watched it gloomily from the front porch, and even Jack got sick of Go Fish and Cole's complaining and went to mope on the porch with Trooper.

Cole was cold. Cole was hungry for food they didn't have. Cole was damp and sandy to his dirty underwear.

He'd fast used up the wood he'd griped about fetching and piling on the porch the night before, and when Brother went out back to get more, he found the wood box open, the wood soaking wet. Without heat, the beach house quickly grew drafty and dank. Cole turned on the kitchen stove's four burners and oven on high and opened the oven door. He sat right in front of it moaning about the pathetic heat and the imagined comforts of "the manor house"—satellite TV, hot delicious food, clean dry clothes, roaring fireplaces, Jacuzzis, saunas, a heated pool—all denied him because Brother wouldn't knock on Eden's door.

"I get it," Brother said dryly. He was huddled in most of his clothes in the un-cursed recliner where he'd spent a restless night, while Jack and Cole slept in the bed under the sleeping bag. "You might get those things because of me, but right now, it's not my fault you don't have them. You're the one who got the wood wet."

"My misery rejects your logic," Cole said. "I'm going up there."

"Right," Brother told him, "and if Lucy's still mad and says she's never seen you before, her mother'll call the cops and have you arrested, and they'll throw away the key."

"The police'll have to wait for the ferry."

"Or maybe since Grayson's a senator, they'll send the Coast Guard or the military—they have helicopters."

"I'll take little Jack up there with me and they'll—"

"—arrest you and put Jack in a foster home."

Cole snarled.

"I don't want to go to a monster home," Jack whined from the porch.

"See what you started?" Cole said.

"You're the one who hasn't quit grousing since you got up. What happened to my friend who was glad I was myself again?"

"I *was* glad till you went all do-nothing again. I don't get why you won't go up there."

"Because if Lucy's right that they're coming, there's no point in all hell breaking loose till the senator and Gabe get here."

"At least hell is warm," Cole said, his palms to the open oven. "You and Gabe have the same face. Nobody's going to question *that*."

"It's not so simple."

"Is too."

"Leave on the ferry then. *It's* got heat."

"Must be nice, having options. I'm only here because you took Jack."

"*Took?*"

"I left him with *Mem*," Cole said defensively.

"Who was dead at the time."

"Which I didn't know, okay?"

Brother took a deep breath. "Look. You and Jack can get on the next *warm* ferry, catch a bus, and go back to doing whatever you want. I'll give you a hundred bucks. You could get your job back at The Elms. It's not like people are lining up to work there."

"A hundred won't get us very far."

"Okay two hundred. That's the best I can do right now."

"It's not," Cole said. "You're just selfish. We're homeless. *Our* situation's worse than *yours.*"

"It's not a contest!" Brother snapped. "Has it occurred to you that the Graysons might not be thrilled about me showing up?"

Cole didn't answer.

"Well, it occurred to me," Brother told him. "I may not like how Lucy's trying to manage and control everything, but she's right about timing. I thought about it all night."

"Poor you."

Brother ignored him. "Assume the Graysons *don't* know about me—and I don't think they do—that's a major shock. Twins aren't something they can easily dispute or deny."

"You don't know *what* they claim," Cole countered. "Maybe they claim Gabe's adopted. And that they honestly didn't know about you. You only know the few things Mem chose to tell you. Let's say you believe the little she said."

"I do," Brother said.

"Okay, me too. But her story's real thin, you know? A whale could swim through the holes in it. Even you've got to admit that."

"Maybe," Brother conceded, remembering what Warren had said about Mem hiding things, *maybe a lot of things.* "But whatever's true, when I show up—Gabe's carbon copy—they've got explaining to do. Maybe *even you* can see that?"

"What if they *do* know about you?"

"Say they *do.* Say they've known all this time, but never made any effort to find me or contact Mem. Not even a Christmas card. They're not likely to be happy I've found them. Plus, my twin's already causing them big trouble. Then I show up and cause more. Did I mention Grayson's a U. S. senator and running for reelection?"

"Your condescension's not appreciated," Cole said.

Brother sighed at the trundling noise coming down the walkway above them. "Gang's all here."

"Jack, honey, what's the matter?" Lucy's voice said.

"They're going to take me to a monster house!" Jack sobbed.

"Who is?"

"Brother and Cole!"

"They are not," Lucy said.

"They are! Brother said so!"

"Jesus Louise Christ," she said, coming through the door. "I could hear the two of you from the walk. Come out here and help me get this wood inside."

Cole stayed willfully put, but Brother followed Lucy out. She was swallowed in a hooded army-green slicker that belonged to someone bigger and taller. She handed Brother her backpack, which he set inside the door. They went to the walkway, where each took one end of the red wagon heaped with wood and worked it down the beach stairs and onto the porch.

"Peace offering," she said. "I brought oatmeal cookies and the makings for sandwiches."

"How'd you know Cole left the wood box open?"

"I didn't. You can thank Millicent when you meet her. I said I was coming down here to study where it was quiet, and she said I'd better take wood because the way Gabe uses the place, there was no telling how much was left. She never comes down here to check. She doesn't like the water. Or the sand. Or the cold and damp."

"Is Millicent *single?*" Cole said to Lucy. "I say we all go up to the main house, introduce Brother, get warm, kiss Millicent, and go from there."

"Oh, God, no! *Not* a good time," Lucy warned. "Why do you think I left? The place is crazy with preparations right now. A special ferry brought over the catering hordes. A *real* monster house."

"Great," Cole said, as Jack started a new wave of wailing.

Lucy closed her eyes. "Jack!" she shouted. "Get the wood that fell out on the porch, and put a sock in it!"

Jack quit and dragged in the log quarter, but made an ugly face at Lucy and Brother as he passed them. He dropped the wood by the stove and plopped down furiously next to Cole.

Lucy looked at Brother. "There's a lot we need to talk about, a lot we need to decide."

There was that *we* again, twice in one sentence.

"I want to go home," Jack pouted.

"Good luck with that," Cole told him, then eyed Brother.

"I want to go home now," Jack said louder.

"No can do, Jackaroo."

"Why not?" Jack demanded.

"Because our house isn't—"

"Don't, Cole," Brother interrupted. "There's dry wood now. Build a fire. Eat something."

"You build it," Cole snapped. "I'm not hungry."

"Me either. I hate it here," Jack said.

"You try to help people," Lucy said, and threw herself in a chair.

They all glared at Brother, like everything was his fault and his job to fix. Was this what it was like to have a constituency? Everybody constantly unhappy and wanting something? Even Trooper's whimpering had grown louder and his pacing more anxious on the porch. Brother went to open the door for him, looked up and down the beach and saw nothing, held the door open, but the dog wouldn't come in. He stood looking at Brother as if Brother should know what he wanted, and then when Brother didn't, he started pacing again.

"I'll take him for a walk to calm him," Brother said, needing to hit reset.

"*Now?* I just *got* here!" Lucy said.

"I won't be gone but a few minutes," he said.

"Promise?" she said. "We—"

"Have a lot to talk about, I know. And I want to hear," Brother told her, but with every *we* she spouted, he was listening less and less.

"Well, if you're coming right back, take this," she said, wriggling out of the slicker. Again, she was impractically dressed in a dress, tights, and a sparkly sweater, more for a party than a beach house. He even smelled perfume. "It's Gabe's, so it should fit you."

"Thanks," he said, and slipped it on. No surprise, it fit him perfectly. He pulled up the hood and hurried out the door, relieved to get away from Lucy's machinations, Cole's pity party, and Jack's tantrum, if only for twenty minutes. He wondered how far away he and Trooper could get, and however far, it wasn't far enough. Had Mem felt this way? She must have. She'd spent her whole childhood here, the daughter of a maid, surrounded by wilderness and water. What a confining place it must have been for a free-spirited girl. Maybe it was Eden to the Graysons, who came and went easily. Even Lucy and Gabe left the island and Satterfield for Washington and school. But to Mem, the island must have sometimes seemed a jail. Today, it sure seemed like one to him.

When he and Trooper got to the exit marker for the refuge parking lot, Trooper took off and galloped up the dune. Brother called to him, but he disappeared, and Brother had no choice but to follow. The ferry horn sounded as Brother reached the top. He ran through the scrub and the refuge lot after Trooper, who sped straight for the dock.

"True!" Brother called, but the dog ran full out until he was maybe a hundred yards from Eden's drive, where he suddenly stopped and growled. Brother caught up, winded, gasping for breath. The rain had picked up, and at first he thought it was just the dog's misery in the wet, but it was more than that. Trooper started to backtrack, his eyes widening and shifting between Brother and the road ahead.

"What is it, True?" Brother said, grabbing his collar.

Brother squatted and put both arms around the dog, but he wouldn't be calmed. Brother managed to move them onto the shoulder, so that they wouldn't be obvious to whatever Trooper thought was coming—because as sure as Mem was dead and the life of that little boy at the rest stop had been saved, something was. Trooper growled again as Brother heard the nearing sound of engines. A long, dark sedan appeared and turned slowly into Eden's drive, a big black SUV right behind it. Both cars' window glass was tinted dark and their lights shone yellow in the bleak day. In the first car, a backseat window was open. As it pulled into the drive, a pale face, something like Brother's own, briefly looked their way. At that distance, in the rain, it was impossible to see for certain if it was Gabe, and moments later the car was gone.

The second car parked across the drive entrance. It idled, but no one got out. Brother waited, wondering if they'd been seen.

He was glad he had hold of Trooper's collar, because suddenly his dog lurched *toward* the ferry. He yanked Brother off his heels and started to bark, this time the excited yips he sounded to greet a friend. A black pickup truck came barreling down the road past Eden and skidded to a sudden stop beside them. Brother's heart leaped to read Scripps' Scrap on the side.

"Turn on the damned cell phone, why don't you!" Kit snapped as her window lowered. "I've been trying to call you since last night. Get in the truck."

"Nice to see you too," Brother said, and rushed with Trooper to the passenger side. Trooper yipped and Frank replied in kind from the rear seat.

"Hurry up!" Kit told him. She was staring in her side mirror at the car blocking Eden's drive. A man got out and started their way. Brother barely got Trooper in back, slid into the passenger seat, and grabbed the door handle, before Kit gunned the engine and they hurtled down the refuge road.

14

"YOU SMELL LIKE A GIRL," Kit said. She sniffed the air, then glanced in the back where Frank and a soaked Trooper were turning in tight, excited circles, happy to see each other and eager to get out and play. "Rich girl and wet dog."

"Sorry on both counts," Brother said. "The coat's a loaner from my new stepsister, and True's as unhappy about being wet as you are. Was that—?"

"Yep."

"And—?"

"Yep, again. I tried to call and tell you. It was all over the news yesterday, because the national press hasn't got anything better to do than hound an eighteen-year-old drug addict."

"Seventeen."

Kit cut her eyes his way. "You're sure about that, are you?"

Brother pushed back his hood and leaned against the

headrest. He and Mem had never been sure about his exact birth day, but he'd never considered the *year* might be iffy.

"Happy belated birthday," Kit said.

"You're sure about that, are you?" he asked. She laughed as he pointed at the turn into the refuge lot. "I thought you weren't coming till tomorrow."

"You sounded like you might do something crazy like tear off after your brother. I thought about it, and in your place, no matter what anybody said, that's what I'd do. So when I heard he was headed home and you weren't answering your cell or, I'm guessing, picking up your messages . . . ?" She put the truck in park, killed the engine, and looked pointedly his way.

"Maybe later you could show me how to do that," he said, embarrassed by his ignorance. There'd never been enough money for a cell, for so many things.

Kit smiled. "Don't worry. I'll coach you into the twenty-first century."

"I'm really glad to see you."

Her smile broadened. "That makes blowing off my exam totally worth it."

"Miss four-point-oh?"

"Hard to believe, isn't it? Charlie actually felt my forehead. But I think he's glad to see me let go a little. He says I must think you're pretty special."

Brother smiled and shook his head a little.

"What?" Kit said.

"Like you said, hard to believe. My luck, I mean."

She looked thoughtful and reached for a folder behind her seat. "I brought something to show you. I found this on a blog after the news stories broke." She took a photo from the folder. It was a picture of Gabe, one arm around a basketball and the other around a brunette, the two at the center of six or eight other boys, maybe after a game. He wore the same smug expression he'd worn in the school picture in the newspaper and looked like he belonged at the center, like he owned it. "Didn't know you had basketball in you? Or tennis? Or lacrosse?"

Brother snorted. "News to me."

"Newsflash: you do. But that 'news to me' is the big difference between you and the boy in that picture. It's what I like about you. Charlie too. What even Mitchell and Carl like about you, even though you're related to you-know-who."

"You told them?"

"Only after they'd seen Gabe on TV and the bark was out of the dog. Carl said to tell you your car will either be fully restored or sold for scrap, depends on you."

They laughed.

"But what I was saying," she went on, "is that I like it that you're not all 'Look how wonderful I am,' like the guy in this picture." She stabbed Gabe's face with her index finger. "This guy's sharp-looking and savvy, but he wears it like bad cologne. I don't even have to meet him to smell it. He might be your twin, but if I'd run into him at that rest stop, he wouldn't have gotten to hello before I put my foot on the gas and kept going. So you talk about luck all you want, but luck's not why I'm here. Right, Frankie?"

Frank barked from the backseat, and Kit nodded at Brother like that made it a fact.

"Before we go back to Cole and Jack and Lucy," Brother said, "what do you say we catch our deaths and let the dogs run?"

"I'm there."

Kit got out and pulled a thick navy sweater and a poncho from behind her seat. She tossed the sweater at him, saying, "One of Charlie's he'll never fit in again," and slipped the poncho over her head. He put the sweater on under Gabe's slicker while she slung a small pack over one shoulder and let Frank and Trooper spill out the back. He saw a ferry schedule on the dashboard, the afternoon departure time highlighted in yellow. He wondered if she'd stay or go but didn't want to ask.

"I brought Charlie's sleeping bag, plus the camper," she said, opening the door to the shell on the truck bed. Inside, carefully nested in quilts and blankets, were his mother, grandfather, and grandmother's urns. The care she'd taken touched him.

"That's so thoughtful," he said.

"Seemed the right thing to do."

The dogs raced each other into the trees, barking in chorus. Brother could hear Frank's ecstatic falsetto as he reached the water and Trooper's answering bass. When he and Kit got to the dune, they stood at the top watching Trooper, wet enough already, barking and running back and forth in the sand, while Frank waded in chest-deep, hopped small waves with abandon, and tossed sea foam into the air with his snout as if it were snow.

"You've got your junkie, and I've got mine," Kit said, shaking her head.

They made their way down the dune where Brother showed her his exit marker, then walked along the refuge shore to give Frank his fix, which took some walking.

The wind drowned out all but the louder sea and everything together cleared Brother's head. He and Kit pointed and shouted to share the sights: a lone egret gliding inland, a dozen loud gulls wheeling over a fish-crowded stretch of sea, pelicans skimming the water (Kit said they looked like the winged monkeys in *The Wizard of Oz*); and after them, three loud, low-flying military helicopters heading back to a nearby base. They joked that they were spies for Senator, keeping an eye on his turf.

On their walk back, Brother told her about meeting Amos and showed her the path.

"Up that trail and right is the little house. It's not heated, but there's water for the dogs."

"Is it closer than the truck?"

"A little."

Kit nodded. "Frank could use a break from mainlining, and I want to see it."

There was no sign of Amos or his keeper. It was chilly in the playhouse, but the walls kept out the wind and rain and muted the sea sound, so they could talk more. Everything looked as it had the day before, down to the empty Oreo bag. Kit took a small towel from her pack and rubbed down both dogs on the porch. They took turns lapping the sulfury tap water from a plastic bowl, gobbled half a bag of treats, then flopped, worn out, on the bare floor and went to sleep, side by side. Kit pulled out a thermos, "For the humans," she said, and poured a cup of strong black coffee, which they shared.

"You've really got this down," Brother said, admiring her organization. "What else you got in there? Burgers and fries? A piano?"

She looked a little embarrassed. "Charlie says Liza's leaving turned me into a pack rat and a planner. He says it's why I used to squirrel food under the bed when I was little and kept all kinds of toys, books, clothes, and other stuff under the covers with me at night, *just in case*. I'm still kinda like that."

"Smart."

"You think so? I got friends who say I make the army look slapdash. They make fun of me for leaving no paper unwritten and no assignment to the last minute, call me an old lady at eighteen."

"You don't look like any old lady," he said, noticing how her black hair curled softly when it was wet, how her dark eyes had a violet cast in the stormy light. Even in a poncho the size of the pup tent, she was something.

"And the scrap yard's no image-builder. This boy I know says I'll turn into one of those crazy hoarders who collects so much stuff they can't even walk in their houses."

"A boy you know, as in boyfriend?" Brother asked.

"God, no. I mean, it's not like I don't date, but my friends are right. I feel old. I mean, compared to everybody else my age. Practically all the girls and boys I know seem about twelve."

"Practically?" he ventured.

She lowered her eyes, looked away.

"I'm sorry," he said. "That's none of my—"

"Except you."

"Mem used to call me an old soul, said that I'd squandered my youth taking care of an old woman with cancer." Kit looked up, smiled a little. "Without having looked in your room, I'd imagine it's like the back of the camper and the rest of your house." He paused to find the right word. "Homey."

"You looked!"

"I promise I didn't. And not because I'm not curious, but because I was too much in my own head, thinking about my own problems."

"Well, yeah!" she said, looking pleased he'd turned the conversation back to himself. She kept it there. "So tell me what's happened since we talked on the phone."

He filled in the blanks, told her more about meeting Amos and getting lost and upset and mad and what Cole had said about him being more himself afterward. "He's a pain sometimes, but he makes me laugh and his saying that made me feel I might . . . I don't know . . . come unstuck. Anyway, what he said made me feel better, even if he went back to griping after."

Kit sipped her coffee, listening closely, as usual.

"Okay," he said when he was done. "Your turn."

She passed him the thermos cup and sat up straighter in her chair, all business. "Okay, but keep in mind that a lot of this comes from gourd-heads on the Net and the evening news."

"Got it."

"Okay, so Gabe was at this Virginia country club rehab place working his thirty-day program and, like you saw in the paper, it was in the news, but under the radar, everybody pretty much minding their manners and business, until you and I and Jack showed up in Satterfield.

"But after that waitress saw you, she was all over the news saying Gabe had violated some court order. Then Gabe and the senator appeared with the head of the rehab place swearing that Gabe had not been anywhere near Satterfield during the specified time, pretty much calling that waitress a liar. So the waitress gets mad and back on the news, swearing on—I kid you not—a stack of Bibles, saying Gabriel Grayson *was so* in Satterfield, that if he says not he's lying through his perfect teeth, that this was a massive cover-up, just like his family covered up all his other messes. Seems Gabe's had some DWIs—*exact number in dispute*—one involving the waitress's kid brother, who was riding with him and got hurt so bad in a crash he still has seizures because of it. Now the media thinks that because your family's covered up stuff before, they're at it again. Justice, I'd've said, if they'd interviewed me, but they didn't. And footnote: that's when Carl calls Charlie, wondering what he really knows about the boy who was in his garage with so many dead people in the back of his car and who's squiring around his only daughter.

"But, back to our main story. Now 'Gabe sightings' have started coming out of the woodwork, at first following your and Trooper's path across our great state. But the busybodies and nutcases have been calling in too, people thinking they saw what they didn't. Upshot: You and your brother are pretty much *everywhere*."

"Great," Brother said.

"And before you go blaming yourself for popping the cork from that bottle, hear me say: This is in no way your fault. This is his own mess catching up with him."

Brother sat back in his chair, not sure which "he" she meant, Gabe or the senator. It was a lot to take in.

"That's why I drove down early. That, and because you turned off the phone. Though as it turned out, I'm glad I came when I did."

"You didn't know they'd be on the ferry?"

"No clue. And I don't think anybody else knows either—yet. Which is good, because it's likely the only reason Frank and I got to *stay* on the ferry. Frank and I were early—you know how I drive. Given the weather, the ferry guy seemed surprised to have any fare at all. Then maybe thirty seconds after we'd left the dock, the two limos pull up. Next thing I know, the ferry's in reverse and we're back where we started. Frank and I were in the truck—because of how he is near the wet stuff—so I don't know if somebody called the pilot over the radio or what. But before the ferry guy can leave, some man gets out of the SUV and they seemed to have a discussion about whether Frank and I'd be allowed to stay on board. I hear the ferry guy say, "It's just some teenaged girl and her beach-crazy dog," since when we'd gotten to the dock, Frank had been so worked up that the ferry guy asked if he was okay, and after I explained, the guy laughed and said he'd had a dog like that once. So crazy Frankie was my ticket to ride. Once again, dogs save the day!" she said, raising her arms and clenched fists in victory. Even weary, Frank heard the praise in her voice and his tail slapped the floor softly.

"So did you see them?"

"I saw Gabe. Once we'd left the dock again, Gabe got out of the car to lean against the railing and look out at the water. He wore sunglasses and he's not so cocky now as in that picture I showed you, more mad, but even so, for a second, I saw what that waitress saw, Brother. To somebody not looking carefully, *he's you*." She paused, looked contrite. "I'm sorry, but it's true."

"I guess I knew that already."

"Studying him, I could see differences, but prepare yourself. The initial shock was completely weird for me, and I can't even imagine what it'll be like for you."

"And the senator?"

"Him I only *heard*. When your brother was at the railing, he lit a cigarette, and suddenly the backseat window in the second car went down and the big man's voice comes booming out, "GAY-brull! Put that out and get IN-side this KAH!""

Brother smiled. "You do a good impression."

But Kit didn't smile back. "Your twin just let that cigarette drop into the water. And for a second, when he turned, I could really see him. His face? Vacant. Not like that picture at all. That boy went to that car like a whipped dog."

"You softening toward the Graysons?"

"No, I am not. I'm just reporting what I saw. Tell me about your stepsister."

"She's okay, but I think she sees me as a way to get attention she doesn't get otherwise."

"Because she's not the favorite son?"

He nodded. "Because she lives in Gabe's shadow. Because she's a girl. Because her mother's unhappy and into herself. Probably a hundred other reasons I don't know. When I showed up, I think she saw an opportunity, a way to gain an upper hand or get even."

"So do you think she's out of the loop or do you think she knows things she's not telling?"

"Both," he said, and paused. "But I haven't told her everything either. For instance, I haven't told about you."

"Hah! I feel like a secret weapon. And not telling her or them everything, that's just smart. Right now, smart is the main thing you have to be." But suddenly she hesitated, looked at him warily. "You haven't kept things from me, have you? Things I need to know?"

"God, no," he said.

"Good. Fine. That's all I need to know."

"No, it's not," Brother said. "I know we've just met, but I'm not only grateful to you, I like you *a lot*. So what I need to say is, when we get back to the beach house and it's not just us and the dogs anymore, and I can't always think out loud with you or talk to you straight and one-on-one like I've done up to now, I hope you'll remember that."

Kit looked at him seriously. "You remember it, too."

But before he could say more, there were voices outside and they turned to the door.

15

"SIR, I'M SORRY, I didn't think anyone would be here. Never seen you here before," said Amos's minder, as Brother, Kit, and the dogs came out of the house and started down the steps. He was the same man Brother'd seen with Amos earlier. He and Amos stood together, elbows linked, on the edge of the small yard. "I'll get us gone fast as I can. C'mon, Amos, old friend, we got to give way to the young people today."

He tugged gently on Amos's arm, but the old man had other ideas, pulled free and went stubbornly toward the steps. He wore the same black cap and brown greatcoat, but today his long gray hair was neatly combed and banded in a ponytail, his stony face clean-shaven, his drool only a trickle. Brother noted the small towel the minder held in one hand, like the washcloths he'd kept handy for the droolers at The Elms.

"Please don't go on our account," Brother said, glancing at Kit, who had both dogs' collars. "We were just leaving."

The minder smiled apologetically and kept trying to steer Amos back the way they'd come, without any success. Amos's bland expression grew cross, his face red, and he made a loud keening sound through his clenched teeth. Like the worst afflicted at The Elms, he had no tolerance for frustration. He wanted what he wanted, and he wanted it now.

"Really, we just stopped in to water the dogs, and they're watered," Kit said. She ordered both dogs to sit and stay, which they did, reluctantly, impatiently wagging twin arcs in the wet ground. She took treats out of her pocket and rewarded them. "I'm Kit, by the way, and that's Frank and that's Trooper," she added, pointing. "I don't think we've met."

"Tommy," the man said, smiling broadly and extending his hand, which Kit shook warmly. "Hey, Frank, and hello again, Trooper," he said, and nodded toward the old man. "This is Amos."

"Nice to meet both of you sirs," Kit said.

Tommy's eyes brightened at Kit's respectful manner. Amos grunted at the sound of her voice, and his blue eyes lighted on her for a moment, then on the dogs and Brother, though he gave no sign that he recognized Brother or Trooper from the previous day. He returned to his determined tottering toward the house, Tommy steadfastly beside him. "Hard to dissuade you once your mind's set, isn't that right, old friend?"

Amos either didn't hear him or pretended not to.

"Good to see you again, Amos," Brother said anyway. "How are things?"

"Most days aren't so bad, isn't that right?" Tommy answered, glancing at Amos for agreement he didn't get. "Like that for most people, I guess, us a little more so. But yesterday was a good day. You opened your own drink," he said to Amos. "And drank it without me helping. New medicine must be working."

Brother remembered the Coke he'd opened and didn't say different. From his time at the nursing home, he knew the joy of small victories—if only for the staff—a pound gained, a laugh or a word after a week of silence. He liked Tommy's optimism, how he kept from talking about Amos in the third person and included him in conversations he likely didn't understand—though who knew? Brother had tried to do that with the old people at The Elms, in case something got through.

"He likes this house," Brother said.

"He does that. About as much as swimming."

"Swimming!" Kit said.

Tommy nodded. "Till about six months ago, we swam in the ocean every day. Surprising isn't it? Now we try to keep clear of the wa—"

"If you could not say that word," Kit interrupted quickly and loudly. "I'm sorry, but the word W-A-T-E-R makes the black dog bonkers."

"You're kidding me?" Tommy said, chuckling over his shoulder. He and Amos had been making steady progress up the steps and were nearly to the top.

"Afraid not," she said.

Tommy shook his head. "It's a strange and wondrous world.

But like I was saying, we used to swim every day it was warm enough, and my friend here swam far better than I ever will. Peculiar to the sickness, the doctor says. Doing that one thing, he hardly seemed sick at all, though recently there's been, well"—he lowered his voice—"a decline."

Brother thought of Howard, a resident at The Elms. He had Amos's same halting walk, mask-like face, and drooling, except when he rode the exercise bike in the common room. Atop the two wheels he'd pedaled like a happy ten-year-old, sometimes for hours, and Brother and the other aides had let him. "The definition of going nowhere fast," one aide had said, but Brother had watched the old man's brighter eyes and faraway smile and thought differently.

Finally Tommy and Amos reached the porch. Amos headed inside while Tommy waited to see if Brother or Kit needed something more. The rain had stopped, and Kit set the dogs free to roughhouse among the trees.

"Take care, Tommy, Amos," Brother called.

Tommy looked at Brother oddly, as if trying to make sense of the young man who stood before him.

"You too, sir! And a pleasure to meet you, ma'am. Good to see you looking so well again, sir," he added. "If you don't mind me saying, you seem a lot better!"

He lingered studying Brother, then all of them looked skyward to the sound of helicopters overhead. Tommy saluted the sky, and said, "God bless."

"Bye, Tommy," Kit said, and went after Frank and Trooper. Brother waved and ran to catch up with her and the dogs.

"Tommy's nice," she said, as Brother fell in step beside her. The dogs circled back to her whistle and trotted ahead of them on the path. "If I were like Amos, I'd want somebody kind like Tommy taking care of me." She paused. "Like you. What you did yesterday? Most people, if they met Amos in a lonely place like this, they wouldn't pause to chat. They'd run the other way."

Brother shrugged. "I'm used to it and Lucy told me he was harmless."

"Yeah, but I'll bet she didn't rush over to say *Hey, Amos, how're you doing?* Which just makes her like most people, either grossed out or scared of people like him. But not you. You stopped to talk and figured out he needed his drink opened and helped him drink it."

"I didn't tell you that."

"Am I wrong?"

He didn't answer.

"That's kind."

"Back there," he said, "what I said—"

"What you said," Kit interrupted, "about being able to think out loud with me?"

"I can and do whenever possible."

"That's about the nicest compliment anyone's ever given me."

"It is?" he asked.

"Yes! It means you trust me and you'll tell me what I need to know to make my own decisions."

"But I hardly know what *I* think most of the time."

"Well, me either!"

"You always seem to know what you think."

Kit sighed. "I'm opinionated, but that's not the same thing."

"Well, you're much better at thinking for yourself and making good decisions than I am."

Kit shook her head. "You've had to keep a lot inside. Hidden from your sick grandmother. Maybe even from yourself. You had to put her first. But from what you've told me about her, she was all about thinking for yourself. And you do fine at thinking, a lot better than most people. Heck, Brother, don't you know? Most people don't think at all!"

"You sound like her."

"And that's about the second nicest compliment I've ever gotten because I know how highly you thought of her and what she meant to you. Thank you."

Brother remembered the ferry schedule in the truck and made himself ask. "So do you have to leave this afternoon?"

Kit looked surprised.

"I saw the ferry schedule on the dash."

"And . . . ?"

He was confused. "And what?"

"And you're hoping I will . . ."

"Stay. *Please.* I'd really like it if you stayed."

Kit nodded decisively. "Then that's what I'll do."

❋ ❋ ❋

At the truck, he insisted on paying her what he owed her, plus extra for gas. She told him they didn't have to settle now, but he wanted to. It made him feel better to square things, even if he had to borrow from her again later—but borrow, he told her, was all he'd ever do. She showed him how to get messages on his phone. "I set it on vibrate for privacy and brought a charger," she said, with a chiding look, "so you can leave it *on*."

She opened the back of the camper and pointed at a cooler. "I've got hot dogs and s'more makings for Jack. Also flashlights. Batteries. Sunscreen, though maybe that's optimistic. Bottled water, a first-aid kit, TP, soap, tissues—"

"Kit," he said, stopping her. "It's time."

Frank gave a low growl as he took her hand in his, but he held on.

"I knew when they came on the ferry," Brother said. "I was selfish, wanted a little more time with you. But after, when we ran into Tommy and he thought I was Gabe . . ."

She nodded. "I know. I wonder if Tommy's called Eden to say it was good to see Gabe so changed for the better, and nice to meet his girlfriend and their dogs. Hush, Frank."

Frank stopped growling as she clipped on his leash.

"How do I look?" Brother asked.

She nodded approvingly. "Charlie's sweater makes a nice difference. A fresh shirt and a haircut wouldn't hurt you," she said, handing him a comb from her back pocket. "But then you'd look more like your brother and less like you. What about Cole and Jack?"

"They'll be fine for an hour or two. Lucy brought wood and food this morning. We'll figure everything out before dark."

"Are we all four going?" she said, looking at the dogs.

"Unless you and Frank want to stay here or hang out on the beach with the whiners."

She laughed. "And miss the senator's jaw hitting the parquet? Front door or back?"

Brother glanced at Mem's urn. "I think she'd want us to go in through the front door, don't you?"

16

THEY LEASHED THE DOGS and cut through the woods to join Eden's drive below the secured front entrance. The afternoon was overcast, but footlights along the drive glowed softly through the grayness and misting rain. At first, having Kit and the dogs with him buoyed Brother's resolve, but the farther they got down the drive, the more his confidence waned. The decision that felt right minutes before now seemed stupid and rash. Only an idiot was fool enough to march up to Gideon Grayson's front door. What was he thinking? At minimum he'd be arrested, as he'd warned Cole, and more likely squashed like a bug. *I knew that woman was hiding something, maybe a lot of somethings,* Warren had said, and Brother now felt sure he was right and wondered what other secrets Mem had found easier to keep to herself.

The drive curved sharply around several large rocks. He saw the lights of the house through the screen of trees and stopped. He studied Trooper. The dog sat and waited calmly, his soft eyes expectant, without worry or fear. If trouble lay ahead, he gave no sign.

"It's okay to be scared and have second thoughts," Kit said quietly. "Even third and fourth thoughts. I would."

Brother nodded. "I never really doubted Mem before."

Kit looked toward the house, as if thinking about whether to say something or not, and then back at Brother. "I didn't know your grandmother, but from what you've told me, I think she was a fine person. As fine a person as Charlie, and he's the best person I know."

"I think so too."

"But everybody has blind spots, things they're good at and things they're not. Charlie's been a great dad to me, but he once told me he didn't think he'd been a very good husband to Liza. He didn't say more, but that was the first time it occurred to me that a person could be good at one and not the other. It sounds like Mem wasn't such a good mother to her daughter, your mom, but she was a good grandmother to you."

Brother nodded.

"The other thing I think might sound weird."

She hesitated, but Brother nodded again for her to go on.

"From what you've said, I don't think anything in the world would've brought your grandmother back here. But I think she raised you to walk down this drive."

"What do you mean?"

"Think about it. All those years she kept tabs on the senator and told you about him. Her independent ways and good manners. Her befriending Warren, who was a good role model for you. How she wanted you to go to college and study the law. Even joining you to a church she didn't hold with and standing up to that minister who thought the exact opposite of everything she held dear. It's like she was trying to prepare you to stand up for yourself against people like the senator. I think she prepared you the only way she knew how."

"I didn't tell you all that."

"And I haven't told you about my two hours shopping with Cole before he hitched down here. I hardly got a word in. Brother this and Brother that. He might be flaky sometimes, but he's a good talker and he thinks an awful lot of you."

Brother snorted, surprised.

"Did he tell you why he left Jack at your house?"

"He told me he freaked because they were losing their house."

"That's not all he told me. He said the night before he left you two got sorry drunk and fought and Jack got upset. He watched you with Jack and knew he wasn't half the brother he wanted to be. He'd seen how smart you were in GED class, watched you take care of Mem and how good you were with the old people at the nursing home, plus how much Jack liked you. He said you were the better man. Better for Jack. That Jack would be better off with you."

"With *Mem*," Brother said.

"No. Cole knew Mem was dying. He said, 'better off with Brother.' But she's a big part of the reason you're who you are. She's a lot of the why."

Brother stood there, trying to take all this in.

"I'm sorry, I wasn't going to tell you that till later. You've got enough on your mind. You want to go back?"

"We're here. Let's go before I lose what's left of my nerve."

And he nearly did lose it five or six times as they rounded the curve and walked the rest of the way to the Grayson's sprawling house. The white columns of its two-story portico gleamed like teeth, above which high windows blazed like all-seeing eyes. There were lighted terraces and balconies; barbered hedges; and rolling, sodded lawns. The compound shone with light enough to illuminate all of Schuyler and the surrounding county. Several vans and expensive cars were parked in the drive.

Kit surveyed everything and whistled. "I read his wife's got more money than he does. Plastic forks."

"What?"

"*Her* fortune. Plastic forks, spoons, and knives."

"Business must be good."

They walked through a dormant low-walled garden and around a stone pool crowded with fat orange fish. Kit held tight to Frank's leash at a fountain where a life-sized stonework Adam and Eve lay asleep like children under an apple tree, no serpent in sight. Through the windows, Brother saw chandeliers, fancy wallpapers, and furnishings that further told people of means lived inside. He looked through the lighted windows for Gabe or Lucy but saw only well-dressed men and women rushing back and forth, up and down the stairs, and through the halls. Everything was rich, imposing, and just so, but it was odd how the whole thing struck him. Compared with the house on the beach and the neighboring refuge, the mansion and grounds seemed gaudy, artificial, out of place.

"Looks like something's going on," Kit said.

They climbed the front steps to the two-story portico that ran the length of the house. Brother stared up at the second floor windows and at a tapered porch light hanging high overhead like a sword.

"You look like a tourist," Kit teased. She sounded so much like Mem that it steadied him. He looked once more at Trooper, who looked blankly back, then pressed the bell.

A chime rang in the house and the dogs' ears pricked at the high sound. Almost instantly, a deadbolt turned and a scowling, officious man in a dark suit and tie opened the door. Behind him, waiters dressed in black and white bustled by with vases of flowers and glasses on silver trays.

"The prodigal returns," the man said in a disapproving voice. He thumbed a short message on his phone keyboard, then looked impatiently at Brother. "Lose your key?"

"No, sir," Brother said, as the man scrutinized Kit and the dogs.

"You're not bringing dogs through here," the man said, "take them around to the kitchen."

Brother stood taller and cleared his throat. "Begging your pardon, sir, but if you would please tell Senator Grayson that Mem's grandson, Billy Grace, would like to see him."

"Mem? Who in hell is Mem?" the man sneered, looking at

Brother in disbelief. "Are you high? Senator's fighting for his political life, and you're already smuggling in your druggie pals and God knows what else." He aimed the last crack at Kit, and Frank started to growl.

"Please, sir, lower your voice," she said, "my dog—"

"You'd best restrain that dog," the man ordered.

"He's just reacting to your tone, sir," Kit told him.

"Are you threatening me, young woman?"

"No, sir. But my dog thinks *you're* threatening *me*, and that upsets him."

A second growl and the sight of Frank's canines seemed to give the man pause.

"Sir," Brother said, calmly, "if you could please tell the senator—"

"I'm not your errand boy," the man snapped. "And I damn sure won't be party to your pranks. Take those curs around to the kitchen."

When they didn't move, his eyes widened and he yelled, "Now!" and slammed the door.

Kit looked at Brother. "That went well."

He smiled grimly. Maybe Lucy had been right about timing. He tried to think what to do next.

Before he could, there were raised, simultaneous voices on the other side of the door, among them the rude man's voice saying Gabe would be the end of them all, and Lucy's insisting she didn't know anything about what Gabe had been doing since he got home or anything about a girlfriend and that Gabe always ruined everything. A woman's shrill voice called out, asking if chaos was going to continually keep her from getting her party face on and would someone please bring her a drink. But everyone fell abruptly silent when Senator's unmistakable voice resounded, shouting that even a hawk wanted peace in his own household. This was followed by what sounded like stomping, a slammed door, and unintelligible whispering between the rude man and the senator, then a silence so pregnant it might have borne triplets, after which the front door swung open and Brother found himself face-to-face with the senator himself.

The first syllable of Gabriel's name died on the senator's lips. Annoyance drained with the color from his face and shock replaced his penetrating stare. The man who scolded presidents and dictators as if they were schoolboys stood before him completely disarmed, and at the same time it seemed to Brother, exquisitely vulnerable. At least the senator looked this way for about ten seconds, when he appeared to remember himself and his face rehardened to its usual stone. Only his dark eyes moved slightly as he took in Brother, feature by feature, as if trying to disprove what he had instantly, instinctively known: that Brother was not his son.

"Sir, my name is Billy Grace," Brother said. "Mem was my grandmother, and I believe I'm Gabriel's—"

"Mem is dead?" the senator demanded.

"Yes, sir, almost a week ago," Brother replied.

The senator's gaze dropped to the floor and lingered there, after which he lifted his eyes and said, more quietly, "She told you to come here?"

"No, sir. I came on my own."

Maybe Brother imagined it, but he thought the senator seemed disappointed.

"Gabriel's picture. It was in the paper," Brother told him. "Before that I—"

"So it was," the senator interrupted, and then fell silent until something seemed to dawn on him. "It was you who was seen in Satterfield."

"Yes, sir."

"And elsewhere?"

"I don't know, sir. Maybe."

"Well. That explains a good deal."

"You couldn't have sprung your surprise at a worse possible time," put in the rude man who'd answered the door.

"Again, sirs, I only found out a few days ago, after—"

The rude man *tsk*ed. "An unlikely story if I've ever—"

"Eric," the senator interrupted, "have you sent that communication to the secretary?"

"No, sir, I haven't had time, I—"

"Find the time now, Eric. And then find something else to do."

Eric glared at Brother but huffed off to do as he was told.

"Your given name is—" the senator began.

"Billy's my given name, sir, but I'm called Brother."

The senator managed a thin smile. "How apt." He regarded Kit.

"I'm Kit Scripps, Senator Grayson, sir, Brother's friend." Kit put out her hand, which the senator shook with a cool, courtly nod. Kit's formality seemed to flip an invisible switch inside him. He squared his shoulders and, glancing at the gathering onlookers in the hall, shifted into full automatic, his televised self. He took a step back and opened the door wider, addressing Brother, but everyone else as well.

"Please do accept my sincere condolences for your loss, for all of our loss," he said, in his most gracious voice, "and do come inside."

"If you'll point me in the right direction, I can take the dogs around back, sir," Kit said quickly.

"That won't be necessary, young lady. In this modern age we do have such things as vacuum cleaners and senate aides to propel them," he told her, glancing at the rude man who was eavesdropping while he tapped his phone in the corner. The man's face reddened. The small crowd in the hall, a mixture of uniformed waitstaff and several others in suits, looked full of questions as Brother, Kit, and the dogs walked inside.

Senator spoke to the onlookers. "You may all return to whatever important work you were doing," he told them sternly, and they scattered like mice.

"If you will wait for me through there, in the library," he said to Brother, pointing to a paneled door beside the entrance, "I will show Miss Scripps and the hounds to the pantry, where they may take refreshment."

Kit took Trooper's leash from Brother, mouthed "good luck," and followed the senator. She and the dogs disappeared into what looked like a dining room on the far side of the large entry hall, leaving Brother alone.

The large hall rose two floors. Brother took in the thick carpets, heavy furniture, and the huge, heady flower arrangements spilling out of two standing vases against the far wall. Everything was spotless and polished to a glaring shine. It was the kind of place he'd seen only on television or in a movie, never in person. This was where his brother lived, what Gabe was used to. He looked up the curved, banistered staircase that led to a railed landing on the second floor. Talk and the clatter of party preparations sounded in the rest of the house. He saw or heard no sign of Lucy or his brother.

The heavy library door shut behind him with a soft whoosh. He hung Gabe's slicker on a hat rack by the door, smoothed Charlie's sweater, and combed his damp hair as best he could with his fingers.

The library lighting was dim, the lamps turned low, the deep red drapes drawn closed. A small herd of cattle had died to cover the red leather couches and chairs arranged in a large central seating area. Parallel walls of bookcases ran the library's length, split on one side by an unused fireplace and on the other by a cabinet holding a half-dozen shotguns and rifles. The bookcases held matching sets of dark leather-bound books, the ones nearest Brother on history or law. The volumes stood like spit-shined soldiers, so perfectly lined up that he wondered if anyone used them or if they were just for show.

At the room's far end was a long trestle table of dark wood

that seemed to serve as the senator's desk. The feet were ornately carved like the paws of a lion, and the empty surface shone. Behind it, on the wall, hung framed photographs of the senator shaking forty or fifty celebrated hands. Brother recognized the presidents, vice presidents, and first ladies of the last fifteen or twenty years along with a number of the famous and others he didn't know. All important people, he saw, by the way they were dressed and where they stood, in front of the Lincoln Memorial or the White House or other momentous places, or because the picture was autographed, and who would hang a signed picture of a nobody?

He walked around to the senator's side of the desk and saw a small, framed photo of his twin at maybe eleven or twelve with a younger Lucy and, he supposed, Lucy's mother, whose painted face, formal clothes, and jewelry explained Lucy's dressing up. Seeing his spitting image beside a man his grandmother hated was surreal, as if he'd had another life he'd forgotten, one that might any minute jump him from behind. But oddly, it reassured him, too. There were mysteries and questions, but whether he and Gabe were brothers wasn't one of them, something he had to prove. He eyed the phone, all seven or eight lines ablaze, and fingered the cell phone in his pocket, his connection to Kit. And then he sat in a chair in front of the desk and waited for the senator to come.

He waited a long time. He imagined the senator speaking to his family and aides, and Brother wished he could hear how the old man explained things. When the senator finally entered,

Brother stood as Mem had taught him, and he saw the senator note this.

"Have a seat, Brother," he said, taking his own chair behind the desk. "William is your *proper* given name?"

"No, sir," Brother answered, and sat again. "It's Billy, though no one's ever called me that."

The senator frowned, something he was good at; his face fell naturally into censure. They sat looking at each other, neither one of them saying anything. Brother studied the senator's once handsome features, slackened by time and gravity; the widow's peak at the front of his dark slicked-back hair, every comb-row visible. He didn't look at all like Brother or Gabriel. But his manner favored someone's and when he laced his fingers together on his desk with his thumbs crossed and his forefingers straight out, in a there's-the-church-and-there's-the-steeple way, Brother thought of Reverend Harvey.

"There are many things you don't know," the senator said solemnly. "Many things, it appears, I do not know myself. It will take time to sort matters out."

"Is Gabe all right?" Brother asked.

"Always an open question," the senator said quickly.

The glib and evasive reply irritated Brother, and his face must have shown it. Little, if anything, was lost on the old man. One eyebrow lifted as if to contest Brother's right to irritation or to ask such questions, but almost instantly the senator said, "Yes, well," and Brother took him to mean that he understood the brotherly concern but that certain things were as they were.

After that the senator went silent again, as if considering carefully what to say. The wide desk between them looked like real acreage then. Brother shifted uncomfortably in his hard, high-backed chair. As the Graysons could plainly afford something better, it seemed calculated to make the visitor squirm. The whole room was arranged to put the senator in control, at its center, and made Brother think of the photo of Gabe that Kit had found on the Web. Senator Grayson sat in his large chair as if on a throne, cozy in a power that no one was meant to challenge.

All this should have cowed Brother, but to his surprise, it didn't. Maybe Mem's rants, what Lucy and Kit had told him, together with Mitchell and Carl's earthy opinions, had cut the big man down to size, given Brother some immunity. A clock ticked on the bookshelf. As Mem had taught him, he didn't rush to fill the silence but waited for the senator to speak.

"What do you know about your origins?" he asked finally. The way he said it, like a dare, made Brother sure he wasn't saying what he meant. Brother thought of high school Spanish class, where he'd had to silently translate the teacher's questions into English before he could answer. He thought what the senator had really asked was, "What do you ignorantly believe about yourself?"

"Sir?"

"About your parentage."

Brother saw no reason to hold back. "I never knew my father. My mother was killed in a car accident when I was three."

The senator nodded. Brother couldn't tell if either was news to him.

"Go on."

"I was raised by my grandmother, Mem."

"Go on."

"She said she'd run away when she was a teenager."

"Yes."

"That she'd run off with a boy called Billy who'd put her in the family way—"

"How like her to bear no responsibility in the matter. Please continue."

"She said she and Billy were childhood sweethearts, but ran off to get married—"

"To my knowledge and according to the records of the State of North Carolina, Mem and Billy were never legally wed." The senator said this with a relish that sent a shiver through Brother. "Anything else?"

"Before my mother was born, my grandfather was drafted and later died in the Vietnam War."

The senator snorted. "Mem always did love fairy tales. Anything else?"

Brother fell silent then, reluctant to have any more of Mem's cherished memories picked off like small game. "That's all I know, sir."

The senator regarded Brother as though he very much doubted that. "You have more composure than your twin," he said, with a reappraising look, "and far better manners."

"It's kind of you to say so, sir," Brother told him, dispatching a lieutenant from Mem's army.

The senator smiled slightly, said, "Mem raised you well."

Brother felt they were playing a game, one he hardly understood, with confusing rules, high stakes, and serious penalties for the losing side. Despite Mem's lessons, he felt at a huge disadvantage.

"All right then," the senator said, "what do you extrapolate *might* be true?"

Brother hesitated.

"*Extrapolate* means—"

"I know what it means, sir. Everything's happened so fast, I haven't had time to—"

"Fair enough," the senator interrupted. "You're also smarter than your twin."

"I doubt that, sir, the school I went to—"

"I'm not talking about schools," the senator snapped. "Any fool can learn names and dates."

Brother waited to see where this was going.

"What if I told you that I'm still extrapolating myself?" the senator said. "What if I told you that though there is not one question in my mind that you are Mem's grandchild and Gabriel's twin, I had no idea that you existed until this very day?"

Brother didn't know what to believe, and this time the senator's face gave nothing away.

"I am as thunderstruck as anyone here." The senator paused. "Saying any more will entail telling you things you may not wish to hear."

Someone knocked lightly at the door, and the senator looked up as a man wearing an earpiece poked his head in and nodded at the phone where a single red light remained flashing.

"Tell her I'll call her back."

"She says—"

"I don't give a damn what she says," the senator told him, with the finality of an ax falling, and the man quickly ducked out and shut the door. "Your decision?"

Brother wanted to know and didn't, but he nodded for the senator to go on.

The senator opened the right hand drawer of his desk, took out a small gold-framed picture and handed it to Brother. It was a faded photo of two sun-browned boys, one clearly older, and two smiling girls, one blond and sunburned, the other brunette and dark, all between maybe eight and fourteen. The four were smiling and holding fishing poles. The brunette held up a small, silvery fish, dangling from a line, her large eyes shining proudly. Mem.

"The younger boy on the left is my brother William, Billy, as Mem called him, as he called himself. Mem is next to him, holding the fish, then my sister, Mamie. The boy on the right you see sitting before you. Mem, Billy, Mamie, and I all played together when we were children. In those days Winter Island was an even more isolated place than it is now, especially for the young. What few children lived here played and learned together, whatever their ages or races or class. Other children came and went with our more transient staff, but Mem's mother, Muriel, was our housekeeper for many years, and Mem lived here from the time she was a toddler until she ran off as a girl, nearly all our young lives.

"Because of this and because we were all more or less the same age, Mem was for all purposes a member of our family. In the early years, when my brother, sister, and I were educated at home, Mem was tutored alongside us. The four of us were close—very close—but Mem and Billy had a special bond. They were joined at the hip, as people say, from the day they met. We four did most everything together, but Mamie used to say that Mem and Billy were so close that they thought each other's thoughts. Our parents, absorbed in their own ambitions and priorities, left us alone. They assumed our closeness would lessen over time and we would drift apart, as children do, especially after my brother, sister, and I were sent off to school, here only at holidays and in the summer."

Brother placed the little picture on the desk and the senator's gaze lingered over it before he went on.

"But Mem and Billy's affection for each other did not wane as they grew older or spent time apart. In fact, time and separation made their bond stronger. Later, the adults saw their error in letting them become so familiar, and their fault in encouraging Mem's aspirations above her station. Mem was, even to those who loved her, a headstrong and difficult girl. She was reckless, always in trouble, breaking bones and rules and hearts. She and Billy shared a deep love of the wild places on this island and the impulsive ideas in their heads."

The senator's voice hardened at this last and he looked

to the door, as if he were thinking of someone or something beyond it.

"Mem was what used to be called a tomboy, barely civilized, and later what she and those fanatical times called a flower child, but what in any day any sensible person would call a willful, wanton girl. When she and Billy became teenagers, certain other things took place between them that the adults further chose to deny. Your grandmother became pregnant with your mother the summer before she turned seventeen. And the morning after this was known, Mem and Billy ran off, and soon because Billy was eighteen and not in college, he was drafted and sent to Vietnam."

There was rising resentment in the senator's voice as he spoke, and Brother couldn't tell if it was the running off or the getting drafted or both that riled him. "Your and Gabriel's mother—"

"Billie," Brother said.

"What?" The senator chaffed at the interruption.

"Her name was Billie too, but spelled with an i-e."

The old man paused for a long, punishing moment, then continued as if he hadn't heard. "The entire circumstances of your mother's birth and rearing remain an utter mystery to me, as does the identity of your father. I didn't know your mother existed until she knocked at our door with *one* out-of-wedlock toddler in her arms. *One* baby boy. Of course, my late wife Mary and I invited her in, just as I have invited you. I had always hoped to know more about Mem's life after she left us. Before that night, I supposed she had done what so many hardhearted girls do when they get themselves in such circumstances."

Brother really shrank from the old man then. He realized how poorly the senator had known Mem, how little he understood her deepest heart.

"There was no mistaking the young woman who arrived here was Mem's daughter—she greatly favored her mother. She claimed not to know Mem's whereabouts at that time. The truth of her story is anyone's guess.

"The night your mother came, my late wife, Mary, who could not have children, went crazy over the little boy, which was exactly what your mother had hoped. While my wife doted on the child in the living room, your mother asked if she could speak with me alone. She sat in that very chair, where you sit now, and without one tear or the slightest hesitation, told me she would sell her child to me for ten thousand dollars."

He stopped there. Brother saw the senator had hoped to shock him, and had, though Brother worked hard not to show it. He half-expected the old man to gloat, to further disparage his mother, but he didn't. At first his restraint impressed Brother, but the senator's refusal to say more also cast his mother in a colder light. There was so little Mem had told him about his mother that he had nothing warm or loving to counter it with. He thought of her sitting here, exactly where he sat, selling his brother to the senator, and shifted uncomfortably in his chair.

"Does Gabriel know?" Brother asked.

"That he's adopted? Yes, though, as a private family matter, it is not generally known."

Brother fell silent, trying not to react. He didn't want the senator to have the satisfaction of knowing his feelings about any of this before he knew them himself. He had a lot to think on, a lot to sort out.

"I suppose some semblance of what I have just told you will have to be told publicly now," the senator went on. He'd said *some semblance* instead of *the truth*, Brother noted. "And in due course, once inquiries have been made, and my wife Caroline and I have had time to discuss it, some formal provision might be made for your future."

"I have to think," Brother said quickly, wanting to get out of there, breathe fresh air. "It's all so—"

"Of course you do," the senator said, rising, suddenly as eager to leave as Brother was. "And I have guests arriving shortly. We're having a small fundraiser here this evening, scheduled long before all the recent nonsense. One hundred or so people will arrive shortly by private ferries. You and Miss Scripps are welcome to attend if you like, and I will think of something to tell our guests, all of whom, fortunately, are long-time contributors or family friends. I understand from Lucy that you are here with friends as well. Millicent, our housekeeper, will provide whatever you need. For now, our home is yours, Brother. We will discuss other matters soon."

Brother understood he was being dismissed. The senator extended his hand and, Mem's ever-polite grandchild, Brother shook it.

"May I please see my brother now?" he asked.

"You may," the senator said with annoyance, "as soon as anyone can find him."

And before Brother could ask what he meant, the senator abruptly strode out of the room and the library door shut behind him.

17

AFTER THE SENATOR LEFT, Brother sat quietly for a few minutes, his head bowed. It was one thing to hear Mem talk about the senator's bullying, read about it in a newspaper, or see it on TV, but it was something else to suffer it at close range. Though he'd held his own and the senator hadn't touched him, he felt like he'd been pummeled. He'd paid attention so acutely his head ached and he'd bitten his tongue nearly off.

He crossed the room for Gabe's slicker, troubled by more questions than when he'd come. Had his mother only wanted money? Then why had she sold one child and not two? Why Gabe and not him? He needed to find his brother, and wondered if he could slip out the door to search without anyone seeing him, just as a starched, unsmiling woman sidled into the room.

Everything about her was gray—her hair, her blouse and skirt, even the ashen cast of her skin; and her grayness made her seem only partly there, as if she might at any moment fade into the wall behind her and disappear.

"Two of you," she sighed.

He put out his hand. "Brother Grace, ma'am."

Her eyes widened slightly in surprise, but she didn't take it. "Millicent," she corrected. "Not ma'am. Not Millie. Millicent."

Brother let his hand drop to his side and tried to remember the little Lucy had said about Eden's housekeeper. She was a good cook; that much he knew firsthand. He thought about Mem's mother, Eden's housekeeper years before, wondered if she had been so shadowy and formal.

"Pleased to meet you," he said, "and thank you for the firewood you sent this morning."

"I'm sorry?"

"When Lucy brought firewood to the beach house, she said—"

"Oh, yes, yes," she interrupted impatiently. "She can't very well learn in the cold."

"And the food Lucy brought us. Thank you for that too."

Millicent's lips pursed slightly—she hadn't known—but she moved briskly on. "We haven't much time. The party security men found your friend and his brother in their sweep."

Cole and Jack. Brother had completely forgotten them.

"Miss Scripps explained that they had come with you," Millicent continued, "which kept us from calling the police. Both boys expressed misery at the present beach house conditions, especially the older boy—"

"Cole."

"—who asked for *asylum*." Her steely demeanor barely wavered, but it was all Brother could do not to laugh.

"So I've put them downstairs, temporarily, in the old playroom. You and your dog may stay there too, for the night, until we can work out something else. Miss Scripps says she has her own arrangements."

"Thank you for that too, for everything," Brother said, and she nodded curtly, one more thing ticked off her list.

"Senator asked me to see if there is anything else you require before the guests arrive."

"Are Kit and the dogs—?"

"This way, please," she said, before he could finish, and walked abruptly out the door.

"I'm sure you're busy, you could just point," he called, grabbing the slicker and hurrying after her.

"No, no. You might go missing too, and we've had enough of that today."

He wanted to ask her if she knew where Gabe was or where to look, but she picked up her pace and soon there was so much distance between them that with the clatter of dishes, voices from other rooms, and a piano playing somewhere, he would have had to run and shout, so he kept his questions to himself. He trailed her through the entry hall, relieved to see no sign of Eric, the senator's rude aide, just a man in a tuxedo with a cello, setting up to play. They passed a big dining room where the chairs had been pulled away from the long table and lined up against the walls. A life-sized painting of Lucy's mother in a red dress hung between the far windows. The table was laid for a buffet with huge empty silver platters, bowls and covered dishes, and a showy arrangement of flowers in the center under a glittering chandelier.

They entered a vast, carpeted living room with floor-to-ceiling windows along the ocean side. There were groupings of sofas and chairs, side tables, and lighted lamps. A grand piano stood at the far end. Kit and a well-dressed older couple chatted around it as an animated man played and talked at the same time. The dogs lay under the piano, asleep.

Kit looked relieved as Brother came in behind Millicent, who frowned at the dogs.

"They're not staying," Brother told her.

"Oh, leave them," said the man playing the piano. Millicent eyed the man in the same way she had the dogs, then hurried off. "Kindest audience I've had all week," the man went on. "I'm George, Senator's personal counsel. That's Catherine and her husband, Jay, family friends. You must be the tabloid fodder."

"I'm Brother."

"Ha-ha," George said with mock delight. "Won't they have a field day with that?"

"It's true," Brother said, and Trooper's tail wagged slightly at the sound of his pet name.

"'The pure and simple truth,'" George sang, "'is rarely pure and never simple.'"

Catherine smiled. "How clever, George. Did you make that up?"

"Oscar Wilde," George said, beaming.

Catherine leaned over to whisper something to Jay that Brother couldn't hear. They glanced at Brother and laughed, while Kit came around to Brother's side of the piano.

"How'd it go?" she asked in a low voice.

"About like you'd expect. He doesn't give anything away."

"I want all the details later."

Brother nodded. "Thanks for speaking up for Cole and Jack."

"You're welcome. Cole couldn't have been more dramatic."

"I heard."

"What now?"

"Is Gabe still missing?"

"Wouldn't you be? I would." She turned to George, Jay, and Catherine and then to the windows behind them. "And I get the feeling nobody's really looking for him."

Brother followed her gaze. It was early evening, but he wouldn't have known from the brightness outside. A red canopy and carpet led from the rear of the house to an enormous spotlit white tent, large enough for a circus and filled with tables and chairs. A band was setting up at the far end. Waitstaff with flowers and glasses on trays moved swiftly and deftly about. The whole household, busy as an anthill, ran on with ruthless efficiency. New and missing sons had caused barely a ripple on its smooth surface.

"We should go over your story," George said to Brother, interrupting his thoughts.

"Story?" Brother said, "I don't think—"

"Very wise," George said. "I'll manage something and let you know."

Kit's phone rang. She glanced at it and told Brother, "Just Charlie. I'll call him back."

"Who's Charlie, dear?" Catherine asked her.

"My dad," Kit told her.

"What's your father's business?" Jay asked.

"Scrap metal."

Catherine looked at Jay and George. "How fascinating," she said, uncertainly.

"Get with it, Cathy," George said. "The future's in garbage. The Chinese are buying it by the boatload."

"But garbage, George," said Catherine. "It's so . . ."

"Trashy?" George said, smiling.

"Maybe so," Kit told them. "But it's a good living."

"Recyclables," Jay offered, nodding. "Very trendy."

"And green," George said, "like money."

The three adults laughed and George began to play something fast and loud, his hands thundering up and down the keys. Brother moved Kit away from the piano, where they could talk. Frank, ever vigilant, lifted his head, then went back to sleep.

"I want to find my brother."

"*Now?* Where're you going to look?"

"Like you said. Away from here."

"It's getting dark. He could be anywhere."

"I don't think so. Tommy said he didn't go to the refuge. He doesn't seem to be here. That doesn't leave a lot."

"Want Frank and me to go with you?"

"It's not that I don't, but I think it's better if I go alone."

"I thought you'd say that. I want to change clothes for the party anyway."

"You brought party clothes?"

She looked at him like he must be kidding.

"Of course you brought party clothes," Brother said. "Will you be okay for a while?"

"Oh, sure. I'll distract the swells with my blue collar while I wait. If I get bored, I'll call Charlie and tell him about the food. They're serving all his favorites: fat, sugar, and starch."

He smiled, loving how relaxed she was with everything. It helped him relax too. "I'll take Trooper and Frank if you want."

"Nah, I may need Frank to keep the lawyers in line," she kidded, shaking her pretty head, and before he thought about it, he bent down and kissed her quickly on the lips.

Frank didn't stir, but when Brother pulled back, Kit was looking over his shoulder.

"I'm sorry. I shouldn't have done that," he said.

"Don't sorry me, I liked it a lot. But Lucy doesn't like sharing her new discovery."

Brother looked around. "I don't see her."

"She *was* glaring at us from the doorway, but not anymore," Kit said. "She's furious we spoiled her surprise. While you were in with the senator, she made it clear *she* was introducing you at the party. And I'm supposed to tell you that she's got clothes laid out for you upstairs."

He cringed. "I'm not going to let her dress me in Gabe's clothes like a doll."

"Too late," she said, eyeing the rain slicker.

"You're right," he said, thinking how it would look if he did find Gabe. "I'll ditch it on the way out. I won't strand you. If I don't find him soon, I'll shower at the beach and come back."

"Just don't be late for your presentation."

"What presentation?"

"Weren't you listening to George? They're in full spin. You're being presented to the faithful at the party. The good son."

"No."

"Yes."

He looked away and saw George playing still, but also watching them closely.

"Awful, I know," Kit said, putting her hand on his arm and turning him slightly, away from prying eyes. "But it might be smart to go along for tonight. There's a lot you want to know and being difficult won't make them chatty."

"I sure am glad you're on my side," Brother said, smiling, but Kit looked serious.

"I know Gabe's your twin," she said, "but he's not like you. I mean, maybe he is deep down, but right now he's not in a good place. If you'd seen him, you'd know. Be careful."

"I will."

She stood on her toes to kiss him, quickly and lightly. And before he could say anything else, she was under the piano, holding Frank's collar and waking Trooper, telling him it was time to go.

❋ ❋ ❋

He left through the kitchen, telling a curious Millicent that Trooper needed to go out. Trooper's company and his few minutes with Kit heartened him until he found Lucy waiting for him on the walkway to the beach.

The cloudy sky had cleared, but the floodlights from the house and party outshone the stars and paled even the moon rising in the sky. Lucy looked so much older in the bright light he didn't recognize her at first. She'd drawn thick black lines around her eyes, slicked her lips deep red, and though her high heels and sparkly black dress might have pleased her mother, to Brother she looked like an over-painted child at Halloween. He remembered the Lucy he'd first met on the beach, the earnest girl who said she wanted to help him, who might know exactly where to look for Gabe. But as he got closer and she moved to block his way, his hope faded that he'd ever see that Lucy again.

"Oh, thank God!" she said in a clipped voice. She was annoyed, wound tight. "Where are you going? Senator says I can surprise everyone and bring you downstairs. He and other people are discussing what we'll say."

Brother's patience frayed. "What other people?"

"People who help Senator decide things."

George and Eric, probably. He didn't want either of them deciding anything to do with his life.

"They're trying not to show it, but they're worried," she went on. "The primary's soon and the woman who'll probably win it and run against Senator . . . people really *like* her."

Mem had liked her too, Brother remembered, saying the

woman was young and smart and might be able to win. She knew what mattered to people, Mem said, and it was too bad she didn't have money, because she would have given the woman what she could. How she'd have loved seeing Senator lose to a female, especially one with a beating heart and brown skin.

"Everything's been so rotten," Lucy went on, "because of *Gabe*. But now, you're here."

The Grayson refrain. *Because of Gabe*, everything his brother's fault. *Pay attention*, Brother heard Mem say, *if and when it suits them, they'll blame you too.*

"Not now, Lucy," he said, keeping his thoughts to himself, his face a blank. He was getting good at that. "I have something to do first."

"What?" she demanded. Was that wine on her breath? "Whatever it is can wait. You have to change. We have to practice."

"I won't be long," he said, not knowing or caring if that was true.

"Liar! You said that last time," she said, fully angry now. "Then you ran off with *that girl*. How many people are you going to invite? What are you up to? I thought we had an agreement, a plan. I thought you were different, but you're not, you're acting like Gabe."

Her face was all fierceness. She'd said it to hurt him, do her worst, but he wasn't going to be drawn in.

"I'll be back soon," he said, and he and Trooper went around her and quickly down the walkway, before he said things he'd regret.

※ ※ ※

The beach was where he would be in Gabe's place. But the beach
house was dark, so he and Trooper walked maybe a half mile up
Eden's shore, where shadowy men were setting up fireworks, then
covered the same distance in the other direction, but saw only
sea, sky, and sand. For all he knew, Gabe might have been on the
dunes, hidden in the dark under the low trees, watching them.
With Trooper along, Brother would have looked like security,
someone to avoid. The wind off the water was cold and he regret-
ted leaving Gabe's slicker behind. As they got back to the beach
house, he heard the horn blasts as the private ferries began to dock
with party guests. He climbed the steps to shower and change.

Trooper barged through the doorway, but froze and woofed a
few feet inside. A lighter clicked and flared from the recliner
nearest the woodstove. Brother started at the face in the yellow
glow, his face and not, as Kit had said. Gabe's was gaunter, more
sunken, his features in sharper, angrier relief. He hadn't bothered
to light a fire but sat in the cold, wearing a coat. He sucked on his
cigarette, clicked the lighter closed. Smoke filled the dark room
and only a ghostly outline and the cigarette's orange ember
showed where he sat.

"If you're one of Lucy's friends, you can get the fuck out."

Brother supposed the voice was his, more or less; he'd never
heard himself outside of his own head. But Trooper recognized it,
or thought he did. His tail wagged and stopped, wagged and
stopped. He pawed Brother's leg, unsure. Finally he leaned uneasily against Brother, quaking and crying softly.

"Is he always such a wuss?" Gabe said.

"He's confused."

"A lot of that going around."

"Turn on the lamp and you'll see why."

"I'd rather you leave."

Trooper scratched more insistently at Brother's leg. "It's okay, True," he said, reaching down to pet him.

"True?" Gabe seemed amused.

"Short for Trooper."

"You're a rent-a-cop?"

"No."

"One of Lucy's little friends? If she said you could be here, she's wrong, as usual. Or did God send you?"

"What?" Brother asked, and then remembered that "God" was what Lucy said Gabe called Senator behind his back. "No one sent me. I came on my own to find you. I'm your brother."

Gabe snickered. "I get it. The latest rehab freak they've brought in to shrink me, tell me his *story*, and preach the tough-love gospel. But here's the thing: Gabe Grayson's sucked at the tit of tough love since he can remember, so too late, I'm immune, sorry. Been there, sucked at that. Tough love doesn't do it for me like it used to."

"Wrong again," Brother said. He heard Gabe's cynical tone in his own voice now and didn't like it.

"Really? Like when I swore I'd never left that nuthouse they shut me in."

"No, you were right about that," Brother said. "I was the one they saw."

"What are you talking about? Who are you?"

"I told you. I'm your brother. Your identical twin. I didn't know anything about you, about us, until last week. Until your picture was in the newspaper. Turn on the light and you'll see."

Gabe got very still. He took several deep drags on his cigarette so the end burned red-hot, then flicked the rest expertly into the woodstove's open door and fell back in the recliner, obstinate, refusing to budge. "I don't believe you," he said.

Brother told Trooper to stay, crossed the room, and switched on the lamp next to the chair.

At first Gabe stared at the beer bottle between his knees. Brother thought he might have to grab his twin's head and make him look, an appealing idea, given how surly Gabe was. He reeked of cigarettes and misery. Four empty beer bottles stood next to the chair, but he didn't seem particularly high, only sullen and angry and determined to stay that way.

"Look at me," Brother told him. "Believe your eyes."

Gabe looked up, glaring, leading with his rigid jaw. A beat later, his eyes widened and his hard features slackened like softened wax. Brother watched his own emotions dawn, one by one, on the near identical face before him: disbelief, shock, horror, outrage, fear, and finally, one he didn't expect or share, something like triumph. Brother had imagined that knowing about Gabe ahead of time had prepared him, at least a little; that the knowledge would blunt the shock. But like Mem's dying, knowing it was coming hadn't prepared him for the fact of it at all. The reality of his double struck him like a fist.

And as if hit by the same blow, Gabe turned away suddenly and wouldn't look back.

Brother waited. He would have given anything to hold Kit's hand. What happened now? Trooper broke the silence, uttered a low stuttering moan.

"It's all right, True," Brother said softly, trying to convince himself as much as the dog.

Gabe snorted. "The hell it is."

There were footsteps on the walkway above the house. Brother heard Lucy's anxious voice and a man's voice he didn't recognize.

"Someone's down there," Lucy said. "I see the light. I can't go because of my heels."

"I'll go," the man said, and then as he hurried down the beach stairs, "Hello? Anybody in there?"

Trooper barked and Lucy called out, "He's there. That's his dog."

"I'll bring him up, ma'am," the man called. "We'll meet you at the house."

Brother saw a shadow cross Gabe's face. Without looking up, he whispered, "Going to rat me out?"

The man climbed the stairs to the house, rapped on the door. Trooper's barking grew shrill and he scratched to go out. "Security, sir! You're wanted at the house."

Brother switched off the lamp and doused the room in darkness. "Coming," he said.

18

TROOPER BARGED OUT AND SHOT UP the stairs toward Eden.

"Sorry, sir. They're anxious for you," the man said. Except for a flashlight, he looked like any other man in a suit. "Anyone else in there?"

"No," Brother said, shutting the door. The man took him at his word.

The lie seemed the least Brother could do. He wasn't sure what he'd expected from Gabe. Maybe he should have waited, given their first meeting more thought, let Gabe hear secondhand about him. Maybe if he'd let Gabe come to him, things might have gone better. Deep down, though, and awkward as it had been, he was glad it was over.

Trooper circled back as they climbed the stairs, and Brother clipped the leash to his collar. When they reached the edge of the party, the security man stopped them. He raised a hand to catch the attention of another man near the rear of the house, pointed at Brother, then said, "Wait here for a moment, please, sir."

Torches burned in Eden's rear gardens, but the night was cold and only a few smokers lingered under the covered walkway from the house to the tent. He searched for Kit through the lighted windows of the main house and the tent's plastic panes, but he didn't see her anywhere.

Gowned ladies and tuxedoed men milled about, talking and laughing loudly in groups or eating and drinking at party tables. Waiters in white jackets served drinks and food from little trays. On the far side of the tent, a band played something bland and jazzy. He caught sight of Cole's red hair in front of the band. He was doing a tipsy slow dance with a woman three or four times his age. He steered her into another couple and then backed her into a potted plant, but the woman chattered on brightly, not seeming to care. Jack sat alone at a table, eating and drinking as fast as he could chew and swallow. Near the tent entrance, Senator stood receiving guests with Lucy, her mother, and an elegant silver-haired woman. Senator said something and the group broke out laughing. It was odd to think of him as someone other people thought funny or someone a woman might love enough to marry. The security man who'd brought Brother from the beach spoke to the senator, and he and the silver-haired woman glanced Brother's way. He wondered who she was. Senator's wife laughed raucously at someone's joke, then waved at a couple across the tent. The red gem on her finger was as big as a grape, likely worth more than he and Mem had ever owned. What did he know about such a world, and what did he want to know?

He spotted Frank, a red bowtie clipped to his collar, and real-ized that the black-dressed, long-legged beauty holding Frank's red leash was Kit. She stood with her back to Brother, shook her head at whatever the man next to her said, then shot something back. Those around her roared. One of them held out a tidbit for Frank, and when he yipped for more, Trooper whined softly and tugged on his leash.

"Excuse me, sir."

A second security man had come up behind them, surprising even Trooper. "Sorry to startle you."

His official manner thawed as Trooper nuzzled him and wagged. The man chuckled as he squatted to pet him. "I used to have a dog like this when I was a kid," he said. "About drove me crazy trying to herd everybody, but I sure miss him. He got a name?"

"Trooper."

"No kidding? I was a paratrooper. How about that?" He picked up Trooper's paw and shook it, then looked up at Brother. "Real nice to meet you, too. I'm supposed to take you upstairs."

"Everybody might appreciate it if I had a shower," Brother said.

The man smiled. "I'll get you where you're wanted. The show-er's up to you."

The man led Brother and Trooper around the house and through a side door. They climbed steps to a long hall hung with framed family pictures, Brother's double in nearly every one: Rid-ing a horse. Playing tennis. One-arming a surfboard twice his size.

"In here, sir," the man said, opening a closed door. "Be happy

201

to mind Trooper while you wash and dress. Your duffel and clothes are on the bed. Sorry about having to look through your things. Orders."

Brother shrugged and started to say how disappointing his toothbrush and dirty socks must have been, but the man was already doting again on Trooper, who basked in the attention. "We'll be right here, sir."

Brother shut the door and switched on the light. Gabe's room. A surfboard leaned in one corner with several tennis rackets and a pair of skis. Swim and tennis trophies gleamed on shelves along the wall. A kite in the shape of a dragon hung from the ceiling, and an old whaler's harpoon topped a lean shelf of books behind the farthest of twin beds. Brother's duffel lay open on the nearer bed, his clothes washed, ironed, and folded beside it in neat piles. To think he'd worried his family might not accept him. Quite the opposite. They were absorbing him with alarming speed.

He took his longest shower in a week; shaved, brushed, and combed. He ignored the white shirt, khaki pants, and blue blazer laid out for him, and tucked a clean if faded black turtleneck into his most presentable jeans. He checked his appearance in the full-length mirror. His clothes weren't fancy, but they were his.

Someone knocked. "You decent, sir? Someone's here to see you," the security man said.

Brother opened the door expecting Lucy, but found the silver-haired woman he'd seen with Senator. She smiled warmly.

"I'm Mamie Grayson Stennis, Senator Grayson's sister. You must be Mem's grandson, Brother. May I please come in?"

Her voice was throaty and kind, what Mem would have called cultured. Like Mem, she was wrinkled and gray but still quite beautiful.

He stepped aside. "Please."

"I'm only here for a short visit. Giddy's anxious for you downstairs."

She came unsteadily through the door and he reflexively took her arm, as he'd so often taken Mem's.

"Thank you," she said. "I'm afraid my legs aren't what they used to be, and this house has so many stairs. A lesser reason I don't linger when I come."

He guided her to the end of the nearer bed and moved his folded clothes to make a place for her to sit. She eyed them, amused. "I see you've met Millicent. Careful you don't find yourself starched and folded."

Brother liked her already. He got the chair from Gabe's desk and sat next to her.

"I won't keep you long. I wanted to tell you privately how sorry I was to hear about Mem. We were girls together. She was my first and best friend for many years. It pains me that we lost touch. I respected her reasons for leaving, but I grieved her loss then and grieve it again now. I'm so very sorry."

"Thank you, ma'am."

"Call me Mamie, Brother, everybody in my family does. You're family now."

"Thank you, Mamie."

"How fortunate I came this weekend to see an old friend.

I seldom come to these occasions otherwise." She tipped her head his way and smiled mischievously, whispering, "I root for the other side."

"You don't live nearby?"

"Oh, no. I live in the Sodom of Chapel Hill," she said, and chuckled softly. "That's what Giddy thinks. I moved there with my late husband. This island is much too circumscribed a place for someone as social as I am. I suffered terribly from it as a girl. I enjoy being a part of the main, as the poet said. But that's a conversation for another day. I hope we'll have many such conversations when we have time."

"I'd like that," Brother told her, and waited to hear if there was more.

She seemed momentarily faraway and a bit sad, the way Mem had seemed when remembering the past, and then regarded him thoughtfully and folded her hands in her lap. "I don't know how you're about to be presented or what you'll be told about your or your brother's history, what I call *Giddy's version*." She gave him a wry, knowing look. "I love my brother in my way, but I oppose nearly everything he stands for."

"Mem did too," Brother said.

Mamie heaved a troubled sigh. "Even as a child, Mem made no secret of how she felt about Giddy. Nor did Billy. Giddy was the oldest. After our father, Gideon *senior*, died suddenly of a heart attack, our mother shunned public life, retired even from her family, and Giddy took over. Before that, he'd managed those close to him, but afterward his controlling ways knew few, if any, bounds. Whether Giddy lets on or not, he remembers precisely how Mem felt about him, and knows from whence you come. She raised you?"

Brother nodded. "My mother died in a car accident when I was little."

"So much tragedy. How did Mem die?"

"Breast cancer."

"Like her mother. Did you ever meet Muriel?"

He shook his head. "Mem hardly ever talked about her."

"No surprise there. Mem and her mother were often at odds. Like many idealistic young people at the time, both Mem and Billy pushed back against all they thought wrong with the world. Our parents, and Giddy, some years older, embodied those wrongs. But Mem and Billy were young and brave and wouldn't be bound by anything, and I admired them for it. Muriel belonged to my parents' generation. She felt Mem should accept her place in the world."

"Her place?"

"The difference, the wedge, between Mem and her mother, Muriel, was that Muriel saw her position as housekeeper as a fixed limitation, but Mem not only refused to be limited by her class or her heritage, I don't think she paid them much mind at all. Except for the great question of her father, of course. She must have gotten her beauty from *him*, because Muriel was the plainest woman you ever saw."

"Mem never talked about her father."

Mamie sighed. "It's like Mem not to have said anything. Of

course, these things don't mean as much as they used to, and thank God."

"What things?"

"Mem's father was a subject of great contention between Mem and her mother. Muriel was tight-lipped about him, even with Mem. They argued over him often and we children heard, because our rooms were at the back of the house, close to theirs. He was foreign, I know that. I remember one argument when Mem was maybe nine or ten and wanting to know her father. Muriel said that even if it were possible, it wouldn't be easy, that he didn't live in this country but had returned to his own—a country she wouldn't disclose, no matter how much Mem begged her. Of course, saying he was foreign might have been a lie, to put Mem off, who knows? As children we speculated wildly about him, positing every conceivable race and nationality across the globe. So many were plausible, with Mem's black hair, beautiful deep eyes, and dark complexion. Her mother was quite fair."

Brother sat back in his chair.

"You didn't know you had such mysterious origins?" Mamie said, smiling broadly.

Brother slowly shook his head.

"Again, so like her not to think you'd want to. She always did breast her cards. Not knowing about her father caused a deep rift between her and her mother. It ate at Mem for the longest time, until Billy found a lovely way of putting the mystery in a new light. 'Not knowing is *much* better,' he told her, 'it makes you a *citizen of the world*.' I *loved* that. You should have seen Mem's face when he said it. She stopped wanting to know after that." Mamie paused, remembering. "I so miss Billy's way of looking at things. Of course, our parents, and later Giddy, weren't so broad-minded."

"So that was another reason she and my grandfather left?"

Mamie looked down at her hands, twirled her wedding rings. "What is it people say these days? It was *complicated*." Brother remembered what George, the senator's lawyer, had said: "*The pure and simple truth is rarely pure and never simple*," but Lucy's carping voice in the hallway interrupted his thoughts.

"We have to go *now!*" she insisted, followed by an urgent knock at the door. "It's Lucy, Brother. They're all waiting."

"I've kept you longer than I meant to," Mamie said. "And I have someone else to see. We'll talk more later. I want to see what Giddy says and does, see if he'll do right by you. He's capable of it, every now and then. If you'll help me down those murderous stairs, we'll go in together. We'll cause quite the sensation," she added, looking excited. "They'll all be certain I've brainwashed you and made you a socialist."

"You sound like Mem."

She started to rise and he helped her. "A lovely compliment, Brother, worthy of Billy."

There was a louder knock at the door. "Sir, they're asking for you," said the security man.

"Coming," Brother called. He shoved his belongings into the duffel and stuffed it under the bed. If Gabe came back, Brother didn't want it to look like he'd moved in.

"Ready?" he said to Mamie.

She placed a cool hand on his cheek. "Mem did a lovely job with you. It gives me some hope for Gabriel."

Before Brother could thank her, Lucy charged in. She looked him over, made a face at his clothes. "There isn't time for you to change," she said, scowling. "We've got to go *now*."

"Lovely to see you too, Lucy," Mamie said, pointedly.

Lucy kissed her hurriedly on both cheeks. "I'm sorry, Mamie, but you know how he is. And *I'm* to bring Brother. *Alone*."

"Yes, I'm afraid I do know," Mamie said, dryly. "I see I've been anticipated and supplanted," she told Brother. "I'll have this nice young soldier take me down. You two run along, and we'll talk again very soon. Good luck." She shot him a look that told him he would need it.

"I'll keep Trooper till you're ready," the security man said from the door.

"What a beautiful dog you are," Mamie crooned as she went out. She took the security man's arm, and the three went off together, Mamie saying, "My husband was a military man."

Brother watched them go, wishing he were going with them.

"From now on I'm not letting you out of my sight," Lucy said. She latched onto his arm and all but dragged him in the opposite direction.

"I can walk, you know," he said, but she pretended not to hear.

As they got to the top of the entrance hall stairs, he heard someone behind them. He glanced over his shoulder to see Millicent in the hall, as if to cut off his escape.

Through the stair rails he could see the crowd below. The

whole party seemed to have moved inside. The music had stopped and except for a few whispers and the clink of ice in drink glasses, the guests were quiet. At the back of the house, he heard Senator's powerful voice growing steadily louder, as if he were moving closer. Brother couldn't hear everything, but he caught enough:

"We apologize for the crowding . . . have brought you all inside for a surprise announcement . . . the greatest gift the Grayson family could have hoped for . . . a mystery has today been solved . . . there will be further details later . . . an extraordinary story, worth waiting for . . . but for now, we hope that everyone present will have another cocktail, more food . . . continue to enjoy the music and the upcoming fireworks in celebration of the newest member of our family . . . another son . . . our adopted son Gabriel's brother . . . once lost, now found . . . if you'll all turn, my stepdaughter, Lucy, is bringing him down the foyer stair . . ."

A murmur swept through the assembled guests, like something borne on a tide. Heads turned. A few people started to clap, uncertainly at first, and then, as others joined in, the applause grew louder. Eyes looked up as Lucy tugged him to the top of the stairs. Brother searched the upturned, expectant faces for Kit or Cole or Jack, but if they were in the crowd below, he couldn't see them.

Lucy smiled wider as they began to go slowly down. She was milking her moment.

"Smile, Brother," she hissed through clenched teeth, poking him with her elbow.

"Go fish," he whispered too softly for her to hear.

As they reached the middle of the stairs the clapping slowed. A few nearer people laughed.

"Is this a joke?" someone said. "Isn't that Gabriel?"

"Maybe it's meant to be metaphorical, maybe he's been born again," a man cracked.

"No, look!" said someone else. "The other one's over *there*."

They all gawked at the back of the room. Gabe leaned against the library door, his dress shirt open at the throat, a surly, couldn't-be-bothered look on his face. The clapping stopped as the guests looked from one to the other, back and forth, confirming and comparing, as if watching a tennis match. Some faces registered shock, others the half-amused suspicion of a prank or a scandal, others confusion, and the rest checked their neighbors' expression for *what* to think. Reaction rippled toward the dining room. Firsthand experience became secondhand whispers and traveled outward as a current of gossip to the farther guests beyond. Lucy held hard to Brother's arm. She peered to her right, toward the living room, as if waiting for a cue, and Brother understood that his presentation had been choreographed and that something more was about to happen. The party fell completely still.

The electrified assembly parted for Senator like the Red Sea for Moses himself. If the old man had pulled stone tablets out of his tuxedo's breast pocket, Brother wouldn't have been surprised. Senator made his dignified way slowly toward Brother, his eyes fixed on his goal. He spoke to no one and no one spoke to him. The whole room stared thunderstruck, barely seemed to breathe, everyone trying to make sense of what they saw.

When Senator reached Brother, he smiled his trademark smile; a work of genius, Mem had said, courtly and contemptuous, both. He eyed Brother like a host about to carve up a turkey. He wrapped his arm tightly around Brother's shoulder, steering him—and Lucy with him—where he wanted them to go. He faced his guests, looking pleased and proud. "My friends, this is Billy, so appropriately nicknamed 'Brother.' Welcome, Brother. Welcome to Eden. Welcome home."

On cue, Lucy gave Brother a sisterly kiss on the cheek, the finishing touch. A few guests started to clap, and when Senator didn't say more, the others quickly joined in to break the awkward silence. Several people even hooted. At the back of the room, Brother caught Gabe's eye, just before he ducked out the front door. Brother wanted to bolt too, but he was locked in Senator's grip on one side and Lucy's on the other, and a crush of applauding and cheering people surrounded him.

Millicent came down the stairs and whispered something in Senator's ear. He glanced up to Mamie standing at the top of the stairs. She seemed to be weighing something, and when Senator's gaze met hers she held it steadily, like a challenge. They stood, staring each other down, until Mamie turned and walked back into the upstairs hall.

Guests took pictures with their cell phones. Near the front door, Brother saw the first security guard working his way to where Gabe had escaped. Senator let go of Brother and waded into the guests, leaving him to Lucy. Those nearby began talking all at once.

"Well, I'd say the fireworks had already started!" one man

joked loudly, and the whole foyer laughed, after which the music started up. Brother wanted air, but Lucy pulled him into the sea of smiling, curious guests. People jostled him, eager to gawk or shake his hand, get his attention, introduce themselves, or congratulate him. This must be what it felt like to drown.

He caught sight of Jack, riding Cole's shoulders over by the dining room, a chicken leg in each hand. For a second, he thought he saw the top of Kit's head. More than anything he wanted to talk to her now, but what he wanted wasn't important to anyone here. He'd never thought he'd miss being a nobody in Schuyler, but he missed it then, and dread washed over him. From now on, he'd never be nobody again.

19

Two hours later Lucy still clung to his arm. He grew annoyed, then angry, then worn out, started to think of her as a growth on his hip, but remembered Kit saying it would be smarter to go along for now and pushed his feelings down. He was polite to everyone he met—as gracious, he couldn't help thinking, as Senator himself.

Lucy steered him from entrance hall to dining room to living room to tent, introducing him until his hand ached, he stank of perfume, and all the VIPs' titles merged: *SecretarySenator CongressmanJudgeAmbassadorDoctorAdmiralGeneralMajor ColonelDeanProfessorReverendSir.* How did anybody remember all this? He'd thought hard work was a double shift at The Elms, but after two hours of Senator's party, he'd never felt more drained in his life.

To his face, the guests smiled and greeted him warmly, expressed their pleasure to meet him, their surprise, their regrets about whatever had separated him from his brother, their fond hopes for his future. But behind the smiles, he sensed suspicions and unease: What else hadn't Senator told them? What would come out tomorrow in the news? Some guests made corny jokes; Brother lost count how many people quipped, *Haven't we met before?* or asked, *So which one of you's the prodigal?* Each time the speaker thought himself witty and original, and Brother smiled and let the person think so. A few people tried to pump him for details before Lucy interrupted and steered him on.

An hour or so into the party, the security man who'd fetched Brother from the beach reappeared with his scowling twin in tow. Gabe loitered at the back of the tent; the security man hovered nearby to make sure he stayed put. People enjoyed seeing them in the same room, Brother noticed, liked looking from one to the other, comparing them. The tent really felt like a circus then, he and his twin the evening sideshow. Gabe glared Brother's way as if to say: *See? Weren't things bad enough without you coming here?* His expression changed, though, after George walked Kit over to introduce her. Brother watched his twin smile for the first time all night, and then Gabe drew her onto the dance floor while looking at Brother to make certain he saw.

The security man who'd taken Brother upstairs happily minded both dogs while Gabe and Kit danced. Gabe held Kit as closely as she'd let him, and he looked happy in his own skin and Brother was suddenly uncomfortable in his.

"I'm done, Lucy," he said as she steered him from a judge and his wife toward another couple. He had to wrench his arm free.

"We're almost through. Don't make a scene," she said, grabbing at him, but he pulled away.

"We're through now."

He headed for George, who was watching Gabe and Kit from the edge of the dance floor.

"I've been watching over your girl for you," George said. "I'm mad for underage feminists."

"Should I worry?" Brother asked.

"Not about me," George said. He nodded at Gabe and Kit. She was listening closely to something his twin was saying as they finished the dance. Other couples on the floor eyed them approvingly. Gabe was a better dancer than Cole, who'd disappeared. Nearby, Jack was squealing "Do it again!" as a giggling woman spun him around and around in front of the band.

"While I have your attention," George said. He took a business card from his breast pocket and handed it to Brother. "You may need that."

"I thought you worked for Senator."

"I work for whoever's paying me," George said.

Brother laughed. "I don't have any money."

"Trust me, that will change," George said. "Call me when it does."

"I see you've met George," Lucy said, joining them. Brother sighed deeply, but she kept her distance this time, eyed George distrustfully, adding, "Senator's weasel."

"Lucy's quite ambitious," George told Brother, then said to Lucy, "My dear, if you want to get places in this world, you should learn to keep things to yourself, like Brother here. Like any natural politician, he's thinking all kinds of things he's not saying. Sizing all of us up."

"I wasn't," Brother said.

"He's a good liar too," George countered.

"Takes one to know one," Lucy said.

"Am not! Are too!" George mocked. "Leave the playground, sweetheart. This is the real world."

Jack started wailing on the dance floor. Brother dodged the other dancers to get to him, Kit arriving a second sooner. Both of them looked grateful to escape, whatever the cause.

The woman who'd been whirling Jack was wiping at a small wet spot on the stomach of her gown. Jack was another matter. His trousers were soaked through and he was crying hard. "I didn't mean it. She squoze me too hard."

"He's had an awful lot of Coke," Kit said to Brother.

"We were just having a little spin," the woman said dismissively.

"As much as he's eaten, you're lucky he didn't throw up," Kit told her, taking her arm. "A little club soda will take that right out. And if we can find a hair dryer, you'll be good as new."

Kit looked at Brother and pointed at Jack. "Butler's pantry and down the stairs."

"What's a butler's pantry?"

"Behind the dining room. You'll find it," Kit called, as she and the woman hurried off.

Brother grabbed a folded tablecloth from a wait station,

wrapped Jack in it from the waist down and carried him out. Jack, still sobbing, buried his face in Brother's chest. "There now, buddy, it wasn't your fault," Brother whispered. "We're going to fix it. Aren't we pals?"

"Ye-ye-yesss," Jack sobbed.

A few people stared as Brother and Jack worked their way through the crowd, but Brother just smiled and said, "Too much excitement."

Inside the house, he hurried past wondering guests and found the stairs to the basement in the bustling pantry behind the dining room. He took Jack down the stairs into a long, paneled basement room with old sofas, chairs, and a huge TV at one end, a pool table at the other. Cole lay asleep on one of the couches, his back to the room.

Jack sniffled as Brother found the little suitcase with Jack's clothes, washed and folded like his own. He thanked Millicent silently. He peeled off the boy's wet things, put them in the bathtub, then ran a soapy washcloth over Jack's bottom half, toweled him dry, and dressed him in fresh underwear and socks. "Want to put on your pajamas and curl up with Cole?" he asked Jack.

"I want to see the fireworks," Jack whimpered. He was exhausted, high on sugar and cola and who knew what else.

"Okay," Brother told him, holding out a pair of clean pants for him to step in. "But why don't you take a little nap, and I'll wake you up in time. How would that be?"

"There won't be fireworks for at least an hour," said a voice behind them, and he turned to Millicent in the doorway. She glanced at Cole on the couch. "He's lucky to have you and Miss Scripps. If you give me his wet things, I'll launder them."

Brother sat Jack on the toilet seat. "Thank you, Millicent. And thank you for washing his clothes so he had clean ones to change into."

"You're welcome," she said. Her eyes lingered on him and for once she didn't frown.

The upstairs door opened and the dogs thundered down the stairs followed by someone in high heels. "Sorry it took me so long," Kit's exasperated voice said. "You'd think somebody'd thrown blood on that woman instead of a little pee!"

Did Brother imagine it or did Millicent almost smile?

"Dogs! Kit!" Jack cried happily. He ran to her and the dogs as Millicent went up the stairs to clean up the next mess.

"Hey, beautiful boy," Kit said, stooping to scoop him up and hug him. Her eyes cut to Cole. "Oh, jeez. Get invited to somebody's house and pass out."

"I am not passed out," Cole said indignantly. "I've danced with a dozen dowagers, and I'm taking a well-deserved power nap."

But Brother didn't want to talk about Cole. He patted Trooper's head and gave Kit a kiss. "Hey."

"Hey, yourself. Had enough glad-handing for a while?"

Brother shook out his right hand. "Feels like it's been in a vice."

"Get used to that. This is your life."

"I haven't decided that yet."

"Yeah, well, good luck opting out. I don't think you get to decide. They've got people to do that for you."

"Let's sit. Jack needs a nap before the fireworks."

She turned so that Brother could see Jack already asleep on her shoulder. They settled on a couch at the far end of the playroom, behind the pool table, the dogs at their feet. The party was heating up overhead, the music, voices, and laughter louder, fueled by drink. The playroom was dark and smelled of ocean and damp, but it was quiet and restful, a good place to hide. He let his head fall back on the cool leather of the couch, closed his eyes. It was good to be with Kit and the dogs again; good just to sit down.

"You want to talk about it?" she said.

"It's not that I don't. But I've been talking for hours."

"I got the better end of that deal. George can be pretty entertaining, as long as you don't turn your back on him."

Brother smirked. He didn't want to talk about George either. "Before we say anything else, could I tell you how beautiful you look?"

She smiled, tipped her pretty head. "Tell me all you want."

Jack's head was in her lap and she was running her fingers gently through his hair. She kicked off her heels and curled her long legs underneath her.

"Okay, I'm ready," she said.

"I was just thinking how I'd like to be Jack right now."

"Keep going."

He sniffed himself and made a face. "I stink with perfume."

"I know, I can smell the Chanel No. 5 from here. And before you go back upstairs, you better wipe the war paint off your cheeks."

Brother rubbed his face and laughed.

"That's better," she said. "You were starting to look all morose like Gabe. For somebody who's got everything, he's one unhappy, mixed-up boy."

"He didn't look so unhappy dancing with you."

"I was telling him about his brother."

"What'd you say?"

"I told him you'd had a hard time in life. But all that did was cheer him up. Sick, huh?"

"What do you mean?"

"Makes him happy you got the short straw."

"That's what you think?"

She narrowed her eyes at him. "I'm going to let that slide because you've had a long day."

"Sorry."

"Apology accepted, and heck no, that's not what I think. But it's how Gabe sees it and everyone else here, too. That's the world they all live in, which, in case you didn't see the neon sign, is the only one that counts. You're rich or poor, winner or loser. Life's more a gray mix to us, like our friend True here. But Gabe thinks he's a rich, well-bred somebody who's got his loser yahoo twin whupped by twenty miles."

"That's all you talked about?"

"No, he tried to talk me out of my dress, but he's not really interested. He just wants to snake me from *you*. Fat chance, but for your sake, I didn't knee him on the dance floor."

Brother laughed.

"I'm not being funny. I happen to think your brother's dangerous as hell."

"Why? He's got me *whupped*."

"You're too smart to be so stupid."

"Go on."

"I guess you didn't find him."

"I found him."

He told her what had happened between them at the beach house, or, really, what hadn't, and how he'd left it.

"So, you'd say he's really angry and shaken and scared?"

"I guess."

"Okay," she said, nodding, "so slip on his pricey shoes. Angry, scared, troubled, over-privileged guy. Made lots of mistakes. Shamed Daddy—and we'll put *daddy* in quotes for now—over and over and cost him plenty, maybe even an election because Junior's messed up *big* this time, nearly OD'd. Plus now maybe the past mistakes he's made that Daddy paved over are going to get dug up, and while people are digging, some others besides. In comes your twin. Clean, smart, and not *too much* of a pain" —she paused for effect— "but a mostly good guy, and more or less the right-living son Daddy dreams of. If you were Gabe, don't you think you'd feel a tiny bit threatened?"

Brother hadn't thought about it like that. "You left out that I was born to an unwed mother and raised by my bleeding-heart grandmother."

"Yeah, and you watch, they'll blame your and Gabe's unwed mother for all Gabe's problems, and, about you, they'll say nature on the Grayson side trounced Mem's freethinking nurture. They'll say you came to Eden *and* to your senses. These people can spin anything."

Brother's head was starting to spin. "You've really thought this through."

"I haven't even started to think this through, but you can bet *they* have. I saw how Senator looked at you from across the room."

"How was that?"

"Like he was salivating. And you can bet Gabe noticed. Don't forget the G-word he uses for Senator. What was it Mem liked to say? 'Pay attention, pay attention, pay attention.'"

Brother was glad for Kit's eyes, ears, quicker mind, and social skills, even if her observations worried him.

"I'm sorry," Kit went on. "As usual, I've said too much. Sometimes when I get going, Charlie just looks at me, shakes his head, and says, 'Girl, you can work that brain.'"

"I like hearing you talk. And I can use all the help paying attention I can get." He reached out, took her hand, and squeezed it. "I met Senator's sister, Mamie. Did you?"

"I was about to, but she excused herself and went upstairs. I met the wife though."

Brother had barely shaken Caroline's hand before Lucy ushered him away. "What'd you think?"

"Tacky. Loud. Lucy in fifty years, if there's no intervention." She lowered her voice. "And between you, me, and the pool table, I'm not sure Gabe's the only one with a little problem."

"Mamie came to see me after I changed. I liked her. You would too. She knows things."

"Ooooooh." Kit's eyes widened. "What?"

"Could you two keep it down?" Cole said hoarsely from the far end of the room.

"Shut up, Cole," they said. Brother leaned over and kissed her, and she kissed him back.

The door opened at the top of the stairs and light flooded in. "Brother, are you down there?" Lucy said. "Senator has a few more people he wants you to meet."

Brother shut his eyes. He wanted to sit on this couch with Kit and just *be* for a few more minutes, talk about her for a change, what *she* wanted from life, dreamed about or anything other than himself, and then keep his promise to watch fireworks with Jack.

"Brother, can you hear me?" Lucy called again. "Millicent said you were down there."

"I need a few minutes, Lucy," he called up the stairs.

"They said now," Lucy said.

"Five minutes?" Brother answered, then whispered to Kit, "It won't stop at a few."

"Just say no," Kit told him.

"It's harder than it looks," Brother said.

"I'll tell them, but they don't like waiting," Lucy said, and shut the door.

"You know she's standing right outside that door, don't you?" Kit said.

Cole rolled over and sat up, blinking. "This is a job for Dowager-man," he said sleepily. "Blue hair's his specialty, but he will distract stepsisters for room, board, and plasma TV."

Kit chuckled. "Atta boy, tag team! You two go, I'll bring Jack upstairs after I shut the dogs in the bathroom. They won't like the fireworks. I'll come find you."

"Promise?"

"Promise."

"C'mon, Brother-man," Cole said, standing. "Let's do this thing."

20

THE NEW PEOPLE SENATOR WANTED Brother to meet instantly blurred with all the ones before them in his mind: the men bloated with their own success and the women, like Senator's wife, over-dressed, hair sprayed stiff, smiles too stretched and white.

Afterward, as he'd expected, Lucy refused to let him go and Cole swooped in to the rescue, prying Lucy off his arm and onto the dance floor.

But once Brother was free, his face became his enemy. He couldn't move five feet without someone stopping him to con-gratulate him and pump his hand. His tiredness became exhaus-tion; his brain threatened to seize. He was hungry and thirsty too, but though food and drink were everywhere around him, whenever he tried to get to either, someone buttonholed him, wanted to chat or take his picture or talk to him about his future. His future. The idea made him laugh. Surviving the next fifteen minutes was as far ahead as he could think.

A fast-talking spectacled man was bending Brother's ear about his story and a book deal, when he felt a hand on his arm and turned to find Millicent.

"If you'll come with me, sir," she said, and Brother, grateful for any interruption, excused himself and followed her through the dining room. He looked longingly at the ice-ringed bowls of fat pink shrimp, the rare roast beef, potatoes topped with cheese, the platters of cookies and small iced cakes. They went through the pantry's rear swinging door into a large, busy kitchen. Servers were arranging fruit and cheeses on platters and heaping salads in bowls. At the back corner of the kitchen, Millicent pointed to a small table set for one, a plate covered with another.

"I haven't seen you eat all night," she said, lifting the top plate. There was pink roast beef, mashed potatoes, string beans, two buttered rolls, and a glass of iced tea. "Senator often gets too distracted to eat."

"Thank you, Millicent. *Again*," he said, and smiled. With everything else she had to do, this was especially kind. Because he wanted to reciprocate, he asked, "Have *you* eaten?"

She started slightly at the question and didn't answer at first, but watched as he sat and dove in on the beef, tender and perfectly rare, though he was so hungry he would have happily eaten scraps. The potatoes were creamy and filling and made him half-human again. Green beans were his favorite. Were they Gabe's too? He ate steadily, trying not to shovel the food into his mouth and to chew before he swallowed.

"You're the first person in this household who's ever asked me that question," Millicent said, but as if he should know better than to ask a servant such a thing. More than anyone he'd ever met, she embodied Mem's advice to listen while others revealed themselves. But she listened so well, was so one-way and shut down, it was unsettling, even creepy. His family's whole history was probably locked up inside her, but inside it would surely stay, as it had stayed inside Mem's mother and, mostly, inside Mem herself.

"I'm not part of the household yet," he said.

She breathed a quick "huh," maybe as close as she came to a laugh. "Would you like more?"

"I'd fall asleep."

"Coffee?"

"Yes, thank you—"

She was off to fetch it before he could add, "If it's not any trouble." She came back with a steaming mug, sugar, and cream on a tray, which she set on the table beside him.

"When you're done, there's a balcony on the third, attic floor that's best for watching the fireworks. I've told Miss Scripps and the little boy. No one else will be there."

"Because?"

"The wind musses their hair."

She said this without irony and waited while he drank. The coffee revived him, not as much as the night's sleep he craved, but enough. She climbed the short flight of stairs in the corner behind them and unlocked the closed door.

"Up the service stairs, turn left, straight through the old

nursery, and into the hall. The unlocked attic door will be in front of you."

Before he could thank her again, someone called her name and she hurried out of the kitchen.

He climbed the narrow stair, what Millicent used, he realized, what Mem and her mother had used years ago. He thought of the spirited girl in the picture of Mem that Senator had shown him, imagined her racing up and down these steps, rowdy and laughing and too full of life for this cramped, stuffy space. He placed his palms on the too-close walls and pressed his forehead there, sure Mem had done the same.

At the top were two tiny rooms hardly bigger than closets, a tinier bathroom in-between. Millicent's rooms, he supposed, and Mem's and her mother's once. The doors stood ajar. One room held a single bed, a small dresser, a nightstand, and a lamp; the other, an easy chair, a bookcase, a folding table, and a small TV on a stand. Mem and her mother had both lived in these rooms that together weren't half the size of the playhouse where he'd met Amos. Mamie had said Mem wouldn't be bound by anything, and it was no wonder.

He followed Millicent's directions into the old nursery, probably Gabe's first room. But for the pale blue walls and a darker blue rectangle where a crib might have stood, there was no sign of a nursery now. A single window faced the rear of the house and in the distance, the sea. The moon hung like a mobile in the sky above it. Two men waited below, by the fireworks, for their cue.

The nursery led to the family-picture lined hall he'd taken

earlier to Gabe's room. He saw where he was now. He opened the door in front of him to a rush of cold, cedar-y air. Old coats were piled on the stairs; Millicent thought of everything. He slipped one on and climbed the steps to a huge attic. From one end to the other stood racks of clothes zipped in plastic and a shipload of dated crates and cartons, the past neatly boxed and stacked. A bank of floor-to-ceiling windows faced the ocean side, and at the center, two open double doors let in the music and voices below.

The narrow balcony faced the water, three floors up. At that height, the wind off the sea blew cutting and cold with nothing to break it, and the translucent top of the white tent was a long way down. The balcony was dark—scant light reached it from the party—and at first he saw no one. He zipped his borrowed jacket as a shrill whistle rose from the beach, then a second and a third. Three glittering stems shot skyward and fireworks bloomed in the sky, red, blue, and white. Guests poured from the house and the tent to watch from the lawn. They oohed and aahed as a second round fired and burst. Husbands shrugged off their jackets and wrapped their wives as the reports doubled and tripled. The sky filled with starbursts in every hue, each series showier than the one before. Brother stood at the rail, thinking explosives the right end to a day of one bombshell after another.

A lighter clicked behind him and cigarette smoke wafted to Brother at the rail. He turned to Gabe leaning against the house, cigarette in one hand, a fifth of something in the other. "I see Millie ratted me out."

"She didn't," Brother said. "She said this was the best place to watch the fireworks because no one else would want to muss their hair."

Gabe threw back his head and laughed. Brother wondered if his own laugh was so full of contempt. "Every now and then that bitch is actually right *and* funny."

Brother said nothing. Millicent was chilly and prim, but she didn't deserve that.

Gabe took a snort from the bottle, met Brother's stare. "You going to tell me I've had enough?"

"Pass," Brother said. Again, the edge in his own voice surprised him.

Gabe smiled. "Good, because I'm celebrating." He drank again, then lifted the bottle and eyed what remained. "Sorry I don't have enough to share. You're the perfect person to celebrate with me."

Brother waited.

"Don't be such a stiff. Ask me why."

"Okay, why?"

"Because," Gabe said with obvious glee, "for the first time ever, *I was right.*"

"I'm happy for you," Brother said tiredly.

"C'mon, you can do better than that. This is a big moment for me. For *us.* Get into the brotherly spirit. Ask me what I was right about."

"Okay. What were you right about?"

Gabe beamed. "I was right about *you.*"

"Me?"

"Yes! And you know what's a million times better than that?" Gabe asked.

"What?"

Gabe bent unsteadily forward and feigned a look of utter astonishment. "God. Was. Wrong."

He laughed loudly, drunkenly, but stopped abruptly when Brother didn't join in.

"I see you're not properly impressed," Gabe said. "That's all right, you're new here. But trust me, that *never* happens. At least, not so it's apparent to the naked eye."

He laughed harder, pleased at his joke, but his laughing threw him off balance, and he staggered and lurched. Brother moved to catch him, but Gabe pulled himself up at the last second and fell against the house.

"I knew," he went on. "I've always known. I tried telling them, but they wouldn't believe me, said I was imagining things. They sent me to doctors, gave me pills. But I still *knew*." He radiated smugness, but underneath there was something else. Pain, Brother thought, *hurt*.

"Knew what?" Brother asked.

"About *you*."

"How?"

"Unlike you," Gabe sneered, "I *remember*."

"What?"

"Among other things, the night she brought us here."

"Who?"

"Are you being purposely dense?" Gabe spat. "Our dear mother. Mommy. What do *you* call her?"

Brother and Mem had talked about her so little. "My mother, I guess. *Our* mother."

Gabe went on as if he hadn't heard. "For the longest time I asked them, 'Where's Mommy? Where's *Brother?*' They said, '*Mary* is your mother now. You have no *brother.*' But I *knew.* Because I *remembered.* Later I told them, 'Send me to all the shrinks you want, but I didn't make him up and he's not my imaginary friend or something I goddamned dreamed.'"

Gabe stood swaying, looking immensely pleased with himself. The rockets fired furiously behind Brother and exploded overhead, but the two of them were watching each other. Brother thought back to the night *he* remembered so clearly, the night his mother left him and didn't come back; the rain, Mem, the blue light of the trooper's cruiser in the road. Why shouldn't Gabe remember *his* last night with their mother just as vividly?

"I believe you," he said.

Gabe studied him. "But you don't remember *us*, do you?" he challenged. "You don't remember her or me. You don't remember all of us coming here that night. I bet you don't even remember how you got your goddamned name."

Brother said nothing, and Gabe waited, relishing the upper hand. "You don't. Who do you *think* gave it to you? The one person on earth who'd call you *Brother.*"

He grinned widely as Brother stood stunned.

"All these years the name and the truth of it has stuck to you,"

Gabe said, marveling, "even though you don't remember a thing."

Brother tried to think what to say. It seemed mean and wrong not to remember his twin, to say he'd believed all along that he was alone, one not two in spite of his name. And then it struck him that maybe he did remember Gabe. That maybe Gabe was the dolphin he'd chased and never caught in his dream. But the dream seemed such a babyish thing, something Gabe wouldn't believe, so Brother blurted instead, "I remember other things."

"What things?" Gabe demanded. "I don't believe you. You're just saying that. Tell me one goddamned thing you remember."

The fireworks above them reached a crescendo, their bursts faster and louder, drowning out any other noise. Brother waited as the colors blossomed red, white, and blue in a spectacular finale overhead, then fizzled and died, glittering earthward. The guests whooped and applauded below.

"I remember," Brother said, as the applause ebbed, "the night she died."

His twin's face instantly fell. He hadn't known. Senator might have told him he was adopted, but not that their mother was dead. It was awful to watch him try to cover his shock and hurt. He dropped his cigarette and, looking down to crush it underfoot, quickly wiped his eyes before he turned the bottle up for a long, final drink. Brother was sorry he'd said anything. This place, this family, *their family* was a goddamned minefield. Every time he turned around he exploded one secret or half truth or outright lie after another. And they weren't pretty explosions like the ones fading in the sky.

"Liar," Gabe said.

"I'm sorry. I might not believe me if I were you."

"If you were *me*," his twin said with the same scorn he'd shown for Millicent. "Well, you aren't. You want to know what else *I* remember?" He dropped the empty bottle, which clinked and rolled without breaking, and lurched toward Brother. Too drunk to control his movements, he overcompensated, reeled backward, and, overcompensating again, pitched forward and fell into Brother near the rail, but Brother caught him, shoved him back. He bounced off the house and fell on his rear. A shiver shot through Brother. He thought how high up they were, how little force the wooden railing might bear. He took a step toward the attic doors in case Gabe got up, came at him again.

"Eeny, meeny, miny, moe," his twin chanted, drunkenly pointing his index finger, alternating between Brother and himself. "Catch a brother by the toe. If he hollers, let him go."

"What are you talking about?" Brother said.

"Eeny, meeny, miny, moe," Gabe finished, pointing at himself. "You hollered. I won."

Gabe tried to get up, but in his state he crumpled like a string puppet. Winners and losers, that's what Kit said, how Gabe sorted people. As usual, she was right. Right, except that staring now at Gabe—drunk, maybe drugged too—Brother knew Gabe hadn't won anything, something he thought Gabe knew himself, down deep. A children's rhyme. That's how their mother had picked whom she kept and whom she gave away. Not gave away, sold. His brother had been *sold*. The thought chilled him. And all he could think was how easily he might have been Gabe and Gabe him.

"Poor little Jack," came Kit's voice, and then Kit through the attic door. "Dead to the world. I couldn't wake him. He'll be crushed he slept through the fireworks."

Seeing Gabe, she stopped short, took a wary step back.

"Tell the little bugger not to worry," Gabe said. "Senator farts them every morning."

Kit looked worriedly at Brother. "Everything okay up here?"

"Everything's goddamned wonderful except that I need another drink," Gabe said, using the house to pull himself to his feet.

Brother moved to help him, but Gabe swatted him away and stumbled inside. Brother held his breath—hoped Gabe wouldn't fall down the steps, break his neck—until the door slammed at the bottom of the stairs.

Kit pressed her warm hands to Brother's cheeks. "You look completely played."

He nodded. "I need sleep soon or I'll be as bad as he is."

She leaned in and whispered, "I have an idea."

21

HE WAS LEARNING all Eden's hiding places and back ways.

He, Kit, and the dogs slipped down the attic steps, ducked through the nursery, and took the service and basement stairs back to the old playroom. They kept two of the jackets Millicent had left on the attic steps. Kit swapped her party clothes for the jeans, boots, and a sweater she'd stowed in a backpack behind the pool table.

"You'd make a good marine," he teased her as they leashed the dogs and left through the basement door.

"Don't kid. If my scholarship hadn't come through, I was thinking about it."

"Really?" he said, remembering her tears at the military-base signs.

She nodded. "Charlie does okay, but college *and* law school, that's steep, even in-state, and I don't want to graduate with a ton of debt. No way I'd want to be a high-paid weasel like George. I want to be a lawyer who helps people, and that kind doesn't make a lot of money."

He didn't want to think about her leaving for college or even going home to Bailey. He knew she'd soon be going back to school, to Charlie, and to everything else she'd put on hold for him. It made him mindful to soak up time with her *now*, store the ease and confidence he felt with her beside him, her hand in his. He tried not to hope too hard for anything more.

They fell quiet and kept to the edge of the party lights as they circled the house and grounds, skirting notice from security and guests. At the truck, she argued for lugging half the contents of the camper to Amos's playhouse, but they settled on a flashlight, Charlie's sleeping bag, one of the quilts she'd used to wrap the urns and her *other* backpack, which, by the heft of it, Brother joked would easily get the four of them through the end of the world.

Away from Eden, his worries eased. Even the heavy pack seemed lighter once they got to the beach, and they all seemed to relax. The walk up the refuge shore allowed Frank a late swim, and gave Brother time to tell Kit some of what Mamie and Gabe had said. He leaned in close to her to be heard over the surf. Soon, they heard the horns of the departing ferries in the distance. Once the last horn sounded, the bright lights of Eden dimmed, the stars reappeared in the sky overhead, and the island returned to itself.

Trooper and Frank ran without being told down the playhouse path, happy to be together and off the leash. They ran shoulder to shoulder up the trail and steps to the little house, playfully racing and bumping into each other. Brother felt for Trooper, who'd be lonely once Frank went home.

"If what Mamie told you is true, right there you've got culture and class, both, maybe race too," Kit said, once they'd finished making their bed on the playhouse floor. "'It's complicated' is the understatement of the year. Maybe not now as much, but *then*." She whistled softly. They'd spread the quilt on the bottom and butterflied Charlie's warmer sleeping bag on top. It was chilly inside the little house but toasty between the dogs and under the down bag. Kit rested her head on Brother's shoulder, as if she'd been doing it for years.

"Nothing's simple here." Brother sighed. "They wouldn't know what to do with simple."

"And everybody watching and trying to control your every move. Is Millicent *everywhere?*"

"Yeah, but I think she likes us a little. She told me Jack was lucky to have us."

"Her lurking's still weird. Lucy's too. It wouldn't surprise me if they were watching us right now." She lifted her head and spoke loudly to the bare walls, "So in case you were wondering, I didn't bring him here to take advantage of him."

Brother chuckled. "I'd be disappointed, if I weren't so tired."

"I want you rested and awake when I take advantage of you."

"I'm looking forward to that, but 'rested and awake' might take a day or two."

"Worth the wait. Besides which, I've got a ten-page take-home exam and an AP history essay to write before Monday. My laptop's in my pack."

"No wonder that thing was so heavy. You're really going to sit here and work?"

"I had about five cups of coffee at the reception."

"What's the essay about?"

"It's extra credit, so I can write whatever I want. I thought maybe I'd write about you."

"Me?"

She nodded. "I had a lot of driving time to think, and you might be American history in the making—or unmaking, depending on how things work out. Plus, how the senator's affected the people in my town. Might be an interesting meditation to look at what happens when people like him hit us where we really live. And who knows? Considering your family, you might be a senator yourself one day."

"Not *me*."

"Oh, fine," she said, suddenly a little testy. She rolled over, unzipped her pack, and pulled out her laptop. "Don't step up. Stick us with Gabe. Thanks a lot."

"That's not what I meant," he said. "I was thinking about *you*. I think Senator Scripps has a nice ring to it. I'll put all my considerable money and influence behind you and hold the dogs' leashes while you change the world for the better."

She laughed and looked contrite. "If you put it *that* way. Sorry. Those party people took it out of me. My cheeks hurt from smiling, and listening to their selfish, entitled talk made me grouchy. Senator and his overprivileged friends don't have any idea how what they do affects people like Charlie and me or you and your grandmother. They say they do, but it's just talk. All they care about is themselves."

"Have I thanked you enough for putting up with everything?"

She sighed. "Yeah, you're real good at that. Mem raised you right, like Charlie raised me. Not like your stepsister and brother, who didn't have good people to raise them like we did."

"Is that sympathy I hear?"

She held up her thumb and index finger with a small space between them. "Half an ounce maybe. I relate to what Gabe remembers about your mother, because of how hard Liza's leaving was on me. And I talked to Lucy some while you were in with Senator. She's not so bad for somebody her age and a half inch deep, which is a quarter inch deeper than a lot of my classmates." She shook her head. "Sad, though. She's working overtime to be like Senator and rise in his eyes, when the truth is that no matter how bad Gabe is or how hard she tries, she'll never beat her brother, because in their eyes, she's just a girl and not blood kin besides. She and Gabe are hard to like, but I feel for them a little.

"Not that they're off my hook," she added quickly, forcefully. "They're old enough to be one hundred percent answerable for being the spoiled, self-involved people they are, even if that's how Senator raised them. Maybe they'll get lucky like you, and something will happen to wake them up—like Mem's dying woke you—maybe any old grown-up minute now they'll see clearly enough to own who they are, good and bad, learn to think for themselves and see there's a world of people out here who'll never scrape up one spoonful of what they've been *handed*, a world that's bigger and more important than their itty-bitty selves. Personally, I don't hold out much hope. Even Gabe's nearly dying didn't wake them. Plus Senator's holding tight to the reins and they all let him."

"You are caffeinated," Brother said, smiling.

"You think I'm wrong?"

"I don't," he said. "And I like listening to you."

"You're making fun of me."

"No, I'm not."

"I held my peace so much at that party, it's nice to let the dam burst, speak my mind, and be with somebody who's awake and paying attention, like your grandmother said."

"You really think?" he asked hopefully. All he felt was tired.

"I do."

"I hope I can stay that way," Brother said.

"Be a shame if you didn't." There was real disappointment in her voice, and he didn't want to disappoint her, not now or ever.

"Part of me wishes we'd met without everything crazy that's happening," he said, "but except for the crazy, we wouldn't have met at all."

She laughed. "Yeah, it's weird, isn't it? For the first time in my life, romance seems like the least complicated thing going on."

He smiled at the word *romance*. "Two things."

"What?"

"I'd like to kiss you, and then I need to sleep in the worst possible way."

She lay back and they kissed for a long time.

"You sleep while I work," was the last thing he heard her say.

* * *

Brother woke to Trooper whimpering softly, nudging him awake with his insistent, cold nose. It was still dark.

"What is it, True?" he whispered. The dog lay facing him, trembling, his head between his paws. Next to him, Frank was quiet but alert and listening, whether because he heard something or because he was reacting to Trooper, Brother didn't know. Kit was curled up on her side, asleep. He wondered what time it was. He held his breath and listened, heard only the ocean in the distance. Seeing Brother's eyes open, Trooper sat up, his tags jingling.

"What's wrong?" Kit said, groggily. She found her phone and showed it to Brother. A little before six.

"I don't know. True's upset about something."

Trooper stood, began to pace, looked from one of them to the other.

"Maybe he just needs to go out?"

"Scratching at the door means he needs to go out," Brother said. "This is what he did right before he saved that little boy at the rest stop. This is something else."

As if to second this, Trooper started to pace *and* whimper, which got Frank doing it too.

Kit sat up. "Your life's hard on my beauty sleep."

"Tell me about it," Brother said. He threw off the warm sleeping bag, splashed cold water on his face at the bathroom sink, and put on his shoes.

The dogs went to the door and barked. Someone came resolutely up the path to the house and climbed the steps onto the porch. Whoever it was heard the barks, because instead of coming in, he knocked and called, "Amos? You in there?"

"Sounds like Tommy," Kit said, pulling on her boots.

Brother peered out the window. Seeing Tommy's silhouette he flashed on the state trooper from the night his mother died, and a chill shot through him as he opened the door. Tommy turned his flashlight upward, lighting his face, then squatted to pet Frank, but Trooper bypassed them both and stood alert at the top of the porch steps, scanning the darkness.

"Sorry, sir. Amos is missing again. I locked us in for the night, like always, but he got out somehow, which he never does. Maybe it's the new pills. I don't know what's got into him."

"How long ago?"

"I don't know. I woke up and the front door was wide open."

"You don't think he's gone swimming do you?" Kit asked, coming out of the bathroom.

"God, ma'am, I hope not. If he's in the water, we won't be able to see him till sunup."

Trooper barked anxiously and Brother and Kit exchanged a worried look.

"What's the matter with him?" Tommy asked.

"He knows things," Kit said, "before they happen."

"What kind of things?" Tommy asked.

"I once saw his knowing things save a little boy's life," she said.

"Well then." Tommy looked hopefully from one to the other. Brother and Kit grabbed their coats and the leashes and they all hurried out.

Trooper shot off the porch and took point, Frank beside him. Kit, Brother, and Tommy hurried after them up the trail. The dogs were waiting when they reached the beach. Seeing Brother, Trooper took off for Eden.

By the time they all reached the beach house, a deep orange dawn rimmed the horizon like a distant fire. Brother and Tommy surveyed the water, but Trooper and Frank made a beeline up the walkway. The door to the beach house was open. Tommy checked inside but came out shaking his head and fell in behind Brother and Kit, running toward the main house.

Destruction met them at Eden's back lawn. The white party tent sat punctured and pummeled, looking like a gigantic beached jellyfish. Someone had worked a stake from the ground and used it to stab, slash, and beat the tent to a deflated and vanquished heap. The main house was dark, but the glass of the rear door was shattered and the door open and canting on its frame. The dogs raced inside through the broken glass. Tommy caught up with Kit and Brother, and all three followed the dirty boot prints, overturned lamps, and strewn flower arrangements through the living room, into the entrance hall, to the library, where Senator's angry voice growled behind the closed door.

"How dare you, after all I've done? After all the money I've paid, and sacrifices I've made! How dare you terrorize my household! We had an agreement. An agreement *you* signed."

Frank stopped several feet back from the door, anxiously watching Trooper, who had his nose to the door crack and breathed loudly in and out. Brother grabbed both dogs by their collars and pulled them to Kit at the rear of the entrance hall. He whispered, "Wait here," and nodded at Tommy, who knocked hard on the door.

"Senator? It's Tommy, sir. Are you all right? Is Amos in there with you?"

"Thank the good Lord," Senator said, and seconds later the door flew open. The old man stood in his pajamas and bathrobe, his hair every which way, his unshaven face red with anger and still swollen with sleep. He glared at Brother. "Why are you here?"

"That's my fault, sir," Tommy said.

"Well, get out!" Senator told Brother. "And take that girl and the damned dogs with you." He cast a stern look Kit's way. Frank sat obediently by her side, but she was doing all she could to hold Trooper, who was pulling so hard at his collar he choked.

"What the hell's the matter with him?" Senator asked.

"He thinks something's wrong," Brother said.

"Nothing's wrong!" Senator shouted, all evidence to the contrary. "Take him outside, now. Before he wakes the whole household."

"Too late," Kit said, turning to the wondering cries of someone upstairs.

"What on earth?" Mamie said as she came out of an upstairs doorway, tying the sash to her robe. A beat later Millicent came hurrying in from the dining room.

"Go back to your room," Senator snapped at Mamie. "You've done enough."

"What are you talking about?" she said crossly.

"Amos," the Senator replied in a harsh whisper. "As if you didn't know."

What Senator meant dawned on Mamie's face.

"Why couldn't you leave it alone?" he went on.

Mamie's eyes hardened. "You should talk," she said fiercely. "I'll dress and come down."

"Stay there!" Senator snapped. "You'll just stir everything up."

"Don't be ridiculous, Giddy," she said. "He's not going to listen to you."

She turned sharply on her heels and returned to her room.

"Tell Caroline and the children to stay upstairs and lock their doors," Senator ordered Millicent.

"Yes, Senator," she said, and hurried up the steps.

Trooper's whining hit a higher, more desperate pitch, and finally, knowing nothing else would silence him, Brother told Kit, "Let him go," and she did.

Trooper shot past Brother and Senator into the library. Frank was crazy to follow his friend, and Kit let go of him too. He barreled through the door behind Trooper, forcing Senator against the jamb to keep from being knocked down and allowing Brother and Tommy to enter and see.

Senator's library was a wreck. The hundreds of books that a day before had stood at polished attention on dustless shelves now littered the floor in ravaged heaps. Some covers had been torn off completely or spines peeled or pages ripped out and wadded up or scattered like leaves—all of it stomped on, as the many boot prints showed. The gun case door glass was shattered, and glass shards and scattered ammunition mined the carpet in front of it. Every photo of the famous had been yanked off the back wall, picture hooks and all, and in places the wall had come off with the nails, leaving the paneling pocked and gouged. Smashed frames, broken glass, and snarls of picture wire rose in strata a foot high on and around Senator's bludgeoned desk, or what was left of it. Against it leaned a shotgun, whose butt end had been used as a club. The sole unbroken lamp burned too brightly. Its shade was gone and the naked bulb bathed the room's most wretched occupant in unmercifully white light. Amos sat hunched behind the desk in Senator's chair, his head in his bloodied hands, his whole body shaking with sobs. He wept loudly, miserably, like a child.

"Oh my God," Brother heard Kit whisper from the entrance hall. She was staring, her mouth open, her eyes wide as if she'd suddenly understood something important. "Oh my *God!*" she said again, this time louder, and she looked urgently at Brother. Frank turned at the sound of her voice, torn between her and Trooper, who had quieted, his worried head resting on Amos's knee.

"Frank, come here. Come here *now*," Kit said firmly, and he slunk reluctantly back to her, though he kept glancing over his shoulder at Trooper.

Tommy crossed the library carefully, sliding on the books to sidestep the glass and shells. When he got to Amos, he bent down and spoke gently. He called Amos "old friend," but otherwise Brother couldn't catch what he said.

"Get him out of here!" Senator ordered coldly.

Tommy looked up, taken aback. Maybe it was Senator's wild hair and rumpled pajamas, but his dress and fury together made him look like someone who'd escaped from a mental ward. His outsized anger at the sick old man seemed to shock even Tommy. Whatever Senator expected from him, Brother saw from Tommy's beleaguered expression that at that moment, getting Amos to go anywhere would be impossible. Even so, Tommy tried. After an awkward silence, he moved in front of Amos and softly coaxed him while trying to lift him under his armpits. But Amos would have none of it. His arms flailed suddenly, and Tommy reared back just in time to keep Amos from hitting him in the face. After that, Tommy stepped to one side and waited. From Brother's time at The Elms, he knew this was all they could do until Amos calmed. Eventually he'd tire, his mood would shift or wane. Even Trooper seemed to understand this, and sat motionless, his eyes on Amos. They all waited except Senator, who huffed impatiently at the back of the room, anxious both for something to be done and someone else to do it. Finally, Amos stilled and focused. His face was blood-smeared, wet with tears and drool, and contorted with anger and hurt that had one single object: Senator.

"Oh, my," said Millicent, who'd returned and stood in the doorway, taking everything in. "Should I call the police?"

"I forbid it!" Senator roared, and even stoic Millicent drew back and looked to Brother and Tommy for direction.

Mamie must have come down behind Millicent, because Brother heard her calm voice in the entrance hall, saying, "That won't be necessary, Millicent. Please, if you would just make us some coffee."

Amos's posture and expression relaxed a bit at the sound of Mamie's voice. He set one hand on Trooper's head. His gaze, though, remained fixed on Senator, who sighed irritably and stood immovable on the room's one clean patch of carpet. Brother looked at Tommy, who ever so slightly shrugged. Some sort of impasse had been reached.

Millicent went to make the coffee, and Mamie took her place in the doorway. She'd put on the clothes she'd worn the night before, and, despite everything, she seemed unruffled, even serene. "Oh dear," she said, surveying the mess, but Brother noted satisfaction in her face and voice, as if a score had been settled.

"Has the bleeding stopped?" she asked Tommy.

"I'm not sure, ma'am," he said. "I can't get hold to see."

"Maybe you could go ask Millicent for a basin of warm water, soap, and a towel?"

"Yes, ma'am." He started for the door, relieved to have something asked of him he could easily do.

"Stay, Tommy," Senator ordered. Tommy stopped and looked as divided as Frank had moments before.

"I think Brother can handle things for a minute or two, Giddy," Mamie said.

Brother was doubtful, but Tommy seized the opening to leave the room. Amos might be old, sick, and addled, but the chaos in the library proved he was plenty strong enough to break someone's nose or worse. Best, Brother thought, to just stand where he was and hope everyone would stay put until Tommy got back. Brother looked at Mamie, keeping her satisfied distance in the doorway; then at Amos, still furious and grieved and refusing to cede the desk; then at the senator, entrenched and justified in his anger at the back of his ruined room but reluctant to call the police. Just then Amos didn't seem at all like a culprit or the local demented hermit but more like a difficult and disturbed member of the family. *Pay attention, Brother*, Mem's voice said. *Pay very close attention.* And then Brother knew what Kit had understood the moment Senator had opened the library door.

"Giddy, come into the hall with me, won't you?" Mamie said. "I think that might make things easier for Brother."

"I won't be thrown out of my own library," Senator told her.

A sound like a growl came from Amos.

"Or threatened," Senator barked at him.

"It might be easier if you stepped out for a moment, sir," Brother said.

"Or handled," Senator told Brother, glaring and standing his ground.

Brother looked wearily over Mamie's shoulder at Kit. "Kit," he called, "would you do me a big favor?"

"Anything," she said.

"Would you and Frank please go get the little wooden box in the camper of the truck? Would you get it and bring it back here now?"

For a second she seemed unsure what he meant, but then she said softly, "Oh. Oh, yes," and she and Frank hurried from view. The front door opened and shut and Brother heard the two of them running up the drive.

He slowly, carefully made his way to Amos. The old man tensed as he approached. Not wanting to agitate him further, Brother knelt beside Trooper. Amos watched closely as Brother checked the pads of Trooper's paws for glass, lifting one paw at a time, feeling the pads and in-between areas thoroughly and gently. He moved and spoke calmly to his dog, saying, "No glass in that one, True," so that Amos might understand what he was doing and know his intent. Trooper looked once at Brother, but after that didn't take his blue eyes from the old man's miserable face for even a second. Trooper's solicitude seemed to calm them all. After a few minutes, Amos allowed Brother to gently take his hands, turn them, and inspect them for cuts and glass. The small wounds had mostly stopped bleeding. With his fingernails, Brother plucked out a few slivers of glass from each palm.

Tommy returned with hand towels and a bowl of soapy water and cleared a space for them on the desk. Brother dipped a corner of one towel in the warm water and started with Amos's face. He went slowly, to give Kit time. He wiped the scratched forehead, pushed back stray strands of hair. The old man closed his eyes. Brother wiped gently around them, cleaned Amos's cheeks, stubbly jaw and neck, then rinsed the rag and wiped each of his hands. Trooper licked them for good measure when Brother was done, while Amos quietly watched.

"You've done this before," Tommy said. He took a bottle of antiseptic and a stack of cotton pads from his pocket. Brother wet a cotton pad from the bottle.

"Yes," he said, looking up. He caught and held Amos's rheumy gaze. "I used to take care of my grandmother, my grandmother, Mem."

He spoke her name precisely, and when he did, the old man's eyes opened wide and flooded with tears.

Brother's heart lifted as the truck roared up to the house. Kit and Frank must have run all the way to the refuge lot. Frank barked, but Kit shushed him and snapped at him to get in the backseat and lie down.

"As a guest in this household this isn't your business, young lady," the senator said as she came into the room, but Kit walked right by him and stopped a few feet from the desk with Mem's urn in her hands.

"I'll be right back," Brother told Amos, and went to Kit.

"What about your mother's and the other one?" she whispered as he took it from her.

Brother held her gaze, shook his head slightly, and whispered, "Thank you."

He knelt with the urn at Amos's feet. The old man was

weeping again, but softly now. Tommy and Trooper stood silently near.

"Mem's last wish was to be with you," Brother told Amos. And then, "I loved her too."

And he put Mem's urn in his grandfather's hands.

22

SENATOR STORMED FROM THE LIBRARY and up the entrance hall stairs. The furious energy in the room left with him, and despite the wreckage, the atmosphere calmed.

For most of the next hour Millicent and Kit quietly cleared a path through the destruction between Senator's desk and the library door. Mamie went upstairs—to pack, she said—but a few minutes later, Brother heard her and Senator shouting, and though he couldn't hear what they said, their sharp tones and two slammed doors told him enough. Lucy and Gabe's rooms were farther down the upstairs hall, but even so, Brother doubted they could have slept through all the smashing and shouting, and he wondered why, even now that Senator was gone and the situation calmer, neither one had come down. Maybe they didn't know. Maybe they chose not to. Or maybe, like Brother and Mem with her cancer, they knew and pretended they didn't.

It was Trooper who finally coaxed Amos to go. At first, Tommy spoke patiently to him while Brother and Trooper sat at his feet, but nothing Tommy said made any perceptible difference. Amos stared at the urn and seemed farther gone than usual. His eyes were closed and he kept so motionless that several times Brother checked to make sure he was still breathing. But when Kit leaned over Brother's shoulder to say the debris was roughly cleared, Trooper lifted his head from Amos's knee and turned around. He looked over his haunch at Amos, who batted away Tommy's attempts to help him, got up from Senator's chair, and went slowly with Trooper out the library door, Brother and Tommy behind them.

Amos hugged the urn tightly in the crook of his arm, the palm of his other hand resting on top. Mem's urn and Trooper were all he seemed to see. He moved mechanically, oblivious to Millicent or Kit, the mess piled in the entrance hall, or his having caused it. He'd already forgotten what he'd done, Brother saw, as those with dementia usually did. Amos's world at that moment was Mem, Trooper, and the next step he took.

Kit stood holding Frank at the back of the entrance hall. Brother met her sympathetic gaze, reached to squeeze her extended hand, and mouthed, *I'll be back soon.* She nodded, and he followed Amos and Tommy out the front door. Frank whimpered as Trooper shepherded Amos across the portico and down the steps. They paused as one at the bottom and then together started down the drive. Brother gave Tommy a wondering look. Tommy shook his head.

It was slow going, but after a time the three of them reached the main road, and Amos headed toward the ferry. When he got there, he went to a flattish stone beside the dock and sat, gazing out at the water. Trooper sat with him, looking where he looked. It was hours before the ferry, as Tommy several times tried to tell Amos, but he stared at the water as if Tommy wasn't there. Tommy turned to Brother and shrugged. Brother shrugged back. It was Amos's ritual, one only he understood. The day was warming, the sky clear blue, the sea calm. Amos seemed in a trance. Brother and Tommy waited in respectful silence.

Brother wondered how much Tommy knew. Brother had come to Winter Island believing there was truth to be learned about Mem and his family, but the longer he was here—the more people he talked to and versions he heard—the less confidence he had that he'd ever learn it. His family, Mem included, seemed to have forgotten the truth, if they had bothered to know it in the first place. They remembered the past to suit themselves. They altered it to fit what they believed, to get what they wanted—or thought they did—or simply so that they could bear it. For now, Eden's truth seemed as elusive as the dolphin in his dream.

An hour or more passed. The sun began to climb, the air grew humid, and sweat trickled down Brother's back. Finally Amos stood, took a last look at the water, and started back down the main road, Trooper beside him.

"Where now?" Brother asked Tommy.

"Guess we'll see when we get there," Tommy said. "I can probably take it from here if you want. I was scared to death he was going to jump in that water."

"What were you going to do if he did?"

"I didn't know. But I was glad you were here."

"Let's get him where he's going, and then I'll go back."

"I hoped you'd say that," Tommy said. "Never seen him like he was today. He wanders, but he's never violent, never done anything like that."

"Dementia's hard to predict, day to day."

"You talk like you know."

"I worked a year at a nursing home. Until last week, I didn't know about my family, and they didn't know about me."

Tommy's eyebrows shot up.

"Yeah, I know. It's been interesting."

"That's one word for it," Tommy said.

They ambled up the road, side by side.

"Sir?" Tommy asked.

"Call me Brother, Tommy."

"Brother, can I ask you something?"

"Sure."

"Whose remains are in that box?"

"Does the name Mem mean anything to you?"

Tommy shook his head. "Mrs. Stennis stopped in to see Amos last night, but she didn't tell me why. Sometimes she'll tell me things, but sometimes not. As a group, they're not real forthcoming."

Brother snorted. The king of understatements.

"Don't get me wrong. I'm well compensated. And I'm not trying to be nosy," Tommy said. "It's just sometimes I think knowing a few things might help me care for him better."

"His wife, to answer your question, my grandmother."

"When did she die?"

"About a week ago."

"I'm sorry for your loss, and his," Tommy said solemnly. "I didn't know he had any wife."

"There's disagreement about whether they were married or not," Brother said. "About a lot of things."

Tommy sighed. "Welcome to Eden."

After another quarter of a mile, Tommy took his phone from his pocket and read the screen. "The senator wants to see you."

"Let's get Amos settled first."

Tommy showed Brother the message. "He says *now*."

"I understand."

Tommy hesitated. "You probably know this, but he doesn't like to wait."

Too bad, Brother thought. "I'll take responsibility."

"You know," Tommy said after a moment, "these phones aren't always reliable."

Brother cracked a smile. "So I've heard."

Tommy's phone vibrated like a pesky insect as they inched their way along, but he ignored it. Now and then, he pointed out landmarks and paths, so Brother could better orient himself. Tommy said the recession and cutbacks had stopped even basic refuge staffing and upkeep. Few people came until the season started, when the ferry ran more, and that was fine with him. Their cedar-shingled house was tidy and simply laid out on one level with bedrooms off a great room, a kitchen at one end, and a living room at the other. Amos went directly inside, Trooper with him, straight to one of the bedrooms. Amos got in the single bed and curled up around Mem's urn, his face to the wall. Trooper hopped up and lay down on a blanket at the foot of the bed.

"You rest now," Tommy whispered, but Amos gave no sign he heard.

Brother looked around the old man's room. An easy chair, a chest of drawers, a closet, a plastic cup of water on the bedside table, a rag rug, little more. Not even a picture. Much like Brother's own room in Schuyler.

"I'd better go," he said. "Is it all right if Trooper stays? I'll come back later and get him."

Tommy nodded. "Seems to calm him."

Brother patted his dog's head. "Thanks, pal," he whispered. "I owe you a whole truckload of treats." Trooper rested a paw on Amos's ankle and went to sleep.

Brother and Tommy exchanged phone numbers. Tommy gave him the combination for the refuge chain so he and Kit could drive in if they liked. He told Brother how to get from Amos's house to the beach so he could take the shortcut to Eden. "That is, if you want to get there quicker," he said.

"For the record," Brother told him, "you didn't answer your phone because it was all the two of us could do to get Amos safely home."

"Thank you."

"You too, Tommy. It was a team effort."

"Sir?"

"Please call me Brother, Tommy. 'Sir' makes me feel like an asshole."

For the first time all day, Tommy laughed. He offered his hand, and Brother shook it warmly. "Take good care, Brother," he said, referring, Brother knew, to the upcoming meeting with Senator.

"I will."

It was past noon when he got back to Eden. Millicent had laid out leftovers from the party in the dining room, but except for Jack, who was trying with limited, oozing success to get his mouth around a fat roast beef and cheese sandwich, no one seemed hungry. Cole dozed on the downstairs couch.

"Where's Kit?" Brother asked him.

Cole opened one eye and closed it again. "She and Gabe went down to the beach."

"Lucy?"

"Hovering hopefully somewhere."

"Thanks for the breather last night."

"I like your sister," Cole said, sitting up. "When she lets go a little, she's pretty nice."

Brother remembered how he'd found them two days before, relaxed and stoned together in the beach house over the plate of cookies.

"I mean it," Cole said. "She even invited me and Jack to Washington."

"Really?"

"Sort of," Cole said, leaning on his elbows. "I mean, I said: 'Brother will probably be visiting Washington and we'll probably come too,' and she didn't say anything. So don't spoil things, okay? Jack and I've never been to the White House."

Brother smiled a little. He knew Cole was trying to lighten him up. "I really don't know what I'm doing."

"I know. Kit told me. I'm sorry, man. You should've come rousted us. Didn't hear a thing on this side of the house."

"Just as well."

"What now?"

"Senator wants to talk to me."

Cole huffed. "I'll bet. You're not going unarmed?"

Brother actually laughed a little.

"I mean it, man. At least take True. Where is he?"

"With Amos. My grandfather." It felt odd, new, good, to call him that.

"You know," Cole said, "the story's sad, but upside? There's something nice about you finding him after all this time, you know? He's in a bad way, but he's still here."

"Yeah."

"Hey, you need me and Jack to come with you? People are nicer around little kids." Cole thought for a worried moment. "On the other hand, they might not want witnesses."

"I feel so much better," Brother said, starting up the stairs.

"Hey," Cole said, and Brother paused. "You may not know what you're doing, but you're doing it, you know? More than most people."

"That's what Kit says."

"She's right. But don't tell her I said so, okay?"

"I won't."

"I'm taking Jack to the beach after he's finished his lunch. Come down for the debriefing when you're done."

Brother climbed the stairs to the kitchen. He didn't hurry. The revelations were coming thick and fast, and he was damned if he was rushing to meet them. He went to the kitchen and chugged a Coke, then drank a second while he ate a thick slab of roast beef stuffed inside half a loaf of French bread. Jack was busy making a second sandwich of mayonnaise, mustard, bread, and huge shrimp with the tails still on.

"You doing okay, buddy?" Brother asked him.

Jack beamed. "I love it here!"

"Somebody should," Brother said, thinking he'd never seen Jack happier. How long would that last? Mem, Amos, Gabe, and Lucy, even Senator had been little kids here too.

He took the back stairs and got his duffel from under Gabe's bed. He changed into clothes he hadn't slept in and brushed his teeth and his hair for the first time all day. He stowed his bag in Kit's truck, still parked in the front drive, and stood before the closed library door. Before he could knock, Millicent came up behind him. She seemed winded and, for once, he noticed a few wrinkles in her uniform and hairs out of place.

"You're to go right in."

Behind the door, Brother heard Eric, Senator's rude aide.

"He's livid you've kept him waiting," Eric snapped as he swung the door open.

"It couldn't be helped," Brother said.

The man smirked, making no secret he thought this was crap, but Brother stared blankly at him until his smirk withered and he left, closing the door behind him.

"Come in, come in," Senator called impatiently.

Millicent had done what she could with the room. The carpet and furniture had been vacuumed clean of glass and debris, the gun cabinet doors removed for replacement or repair. Senator's books stood again on the shelves, but Brother saw sizable gaps in the sets, like missing teeth, and pages sticking out of the surviving volumes. No doubt new sets would arrive in days.

Senator sat shaved, combed, and dressed in a suit and tie behind his battered desk. Sizable, splintered craters pitted the carved wood of the legs and top, and Brother doubted it was salvageable. Behind the senator, the gouged paneling looked like it had been sprayed by gunfire. Without the photos of the famous, the wall looked shabby, Senator smaller. Maybe Amos was addle-brained, the damage helter-skelter, but the sight was a powerful commentary. Sitting between the hammered wall and desk, the senator looked like a general who'd lost the war.

But loss or no, his anger remained, and waiting had fueled and focused it. His shield of good manners had been set aside; his eyes seethed in their sockets. His hostility might have unnerved Brother, except for the fresh memory of Amos curled around Mem's urn. Senator might manipulate or rage, but the events of the morning had pushed Brother far beyond even Senator's considerable range.

"Sit," Senator said, as though he were scolding a dog.

But Brother remained standing. "Gabe should be here."

Senator's eyes narrowed. "And yet he isn't."

Brother couldn't tell if he meant Gabe didn't want to be here or wasn't invited. He pressed the point. "Because?"

"Sit down, *please*," Senator insisted.

Brother did, but not in the uncomfortable chair in front of Senator's desk. He sat facing Senator, on the far end of the nearest sofa.

"Your brother sits there," Senator said, as if choosing his twin's place said something cowardly about him.

Out of range, Brother thought, *which makes him smarter than you think*. In no mood to spar, he sat quietly and waited.

"I am not permitted to discuss many things by legal agreement," Senator began. "Nor is Mamie. To her credit, she has, thus far, kept her word."

"What agreement?"

"Our agreement with Amos."

"You mean Billy."

"A childhood name for a boy who no longer exists."

"I don't understand."

Senator looked to the back of the room.

"Hello, Brother," a familiar voice said, and Brother turned. George stood in the back corner, reading something on his phone. He slipped it into his pocket.

"When Amos William Grayson returned from Vietnam," George said, "his physical injuries—head injuries—were quite serious. Even after months in the hospital, it was clear that the doctors had done what they could. Amos would continue to decline and, in time, would be unable to care for himself. He asked Senator for refuge and care here, at Eden, for leave to live here anonymously and in peace, and an agreement was struck."

The door opened and Mamie came in with Millicent behind her.

"I tried to tell her, sir," Millicent said.

"It's all right, Millicent," Senator said. "So nice of you to join us," he told Mamie acidly.

"Leave us, George," Mamie said.

"Yes, ma'am."

"Stay, George," Senator told him.

George looked apologetically at Mamie. "He pays me."

"I hope it's enough," she said.

Senator sighed. "Sit down, Mamie."

"I'll stand. Did you tell him?"

"You're the one who goes around upsetting people by saying things better left unsaid."

"Tell him or I will," Mamie said.

Brother looked from one of them to the other, wanting to shout at them both. Couldn't they put their differences aside to have a simple conversation? Mem and Reverend Harvey had gotten along better.

When Senator said nothing, Mamie asked Brother, "Has he told you about the agreement?"

"Yes," Brother said.

"Has he told you what Amos was forced to agree to?"

Brother shook his head, but he had an idea.

"He wasn't *forced* to do anything," Senator said.

Mamie pursed her lips. "Giddy told Amos that he could live here, cared for, as long as he had no contact with Mem," she said. "Never seek her or see her or write her or even let her know he was alive. In exchange, he could live here and be cared for until he died."

Brother didn't understand. "Didn't part of the island belong to Amos?"

Mamie looked approvingly at him, but Senator glanced uncomfortably at George.

"After Amos and Mem left, the island became Giddy's," Mamie said sharply. "Amos was disinherited, and my share of things was lessened considerably for supporting them." She looked at Senator. "You drove them off and then you turned Mother and Father against them."

"Mem and Amos did that themselves," Senator scoffed. "Eden was Father's and, after he died, Mother's to do with as she liked."

"You fanned those flames, Giddy. Like you always do when you think you're right or want something," Mamie countered, and turned to Brother. "The night before Mem and Billy fled, Giddy told Amos that if he ran off with Mem, it would kill our father within six months."

"And we buried him the following spring," Senator said smugly.

"The two things had nothing to do with each other."

"We disagree," Senator said.

"Amos was shattered," Mamie told Senator, "by a war your jealousy and coldheartedness condemned him to fight, a war you avoided fighting in yourself."

"We have each served our country in our own way," Senator said defensively.

"His service in a war and yours in the safety of the Senate do not compare."

"This is an old argument, Mamie," Senator said wearily, "these subjects upon which we will never agree."

He looked at Brother, who had been listening carefully. Jealousy, Mamie had said, Senator's jealousy had condemned Amos. What had she meant?

"What is pertinent to our discussion," Senator said, "is that when Amos returned he could not care for himself and I arranged for that care."

"Mem would have cared for him," Brother said.

"The way she cared for your mother?" Senator snapped. "Mem couldn't even care for herself."

"She raised and cared for me," Brother said with a quiet firmness.

"And yet here you are. You and your friends, whom I've fed and sheltered for several days," Senator told him pointedly.

"Only because you didn't want them talking to the press," Mamie said.

"I didn't come for a handout," Brother said.

"Didn't you?" Senator snapped. "What sort of idiot do you take me for?"

George cleared his throat from the back of the room. A caution to Senator, who glanced at George and shifted uneasily in his chair.

Mamie breathed deeply. "You never take responsibility for anything, Giddy, not unless it's on your terms and benefits you. Not one thing that goes wrong because of your actions is ever your fault. There are never consequences to *your* actions, only to the actions of *other people*. When Amos came home, you didn't even look for Mem and their child."

"I gave her illegitimate daughter a great deal of money," Senator said, enraged, "and raised that daughter's bastard."

"*Senator*," George warned urgently, cutting his eyes to Brother, but Mamie cut him off.

"You were glad enough for that daughter and her little boy when you and Mary couldn't have children of your own!" she said, shrilly. "*A bargain*, you said—I heard it with my own ears. *A gift from* God. It's only now, when Gabriel's struggling and out of your control that you talk about him like that. Are you blind? Can't you look at the difference between Brother and his twin and admit that Gabriel is in large part what you've made him?"

"Nonsense," Senator said.

"Is it? You've been wrong from the very beginning, Giddy, and that error continues to grow, multiply, and bear very bitter fruit. You thought if you forced Amos and Mem to leave the cocoon of Eden, to see how brutal the world is, that they'd have to face facts, see what dreamers they were, and afterward they'd crawl back and admit you were right. You claim to have loved Mem, but when she wouldn't love you back and loved him instead, your jealously turned you against her and your own brother. When Amos came back you couldn't bear the thought of him and Mem and their child here together, where they might have found some happiness, where their little daughter might have grown up very differently. You say you loved Mem; maybe think you love her still. Tell me, Giddy, what kind of love is that?"

Brother looked at Senator in disbelief. "You loved her?"

"Giddy was sure Mem chose the wrong brother," Mamie said. "Was certain that sooner or later, she'd realize her mistake and come running back."

Senator reddened. His eyes grew moist. "Amos was naïve and weak."

"He was peace-loving and kind," Mamie countered.

"And look what it got him!" Senator shouted.

"Mem," Brother said softly.

"What?" Senator snapped.

Brother answered him calmly. "It got him Mem."

"Don't bother, Brother. It's like talking to a stump," Mamie said, disgusted, heading for the door. "I need some air."

When the door shut, Brother waited to see if George or Senator wanted anything more, but Senator only stared stubbornly at the draped windows, while George took out his phone at the back of the room. Brother marked Senator's tightened jaw, the righteous certainty in it even now, after all these years, the lack of insight or forgiveness. It wasn't hard to imagine Senator loving the vibrant, funny, and beautiful Mem. Maybe he'd loved in her what he didn't have himself. But it was impossible to think Mem could have ever loved him back.

"I'll be going then," Brother said, wanting, like Mamie, to be out of that dark stuffy room. He wanted to talk to his own brother.

"Before you go," George said, "Senator would like to speak with you about your future."

Brother glanced at the senator, who continued to say nothing, wouldn't even look at him.

"Perhaps there are areas of mutual advantage," George went on, "areas where you and Senator might help each other. For your grandfather's continuing benefit, of course."

Brother knew whatever George was about to offer would be heavily weighted to benefit Gideon Grayson and no one else.

"You could stay here," George continued, "until you have your bearings—indefinitely if you like. Senator and Mrs. Grayson will be returning to Washington and Gabe and Lucy to school," George said. "At some future date, you might consider college. Your brother will be attending Yale in the fall. Sooner or later perhaps, something like that might interest you."

Brother didn't need Mem's voice to tell him to pay attention. Maybe they were testing him, seeing if he'd meant what he'd said about not having his hand out. But his stronger impression was that he was being offered a bribe for which a great deal would be asked in return.

"He's waiting to see what it's going to cost him," Senator said finally. He turned to Brother, his composed and stonyhearted self again.

"There would be papers for you to sign," George said. "A legal agreement."

Brother looked from one of them to the other. He wasn't sure which one of them to talk to—their own tag team—which they'd probably intended. "What sort of agreement?"

"That you will honor Amos's wish for sanctuary here," George said.

Not sanctuary, *exile*, Brother thought. "You don't have to worry about that."

"You might change your mind," Senator said.

"No."

"His wish for sanctuary," George said, adding, "*and all that entails.* A nondisclosure agreement."

Brother didn't know precisely what that meant, but he could guess. They wanted his silence in all things that might affect the senator's reputation and reelection. His silence about his grandfather, Mem, his mother, Gabe, everything. They wanted him to wear a muzzle and a leash. Is that why Gabe and Lucy hadn't come down that morning when Amos had broken in? Had they already signed, struck their own deals?

"Miss Scripps and Mr. Hogan would be asked to sign agreements as well," George added. "Compensation could be arranged."

Brother stood abruptly. It was bad enough that the senator was trying to buy Brother's silence, but he wasn't involving his friends.

"We've offended him, George," Senator said.

George nodded. "I see that."

Senator smiled ruefully. "We'll give you a few hours to think about it. You really are your grandmother's child."

"Thank you, Senator, that's very kind of you to say," Brother told him, and he sincerely meant it.

And then, before he exploded, he hurried out the door.

23

"WHAT KIND OF COMPENSATION?" Cole asked when Brother told him and Kit what had happened.

Cole lay in an old folding chaise in front of the beach house, wearing only shorts and with a towel over his eyes. His front side, and only his front side, was already turning red. Brother stood over him.

"No idea," Brother said. "You should turn over."

"I told you," Kit said from a chair a few feet away. She was reading a textbook propped up on her bare legs, Frank in the sand beside her. For once Frank seemed less interested in the water than in scanning the beach for his friend Trooper. Twenty or thirty yards away, Gabe was belly down on a towel, his head on his arms, apparently asleep. Jack had dug a moat around him and was filling it cup by cup with seawater.

"Which is why I didn't do it," Cole said to her. He lifted a corner of the towel to look at Brother. "What'd they offer *you*?"

"Yale was mentioned."

"Whoa. They've swept major dirt under the Oriental rug."

"You know I'm not signing anything," Kit said.

"Always the ethics queen," Cole told her.

"Just filling a local void," she said.

"You should take the deal," Cole said. "Sign their papers and then do what you want."

Kit heaved a huge sigh, but Brother knew what he thought about that. Amos had taken the deal. So had his mother. Gabe and Lucy took it every day. Brother couldn't see that taking the deal had done any of them much good.

"No," he said firmly.

"Okaaaay," Cole said wearily. "Everybody's clear what they're not doing and what they *don't* want. So what *do* you want, Brother-man? You can bet Senator knows what he wants."

Kit looked at Cole like he'd said something important. "He's right," she told Brother.

"Call a press conference," Cole said. "Kit says Cole's right about something."

Kit rolled her eyes and Brother walked over to where Gabe lay. He faced away, his head resting on his forearms, his browning back no doubt the image of Brother's own. Brother still hadn't gotten used to seeing his double in the flesh. A definite out-of-body experience.

Jack came running up from the sea with a beer cup of water and emptied it into the moat around Gabe. "Gabe's an island!"

"I get that," Brother said.

"And, guess what! There were sharks again! Way out there," Jack said excitedly.

Brother squinted at the horizon, once again not seeing anything but ocean. "Gone now."

"I told him," Gabe said, without moving, "all the sharks around here are on land."

Brother laughed a little.

"I wasn't joking," Gabe said. "Is God back in his Eden and all right with his world?"

"The library's still a wreck," Brother said.

"My hangover heard."

"But you didn't come down," Brother said.

"Not my business."

"The hell it's not," Brother said.

"Hell, hell, *hell!*" Jack shouted at the top of his lungs.

"Jack!" Kit called out. "Come here for a minute!"

"I don't want to!" Jack yelled back.

"Come anyway!" Kit said.

"Go on," Gabe told him in a mocking voice. "Run to Mommy."

Jack's face darkened, and for the umpteenth time in two days, Brother wanted to grab Gabe and smack him.

"Go see what Kit wants, buddy," Brother told Jack.

Jack stuck out his tongue at the back of Gabe's head, dropped his cup, and ran to Kit. Brother waited till he was out of earshot. "His mother's dead."

"Join the club," Gabe said.

Brother winced. "Look, I'm sorry I told you that when and how I did. Don't hurt him because you're mad at me."

"Why'd you come over here?" Gabe said irritably, turning to look at Brother. He squinted in the bright sun.

"I thought we could talk."

"We done now?"

"Fine, never mind," Brother said.

"Take his offer," Gabe told him. "You're lucky he's offered anything and at least you'll lose in comfort. You will lose. God always wins. Your grandmother must have been some piece."

Brother didn't take Gabe's bait, but for a moment, he let himself enjoy the fantasy: The crunch of Gabe's broken nose. Two of his perfect teeth joining the shards of shell in the surf. Frank tearing a sizable chunk from Gabe's entitled ass. Then the fantasy degenerated into police and Brother's certain arrest and headlines about a modern-day Cain and Abel duking it out on the shores of Eden.

"How'd you know he offered anything?" Brother said, ignoring the rest. "He told you?"

Gabe snorted. "*Please*. He doesn't tell me anything. Maybe you haven't noticed, but the Grayson family doesn't actually talk— not to each other. But I live here, hear things."

Brother took the opening. "About our mother?"

"I told you all I know." Gabe was quiet for a few moments. "She's really—"

"I'm sorry," Brother said.

"And our father?"

"Mem—*our* grandmother—said she saw the back of his head. Or the back of the man's head our mother claimed was our father. At night." He shrugged. "You?"

"Big fat zero," Gabe said. "God doesn't know either. Fuck him."

Brother didn't know if *him* meant the senator or their father, but it was pretty much how he felt either way. "You knew about Amos?"

"Enough that this morning wasn't a total surprise. Bully for Amos. Mamie came to talk to me after, until God barged in and they had a row. End of story. Happy now? Family reunion over?"

Gabe turned away, rested his head on his arms.

"I don't want *us* to be like Senator and Amos," Brother said.

Everybody knows what they don't *want*, Cole had said.

"I want something better," Brother added. "I thought maybe, with some effort, we might be different, do better than they've done. Considering how completely they've screwed up everything, that shouldn't be too goddamned hard. That's what I came over to say."

Gabe rolled over, sat up, hugged his knees, and looked out at the sea. "I meant what I said about his offer. You should take it, Brother. As for doing better than they've done? If you're hoping for some sappy happy ending, I can't help you."

Can't or won't? Brother wondered. But Gabe had called him Brother. Maybe the rest was the drugs and over time he'd get them out of his system, but that was up to Gabe.

"Just think about it," Brother said, and started back to Kit and Cole.

"You know how I comfort myself?" Gabe called after him.

Brother stopped.

Gabe looked him in the eye. "One day, he'll die."

"Some comfort," Brother said.

Gabe smiled. "You'd be surprised."

* * *

"I need a swim," Brother told Kit. He slipped off his shoes, pulled his T-shirt over his head, and emptied the pockets of his shorts, setting everything next to Kit's chair.

"Woo-woo," Kit said, glancing up. "Want company?"

"Later, I definitely do," he said. "But right now, I need to think."

The sea was bracing, exactly as Brother had hoped. Any other day, he'd have waded in a little at a time until he got used to the chill, but today he strode straight in and dove under the first wave. The cold and force of the surf immediately cleared his head, and as he paddled out where it was deep, the saltwater buoyed him. He started his stroke, let the current take him. He gave himself over to its pull and felt it carry him farther out. After the last few days, it was a relief to give in to the rhythm and force of the water, let it take him where it would. Maybe Cole and Gabe were right. Maybe he should take the offer. Maybe Senator would get his way no matter what he did.

But the deal bothered him and not because he had Kit's sky-high principles. He wasn't sure he did. The offer was too easy, open-ended, wildly generous. Brother remembered the worried look Senator and George had exchanged, thought how accommodating everyone at Eden had been to him and his nobody friends. Senator wasn't generous unless it bought him something or somebody, gained him a huge return.

Kit was right. Mem's odd lessons had prepared him to walk up Eden's drive. Even now, in this ocean, this current, because of Mem's lessons in the deep end of the community pool, he knew the risks and what to do. He knew not to give in to the current, but also not to fight it. *Here in the pool it doesn't matter,* she'd said, *but in the ocean you have to be mindful of rip currents. If you're caught in one and do nothing, you'll be fast carried out too far, farther than you can ever swim back. But if you swim hard against the current, you'll tire and drown. The smart thing is to swim along the shore, till you swim out of the current, then swim in to dry land.*

When he made his way back to the beach, he bent down and kissed Kit for a long time.

"Better now?" she asked.

"Much."

"You're salty."

"Don't mind me," Cole said.

"Why don't you make sure Jack's not playing with fireworks or something?" Brother said.

"He was just here," Kit said. "Jack!"

"Yo ho ho and a pack of gum!" Jack cried from the walkway. He was wearing the pirate eye patch Kit had gotten him at the mini-mart the first day they'd come.

He came racing down the steps, and Brother and Kit saw

Mamie on the walkway, waving, and calling, "Yoo-hoo! I'm ready!"

"I offered to drive her to the ferry," Kit said. "She left her car with all the others on party night."

"I'll go with you," Brother told her. He lifted the towel off Cole's face.

"Hey!" Cole said, grabbing it, putting it back.

"We're leaving. Watch Jack."

"Lighten up, man," Cole said, putting the towel back. "I'm not the best brother, but I'm not the worst. In that race, I wouldn't even *place* around here."

"Oh, good," Mamie said to Brother when he and Kit got to the walkway. "I hoped to speak to both of you before I left. I want to apologize for our family. I wouldn't blame you if you left and never wanted to see any of us ever again. Whatever happens, I'm hoping you'll visit me."

"You don't need to apologize," Brother said.

Mamie smiled. "That's good of you to say, though I don't believe it for a minute. I'm very glad you've come. Both of you are welcome to visit me anytime, you and your dogs, separately or together. My abode's considerably more humble, but you're welcome to stay as long as you like." She looked up and down the beach and sighed. "Eden's beautiful, but it's so terribly *fraught*."

"That's the word for it all right," Kit said, "and I'd love to come visit you."

"Thank you," Brother said. "Me too."

"Good. I'll dust off the photo albums, and we'll swap stories of happier times."

"I'd like that," Brother said.

"I wanted to warn you. I feel sure that Giddy and that man he's hired who's such a . . ." She paused to search for the right word.

"Weasel?" Kit offered.

"Oh, that's marvelous!" Mamie squealed, clapping her hands together.

"Lucy's word," Kit said.

"That girl's going through a bit of a phase right now," Mamie said. "She's drawn to Giddy's power because she doesn't have any of her own, but I think she has unfathomed depths. I was a much shallower creature at her age, so I'm not conceding her future, especially now that she has both of you in her life. Anyway, Giddy and that *weasel* will likely try to buy your allegiance or silence or cooperation. It all amounts to the same thing. They'll want you to fall in line and do whatever they say."

Kit and Brother traded a look.

"I see, as usual, I'm behind the times," Mamie said wryly. "Don't let Giddy or his minions bully you. They've bullied me for years. But he couldn't bully Mem—she wouldn't have it—and there's a lot of her in you," she said to Brother. "Perhaps that's the thing to remember."

"Do you have a bag?" Brother asked, and offered Mamie his arm.

"Mem taught you that, didn't she?" she said, hooking her arm into his. "You know, after the hateful things Giddy said about Mem and your mother in the library, I wanted to say that I think it was impossibly hard for Mem raising your mother alone after

Amos didn't come back to her. Not only difficult but painful, as young and inexperienced as she was. But she's done a beautiful job raising you."

"Thank you."

"My bag's on the portico."

They skirted the house, walking arm in arm, Brother on one side of Mamie and Kit on the other, Frank in the lead. As they passed the back garden, Brother saw the white tent had been cleared away, leaving what looked like a putting green. He saw no sign of anyone at the house.

"I've already said good-bye to your wonderful dog at Amos's," Mamie was saying as Brother opened the camper to set her bag inside.

"How is he doing?" Kit asked.

"The same, I'm afraid. But I think Trooper's a wonderful nurse and—" She stopped short and fixed on something inside the camper. "Oh, my."

Her eyes teared and she rocked slightly; Brother took her arm again, afraid she might fall. "I'd completely forgotten that," she said. "She kept it all this time."

Kit and Brother leaned in to see what Mamie was looking at.

"May I?" she said, and without waiting for a reply, she reached in and picked up the seascape urn, the one Mem said held his grandfather's ashes. With all that had happened that day, Brother had forgotten about it. Mamie turned it in her hands and looked at every side.

"I gave her this," she said. "Right before she and Billy left.

Mother was furious when she found out, but Mem loved this jar. She said those little specks in the ocean were dolphin fins. She swam with them, did she tell you? It's a collector's piece, really. Quite valuable."

"She said my grandfather's ashes were inside it," Brother said. "That he'd died in the war."

"Poor Mem. I suppose that's how she comforted herself when he didn't come back to her," Mamie said. "A lie, but a lie that was true. We did lose him in that war." She set the urn carefully back on the quilt in the camper, her hand lingering on its lid. "Mem was such a determined person, I always wondered why she didn't come here looking for him after the war. I think Amos wondered, too."

"You should keep it," Brother said.

"Wouldn't dream of it," Mamie scoffed. "It's yours now. And if you'll take some very unsentimental advice, you'll have a restorer unseal it and empty out the silliness inside; get it appraised and sell it. I can give you a dealer's name. It should give you a nice start."

"What *is* inside it?" Brother and Kit asked at the same time.

Mamie smiled sadly. "Merely a young girl's parting gift to her favorite brother and her friend, his bride-to-be. A bit of sand and my prettiest shells in a treasured jar. A little piece of Eden."

"I think I'm going to cry," Kit said, taking Brother's hand. "And I'm definitely coming to visit you."

"Oh, goody," Mamie said, and kissed her on both cheeks. "When are you leaving?"

"Tomorrow."

"You are?" Brother's stomach dropped.

"I've got to. I'm major behind. As it is, I'll have to pull two all-nighters to get caught up."

"Oh, look at him, he's crestfallen," Mamie said, placing her hand on Brother's cheek. "I have two parting words for you love-birds: Amos's house. The days of a live-in registered nurse and physical therapist are long gone, so he and Tommy have lots of room. Giddy never goes there—part of the legal agreement. I know Amos would like it. Sadly, no one visits him but me."

She took a small envelope out of her pocketbook and slipped it surreptitiously into Brother's hand. "I've put all my information in here, along with the name and number of Amos's lawyer, which I'm forbidden to give you by the damned agreement, but I'm giving it to you anyway. I think it would be *very* beneficial for you to talk with her." She gave Brother a long, meaningful look and then took both their hands. "I expect I'll be hearing from George about what I've said already today, but the two of you have inspired me. In for a penny, as they say."

He put the envelope in his pocket, thinking again of George's warning looks to Senator.

"You may come to think differently," Mamie went on, "but for me, Eden's never been so much a place, as a time. Mem's and Amos's time is long past. This is your time. People like Giddy and George can take it from you, but only if you let them."

The ferry horn sounded, and Frank barked from the backseat.

"Oh dear," Mamie said. "I'll miss my ferry."

"Not with this one driving," Brother teased, pointing to Kit, who swatted him.

But she was true to his word and as she gunned the engine he felt energized, more sure of himself, as the beginning of a plan—an idea of what he wanted—started to take shape in his mind.

24

AS HE AND KIT WATCHED the ferry leave the dock, he told her what he was thinking.

"I'm proud of you," she said. "I mean, it's not like you're a pro planner like I am, but that may work in your favor. You've got a more organic approach that keeps people guessing. But if I don't see or hear from you in an hour, I'm coming back with the Marines." She pointed at Frank.

He laughed and she kissed him and wished him luck as she dropped him at the top of Eden's drive—*his gauntlet*, she called it. She sped off with the refuge gate code to collect what they'd left that morning at the playhouse. He'd go back to Eden, touch base with Cole, tell his family—what? He was still trying to figure that out. Then he'd meet Kit and the dogs at the playhouse, after which they'd go to Amos's, as Mamie had suggested. There, they'd have time alone before Kit left in the morning. That was his hope anyway, his fledgling effort at a plan.

He walked down the drive alone, but unlike the first time he'd come, he felt steadier, even sure. It seemed the opposite of the way he ought to feel after the earthquake of Mem's dying, the aftershocks of recent days and, especially, the morning with Amos. The last week had shaken him to his core, but it had also righted something inside him. His inner compass seemed truer, his priorities clear. Much that hadn't made sense to him made sense to him now. He understood what mattered to him: Kit, Trooper, his grandfather, Cole and Jack, and maybe his brother, and what didn't—most everything else.

His present goals might be small—getting to spend a few hours with a girl he cared about, a little time with his sick grandfather—but they were things he really wanted, looked forward to, and when was the last time he'd felt *that*? But as he came around the curve of the drive he saw that, as usual, his family wasn't going to make things easy.

Lucy stood waiting in the drive. He thought of Cole's comment that having siblings meant he'd lose his temper every five minutes, and reminded himself that she'd been helpful to him and his friends, at least to start.

"Thank God," she said with a sigh. "We're all leaving in a little while."

"How? The last ferry—"

"Helicopter."

Of course, a helicopter.

"We're all going back to Washington together. Senator wants it to seem like a family thing."

Brother nodded. *Seem* not *be*.

"After the formal announcement about you," she went on, "we'll be better able to keep the media under control if we're there. I don't have school till week after next. I could show you around. You could meet *my* friends. You'll like them."

She looked so hopeful, he felt bad about disappointing her. He thought of what Mamie had said about her. In a way, she was as alone in her family as he was.

"I guess they've figured out what to say about me," he said.

"George was probably up all night."

"Well, *I* haven't figured things out."

"I didn't know," she said quickly. He guessed that was mainly what she'd been waiting to tell him. "About Amos, I mean. Really, I didn't."

"I believe you."

"I'd have told you, if I had."

He wasn't sure why he doubted *that*, but he did. She was good at withholding information when it gained her advantage, the way she'd withheld where Gabe was in rehab or when he was coming home. She'd learned guile from Senator. "I'm not going with your family."

"We're *your* family too. You're one of us now."

True, he thought unhappily, though it hadn't really sunk in before then. "I'm not going all the same."

"You know, *you* came here looking for *us*," she said crossly, "and started everything."

"I didn't start anything. I wasn't even born when it started."

"You know what I meant," she said. "And you can't stay here. Once the press finds out, the place will be swarming."

"I know."

"So what are you going to do?"

"Not sure yet. I've still got a lot to think about."

George stood in the front doorway, a phone to his ear. "Lucy, I need to speak with Brother now." George looked like a man who hated children but who found himself running a daycare for bad kids. Lucy went in reluctantly; George didn't even look at her as she went by. Her hovering annoyed Brother, but he didn't like how they treated her as if she didn't count.

George finished his call and started to say something, but his phone rang again and he raised a finger for Brother to wait.

Brother walked on around the house and—no surprise— George cut through and intercepted him at the putting green.

"You took Mrs. Stennis to the ferry?" George asked.

Brother nodded.

"I saw you talking in the drive. What was in the jar?"

George was fishing, which meant he hadn't heard what they'd said.

"Seashells," Brother answered truthfully.

"I've never really been a beach person," George said, relaxing. He looked around, zeroed in on the putting green. "You like golf?"

"Sure," Brother said, though he'd never touched a golf ball in his life.

"That's great," George said. "We should play when things settle. What's your handicap?"

You, Brother wanted to say. *You and Senator are my handicap.* With the talk about golf George had dropped his guard, as though everything was fine now, the morning forgotten. They assumed Brother would go along. They'd moved on. He should too. Kit was waiting.

"I need to talk to my friend, Cole," Brother said.

"Yes, I need to talk to him, and Miss Scripps too."

Good luck with that last one, Brother thought.

"Before you go, Senator wants you to familiarize yourself with the substance of the press release. The paperwork will come later."

"The press release," Brother repeated.

"About you." George took his phone from his shirt pocket, tapped it a few times, and read, "Gideon and Caroline Grayson are surprised and delighted to announce their newest family member, William Grayson—"

"Billy Grace," Brother corrected.

George ignored him. "—twin brother of their adopted son, Gabriel, who this week appeared unexpectedly at their home on Winter Island, North Carolina. The twins were born eighteen years ago to their single mother, the illegitimate child of the senator's late brother and the daughter of the Grayson family housekeeper. The mother, seeking funds to sustain a drug addiction, sought to sell three-year-old Gabriel to Senator and his late wife, Mary, but hid the existence of William—"

"Billy."

"—for later gain. The mother died tragically in a car accident, before either scheme could be realized. The Graysons magnanimously fostered Gabriel but remained unaware of his brother until this week. They were stunned but overjoyed when William—"

"Billy."

"—appeared, destitute and homeless, at their front door. The Graysons plan to formally adopt and to educate William, et cetera, et cetera."

Brother didn't correct him again. George looked up from his phone, pleased and smiling.

These people can spin anything, Kit had said, but she'd been wrong about that. They didn't just spin; they twisted and contorted and flat out made things up. Senator had admitted to Brother that he'd paid for Gabe that first day in the library. And whatever his mother's weaknesses and mistakes, she'd left both Gabe and Brother with people fit and willing to raise them. Maybe she hadn't won any mothering medals, but she didn't deserve scorn from Senator.

"You'll have to excuse me, George," Brother said. "I have things to take care of."

"What things?" George said. "We can help you with that."

"I'm good, thanks." George wore him out with his slick, easy answers for everything.

"The press release?"

"I'll let you know."

George seemed confused. "He's made you an extraordinary offer."

Brother nodded. People kept telling him that.

"Especially for someone with your prospects." George went on more sharply. "It's not like *I* was born to all this." He waved his hand toward the house, the beach. "I came from nowhere and not much. None of this was handed to me like it's being handed to you."

"I understand."

"Do you?" George asked. Brother had his full attention now. "We don't need you on board, you know. It's all in how we decide to tell your story."

As Kit had predicted: what he decided didn't matter. They'd write his story how they liked. *Destitute and homeless*, George's press release said, already casting him as a lowlife and themselves as saints. What words would they use when he really said no? Vagrant? Dropout? Drifter? Trespasser? Opportunist? His desperate, addict-mother's son? All believable from their hateful point of view. He'd come up with a list in seconds. Think what they could do with money and time.

"I understand, George."

"The offer might expire."

"I know."

"In fact, it might expire soon."

"I get that too."

"We need an answer now."

Brother took the time to breathe, check his temper, and said, "I'll think about it, George."

George looked stunned, like someone sure he'd been holding a winning hand.

"Brother."

Brother hadn't noticed Millicent in the back doorway. *What now?*

"If I could have a word, please."

He nearly snapped at her. But none of this was her fault. At least what she wanted would get him away from George.

"I was just going down to the beach, Millicent," he said, "to see about my friends."

"Please," she said. "Before you go. It won't take long." She cut her eyes to George, seemed nervous, but George was already tapping on his phone again and didn't see.

She led him through the living room, missing some vases and lamps, but otherwise spotless again.

"Millicent, I—"

"This way, *please*," she said in a pleading tone he hadn't heard her use before. They crossed the dining room into the kitchen and climbed the service stairs. She opened the door to her little sitting room. He paused, confused, in the doorway.

"Please, sit down," she said in an urgent whisper.

Across from her armchair were two folding chairs. He sat in one, leaving her the comfortable seat. She shut the door and sat, smoothing her skirt. With the door closed the room seemed tiny and close. Their knees nearly touched. She clasped her hands tightly on her lap. "I asked Gabriel to join us." She lowered her eyes. "I won't repeat what he said to me.

"I've decided to give Senator and Mrs. Grayson my notice," she went on, after a pause. "I've been thinking about it recently, because of my age, but after this morning . . ." She looked up and past him out the small window behind his chair. The shade wasn't drawn, and the afternoon light was stronger than the deeper gloom of the main house. The brightness didn't flatter her. She was older than he'd thought and looked exhausted.

"I understand."

"I think you do," she said, smiling sadly at him. "More than Gabriel, and he and I came to Eden at about the same time."

He hadn't considered. "A long while."

She shook her head dismissively, as if that wasn't the point. "I was here the night she came back for him."

"Who?"

"Your and Gabriel's mother."

Brother sat back in the chair.

"I didn't realize she was your mother until today," Millicent went on. "So much I didn't know." She stopped. He thought how hard this must be for someone used to keeping everything in.

"I was hired shortly after Gabriel's adoption," she continued. "They hadn't anticipated how much work a child would be and needed more help. I think both Mrs. Graysons liked the idea of children more than actual mothering. So I was hired to help and came to Eden a few days ahead of the first Mrs. Grayson's return, with Gabriel, from their second home in Washington. Gabriel was sick, and Mrs. Grayson had stayed with him there until he was better. Senator was already here; he had come ahead. He was in his library, making calls and working on a speech.

"The young woman knocked just after lunch. I hadn't been told anyone was expected. It was raining, and she didn't have an umbrella, had gotten drenched walking from her car. She was quite young, hardly older than you or Miss Scripps, and very agitated. 'Tell Senator Mem's daughter is here.' That's what she said. All she said. I left her in the hall and went to tell Senator. The name she'd given greatly upset him. He wasn't expecting her, and at first he snapped at me, said he wouldn't see her. Then he said for me to tell her to wait.

"I did, and went to get her a towel to wipe off the wet. When I got back she was looking at everything as if remembering something, so I asked her if she'd been here before. 'A month ago, of course,' she said—as if I knew what she was talking about—'and once, when I was little, with my mother. She and my father used to live here. His name was Billy. Did you know Billy?'

"I didn't, I told her, I'd just started. I had no idea what she was talking about. I'd never heard anyone talk about Billy or Mem—not then or since—not until you arrived. And I didn't press her. The agitated way she spoke unnerved me a little, made me think she wasn't right in her mind."

She stopped short and turned a little, as if she heard something in the hall, but then went on.

"Senator took her into the library and closed the door. I went to make coffee and brought a tray. I was about to knock, when I heard her sobbing, upset. She said she'd made a terrible mistake, and she wanted to undo it. That she'd only done it because her mother was so sick and needed money. She said she and her mother had left with nothing when they'd come here the first time, when she was a little girl, the day Senator told them that her father, Billy, was dead. She'd signed the papers, yes, but now she was sorry. She couldn't bear it, had changed her mind. She'd brought back the money, all of it, didn't want it. Senator interrupted her then, shouting, 'If you don't want the money that's your business, but what's done is done. There is nothing and no one for you here, and I will ask you to leave.' I heard him coming to the door, so I stepped back with my tray.

"People don't think about servants. They forget we have eyes and ears like anyone else."

Her eyes were moist. Eyes and ears and feelings, Brother thought.

"I wasn't privy to much more. He went upstairs and didn't come down again until she'd gone. I got her some tissues, and I remember she asked me, 'A person would have a good life here, don't you think?' I had no idea what she meant. Then she thanked me and left. She must have sat in her car at the dock and waited for the next ferry. I never saw her again."

Brother closed his eyes, could imagine the rest. His mother was upset. It was raining. The roads were slick. Had Mem known what she'd done? Refused the money? Is that why Mem never talked about her? He'd never know. But one phrase loomed in his mind: *when they'd come here the first time . . . the day Senator told them that her father, Billy, was dead.* Mem and his mother had come looking for his grandfather while he lived and pined for both of them not half a mile away. Two teenagers fall in love, a third hates them for it and grows up to make the whole world pay.

"That son of a bitch," said a voice outside the door. Footsteps hurried away.

Gabe.

25

BROTHER SHOT FROM HIS CHAIR, knowing exactly where Gabe was headed.

As he ran through the nursery and down the entrance hall stairs, he heard Gabe and Senator shouting over Eric's righteous nasal snarl—he wouldn't mind if Gabe throttled that jerk. His heart both leaped and sank to hear Kit's voice, and Cole's too, asking where Brother was, and Jack shrieking in falsetto, "Gabe said, 'You son of a bitch!'" at the very top of his healthy five-year-old lungs, the whole uproar punctuated with the barks and squeals of two worked up dogs.

When he got to the library, Cole and George were restraining a raging, red-faced Gabe at the center of the room, Cole doing most of the work. Gabe struggled hard, spitting obscenities, and easily threw off George, but Cole, who had once wrestled an enraged 300-pound Alzheimer's patient to the floor, held on. Brother, watching, couldn't help thinking that Senator's white-collar weasels had no real-life skills and that Senator might be dead now except for Brother's "destitute, homeless" friend. Not that Senator would ever thank Cole, but Brother was proud.

At the back of the room, Senator and Eric argued about calling the police, Eric shrilly in favor, Senator thunderously opposed. George backed away to a safe corner, urging everyone to please calm down, but no one paid him any mind.

"Let me goddamned go!" Gabe roared. He twisted and thrashed to free himself, but Cole was bigger and stronger and kept Gabe's arms behind his back, trying without success to steer him to a sofa. Cole caught Brother's eye, as if asking if he had any bright ideas.

Kit had Trooper by the collar and Frank on a short leash but managed to sidle over to Brother in the doorway. "Often as hell breaks loose," she said, "they ought to rename this place. What *now?*"

"Gabe's really mad!" Jack said, running up, just as Lucy came down the front hall steps to crane around Brother and Kit. Upstairs, Caroline called for Millicent to please go see what in blazes was going on in the library.

"He's strung out again, isn't he?" Lucy sneered. "I knew it."

"Shut up, Lucy!" Gabe shouted. "As usual, you're on the wrong side!"

"He sounds pretty sober to me," Kit said. "Wrong side of what?"

"Mem did come for Amos after the war," Brother said.

"Senator told her he was dead. Our mother only gave up Gabe for money to pay Mem's medical bills. But then she wanted Gabe back, and Senator said no."

"Who told you that?" Lucy demanded. "Is that what Gabe said? You can't possibly know any of that."

Brother turned to Millicent wearily climbing the stairs behind them with a tray. Kit and Lucy followed his gaze. "It's true," he told them.

"Tell him to let me go!" Gabe yelled in Brother's direction.

"Don't you dare!" Eric shrieked from the back of the room. "Haul him outside right now, and stay out there with him!"

Cole looked at Brother. "Who's that ass-wipe talking to?"

"You, I think," Brother told him.

"What a swine," Cole said.

"Insult to pigs everywhere," Kit muttered under her breath.

"Let him go, Cole," Brother said.

Cole smirked at Eric and let go of Gabe, who shook out his arms and glared at Eric, George, and Senator, as if he were trying to decide which one of them to tear apart first.

"Have you completely lost the little left of your mind?" Senator shouted at him. He drew himself up and stood haughtily behind his desk as though he were chastising the entire Senate floor. "Are you drugged? I thought I had been perfectly clear that even a whiff of any further nonsense from you would have dire and permanent consequences."

Brother saw Gabe stiffen.

"Now if you will all get out of my library," Senator ordered, and took up some papers on his desk, as if their leaving were a foregone conclusion.

"No!" Gabe shouted.

Senator looked at him in complete disbelief. He wasn't used to being told no even by powerful adults, much less a delinquent teenager, Mem's grandson to boot. He spoke to Gabe in a low, seething voice. "This is your final warning. Unless you wish to have your freedom and future severely curtailed, your trust revoked, I advise you do exactly as I say. Leave my library now!"

He stood stone-faced, waiting, fixing Gabe in his most withering glare. *Enough to scare a body to death*, Mem had said. Brother waited for Gabe to answer, but he didn't—or couldn't. He lowered his eyes, his shoulders dropped, the glare and threats having their bullying effect.

Brother hurried to Gabe's side. "*No* is a simple word, sir," he said to Senator.

Senator's glare shifted to Brother.

"With a straightforward meaning," Brother went on.

Still Senator said nothing.

"It means—"

"I know what it means, you ungrateful little bastard."

Frank emitted a low growl.

"I'm pleased to hear it, sir," Brother told Senator in a steady voice. "Then there won't be any misunderstanding." He paused. "And so there won't be future misunderstandings, I'll speak for myself too. No."

Kit stepped up with Frank and Trooper to stand at Brother's open side. "No," she said.

Cole sighed slightly, lifted Jack, and stepped up beside Gabe. "No," he said, "for me and my brother."

Only Lucy held back, looking cross and uncertain in the doorway.

Senator's piercing eyes landed on each of the naysayers in turn, burning lastly into Gabe. "And you? Your final word."

Gabe lifted his eyes, looked directly at Senator, and said, "My mother came back for me."

26

"WHAT A DAY," Kit sighed.

Brother set the last of their things inside the door to Amos's house and joined her in the porch swing.

A soft, steady breeze stirred the pottery chimes. Trooper lay next to Frank in one of two side-by-side hollows they'd dug in the sandy dirt at the edge of the small yard. He watched Brother settle, but then his blue eyes closed and he was sound asleep again.

"You missed the joyous reunion," Kit said.

"Tell me."

"Maybe two minutes after Frank and I got to the playhouse to get our stuff, Trooper practically flew up the path. You'd've thought they hadn't seen each other in months. They chased each other nonstop around the yard for twenty minutes like two little kids."

Brother enjoyed that picture. He leaned in and kissed Kit for a long time. She'd gone inside to shower while he unloaded the camper. Her hair smelled like roses.

They had the house to themselves. Tommy had coaxed Amos into going for a walk, though he still clung to Mem's urn. Cole and Jack had hiked off, singing the sailor song, to spend the night in Kit's tent. They'd taken the sleeping bags and the hot dogs and s'more fixings to the beach for a campfire and some long-overdue brother time. "They don't allow camping or fires on the refuge," Tommy'd said, "but since the recession, there's nobody to say 'boo.'"

Brother and Kit rocked quietly for a while, listening to the chimes, the birds, the far surf. It was good to be still. One of the best things about being with Kit was how they could be quiet together, not have to fill every silence.

"What do you think Gabe's going to do?" she asked after a while.

Brother shrugged. He'd followed Gabe upstairs while Kit put the dogs in the truck, tried to ask him the same question. But Gabe was tossing random things in a suitcase and wouldn't talk. Been there, Brother thought, remembering the time right after Mem died. "I don't think he knows. He's shell-shocked. I told him where we'd be."

"You think the senator'd really cut him off?" She shook her head. "Stupid question. Of course he would. Being a have-not will be hard for Gabe. Eden's ease is all he knows."

Brother thought it strange he had more experience of the real world, an edge in that way over his advantaged twin, but he supposed it was true.

"Lucy?" Kit asked.

"Right before she slammed her door in my face, she said I was *just like Gabe*."

Kit scanned Brother up and down and stifled a laugh. "Well, *yeah*." She instantly looked sheepish. "Sorry, I couldn't resist."

Brother smiled a little.

"Hidden depths, Mamie said," Kit reminded him. "Lucy knows George is a weasel. Baby steps."

Brother nodded, remembering himself at fifteen. Mem had been in remission. He'd been in school, with prospects, a different person. Nothing about now was part of his wildest nightmares or dreams.

"While I was in the shower," Kit said, "I was thinking that when your grandmother and grandfather left Eden they were younger than we are. Your young mother didn't fare much better, and who knows what ever happened to mine."

He took her hand. Mem had always been so youthful it wasn't hard to think of her as sixteen, but Amos was so ravaged, he was harder. Brother tried to remember more about the old photograph Senator had showed him the first time they'd talked, but he couldn't recall much more than two boys and two girls with fishing poles, and he had no picture of his mother.

Kit rested her head on his shoulder. "We'll be different, won't we?"

He liked her saying "we," but it was odd hearing her unsure. She was always so confident and certain of everything.

He squeezed her hand. "Did your mother go to college?"

She gave him an *are-you-kidding* look. "Liza didn't finish high school. Charlie did, barely."

"Aren't you top of your class? Going to college? Full scholarship?"

"Then law school."

"You're already different," Brother said.

"I haven't done it yet."

"You've laid the foundation."

She sat up straighter. "I have."

He liked her looking to him for reassurance. Till now, she'd been so confident it scared him a little. He liked that she had the occasional doubt.

"And you stood up, spoke truth to power," she said. "You and Gabe both."

He tried not to think how Senator punished people who stood up to him. They had stood up to him. They could do it again.

Kit chuckled.

"What's so funny?"

"I was just thinking how proud Carl and Mitchell will be. You'll be a hero in Bailey, you and Gabe too. They might even give you a parade."

They looked at each other and started to laugh. Another thing he liked about her. She found the light in the hardest, darkest day.

"Tommy's sweet," she said. "He made up two rooms for us." Brother's lightness dimmed a little. "That is, he said if we *wanted* two rooms. He said he didn't like to presume. Neither do I."

"That makes three of us," Brother said.

Neither said anything. Brother didn't have words for this. Just the powerful sense they were paying full attention and, as Mamie had put it, that this was their time. He squeezed her hand and she squeezed back. They looked at each other and smiled shyly, then stood up and went inside. Not even Frank stirred. At first they were awkward, tentative, took exquisite care, as if they were each remembering the long day and thinking of all the ways the world could hurt them. But Eden retreated as they loved and slept, loved even as they slept, curled around each other like waves.

27

IF BROTHER HAD SEEN a more beautiful morning he couldn't remember it. Hungry dogs woke him early and he left Kit, naked and beautiful and sleeping, fed the dogs, and walked them down to the refuge beach, where he found the empty tent and Jack in his pajamas already building a second castle.

"Where's Cole?"

"He went down to the little house to take a shower," Jack said.

A night rain had cleaned the air, washed the sand dark and smooth except for holes crabs had dug and, when the water retreated, the air holes of creatures teeming underneath. A light breeze came off the sea, freed the sea foam the waves churned, sent clusters of iridescent bubbles flying toward shore. Jack and the dogs chased them, Jack laughing and slapping them between his palms with a squeal, and the dogs leaping in the air to bite them, thinking it a great game. Brother held them while Jack tossed bits of stale hot dog buns to a dozen gulls flapping over his head. They caught the bits midair and even when the bread was gone they waited, sharp-eyed and ever hopeful, at a dog-safe distance.

Afterward, Brother left the dogs with Jack and walked the short distance to the beach house to see what was keeping Cole. Once Kit went home to Bailey, if Amos's lawyer approved, he wanted to walk here with his grandfather on the shore of the great mother and just *be* for a while. With Mamie's and the lawyer's permission, he and Trooper would stay with Amos for the near future, think and plan. And he wanted to ask the lawyer about that worried look George and Senator had exchanged. Tommy needed to visit his daughter in Florida, and Cole and Jack could stay and help Brother if they wanted. Even when Tommy got back from vacation, he might need more help keeping up with Amos, at least for now. Kit would finish her senior year and graduate, get ready to go to college in the fall. She and Frank would visit often, though she planned to spend part of the summer canvassing for Senator's opponent and hoped Brother might come along.

A week ago his life had been a dead end, and now it was just beginning.

He climbed the porch to the beach house and heard the shower running through the screen door.

"Cole!" he called as he went inside. The bathroom door was open. The water stopped and a red hand pulled back the moldy curtain.

"Promise you won't say anything," Cole said.

"About what?"

Cole stepped out of the shower. He was deeply, painfully red on his front side, except for a white void where his shorts had been. "I've taken three cold showers. I'll never hear the end of it from Miss Know Everything."

Brother tipped his head and studied Cole's sunburned nakedness. "Red. White. Red," he said, laughing. "All you need's a maple leaf and you'd be a walking Canadian flag."

"Very funny," Cole said. "It hurts like hell." He looked at the unmade bed. "Where's your brother?"

"Gabe was here?"

"Sleeping," Cole said, pointing at the bed. "I woke him when I came in."

Brother had heard the helicopter come and go sometime during the night. He'd assumed both Lucy and Gabe were on it, maybe Millicent too.

"You didn't see him?" Cole asked. "He said he was going for a swim."

Brother walked outside to look. He scanned the sea, saw Gabe's dark head in the deeper water, the strong practiced stroke, better and steadier than his own. Brother's coming had changed a lot for both of them. There was deep water between them, but Gabe was still here, and that seemed like a start.

Brother heard the dogs barking and Jack squeal. He squinted up the refuge beach, saw the familiar awkward gait, the old man headed determinedly his way and once again, alone. Brother stood, shaking his head. He started up the beach to intercept him, but stopped suddenly, shading his eyes. What was he wearing?

The dogs got to Amos first. The old man stopped and bent stiffly to pet them as best he could with Trooper in full herding mode. Jack reached Amos then, excitedly shouting something at Amos that Brother couldn't hear. Jack's pitch rose. He waved his arms and cackled, actually cackled, which he kept up while pulling his striped pajama top over his head. He let the wind take it to the dunes, and then pulled off his bottoms. The breeze filled them and took them like windsocks, and the now naked boy laughed louder, hopped like a rabbit, then bent over and wagged his bare butt at Amos for the utter, ridiculous joy of it. He took Amos's hand and pulled him toward the water, and Brother realized they were both naked. Together they waded in the chilly sea, as Frank yipped and leaped beside them, and even Trooper joined them in the shallows. Then the old man and boy and Frank the water dog began splashing each other, seeing who could get the other wetter first. Jack was the most agile, so Amos and Frank got the worst of it. But Amos was laughing. Amos. Laughing.

Jack tugged Amos into the water up to their knees, Jack chattering on, his patience with the old man's slowness exquisite.

Brother took out his phone and dialed Kit. She answered sleepily.

"Quick, come down to the beach," he said, laughing. "You're missing it."

"What? What am I missing? I'll be right there!" she said, and hung up.

Not a minute later his phone vibrated.

"It's Tommy, Brother," the anxious voice said when he answered. "Have you—"

"Yep. Wading on the beach between you and Eden. Wearing his birthday suit."

"Oh, thank Jesus. I'll be right there."

"Take your time," Brother told him. "I've got him till you get here."

Behind him, the screen door of the beach house slammed.

"What's going on, Brother-man? Did you find Gabe?" Cole shouted. He came toward Brother, walking stiffly from his burn. He squinted, looking where Brother was looking. "Are they—?"

"As jaybirds," Brother called back.

Amos and Jack were laughing uncontrollably now, the one restarting the other, swaying and dancing to music only they could hear. The day before was completely forgotten—the curse of Amos's sickness, but its blessing as well. There was nothing now but joy.

The dogs suddenly left Jack and Amos and raced up toward the refuge, and Brother saw Kit running his way.

"There he is!" she shouted, pointing. She wore her bathing suit and a T-shirt. God, she was beautiful. Tommy huffed and puffed some distance behind her, his arms full of what looked like towels and clothes.

Brother ran to meet her. He pushed her hair back from

her laughing face and kissed her until Tommy chugged up, winded.

"I'd just got him out of the shower and went to the dryer to get some clean towels," he said apologetically, and looked at Kit. "I'm sorry, ma'am. I'll get him covered."

"Leave the man be!" she said, swatting the air. "It's a nice change from yesterday."

Trooper started barking and Jack shouting, "See! See! See!" and jumping up and down. Amos was pointing at something in the water. Brother followed his shaking arm and saw the dark gray fins, five of them close together, the sinuous circular dives, the perfect arcs of their backs appearing and disappearing in the deeper sea, a dark head, the image of his own among them.

"Look!" Jack shrieked. "Sharks! They're eating Gabe!"

"Don't think so, fish-boy," Cole called as he hobbled up.

"Dolphins!" Tommy yelled. "See the rounded fins? Dolphins having their breakfast. Get 'em here all the time."

Brother took Kit's hand. He drew her close as they watched the dolphins submerge and surface in the water, their wheeling freedom, his brother welcome, accepted as one of them.

They were all here now, everyone he cared for. Even Mem was here in spirit with the dolphins, as Jack had tried over and over to tell him. He thought of his dream, the lone gray swimmer he'd chased all those nights in his sleep, always too fast, forever receding. No wonder he'd never caught it. Nobody could. It wasn't a dolphin or even his twin he'd been chasing; it was the past.

"I told you so, I told you so!" Jack chanted, not caring about his error, as he, Amos, and now Cole watched from the surf. Even Tommy tossed the towels and clothes on the sand and stood, resigned and smiling, letting Amos be.

Brother pulled Kit toward the water, saying, "Let's go for a swim."